Severed Kingdom

Titles by J. L. Jackola

Unbound Prophecy Series
Ascension
Descent
Surfacing
Submerged
Riven
Adrift

Unbound Kingdom Trilogy
Severed Kingdom

Severed Kingdom

Unbound Kingdom Book One

J.L. Jackola

Tivshe Publishing

Copyright © 2022 J. L. Jackola

Library of Congress Control Number 2022907921

ISBN 978-1-954175-35-8

Distributed by Tivshe Publishing

Printed in the United States of America

Cover design by Dark Queen Designs

Map design by Worldwyrm

Visit www.tivshepublishing.com

To the curious ones - never stop questioning.

OLD TENEBRON
BORTEES
HOLY LANDS
Western Coast
NOBESN

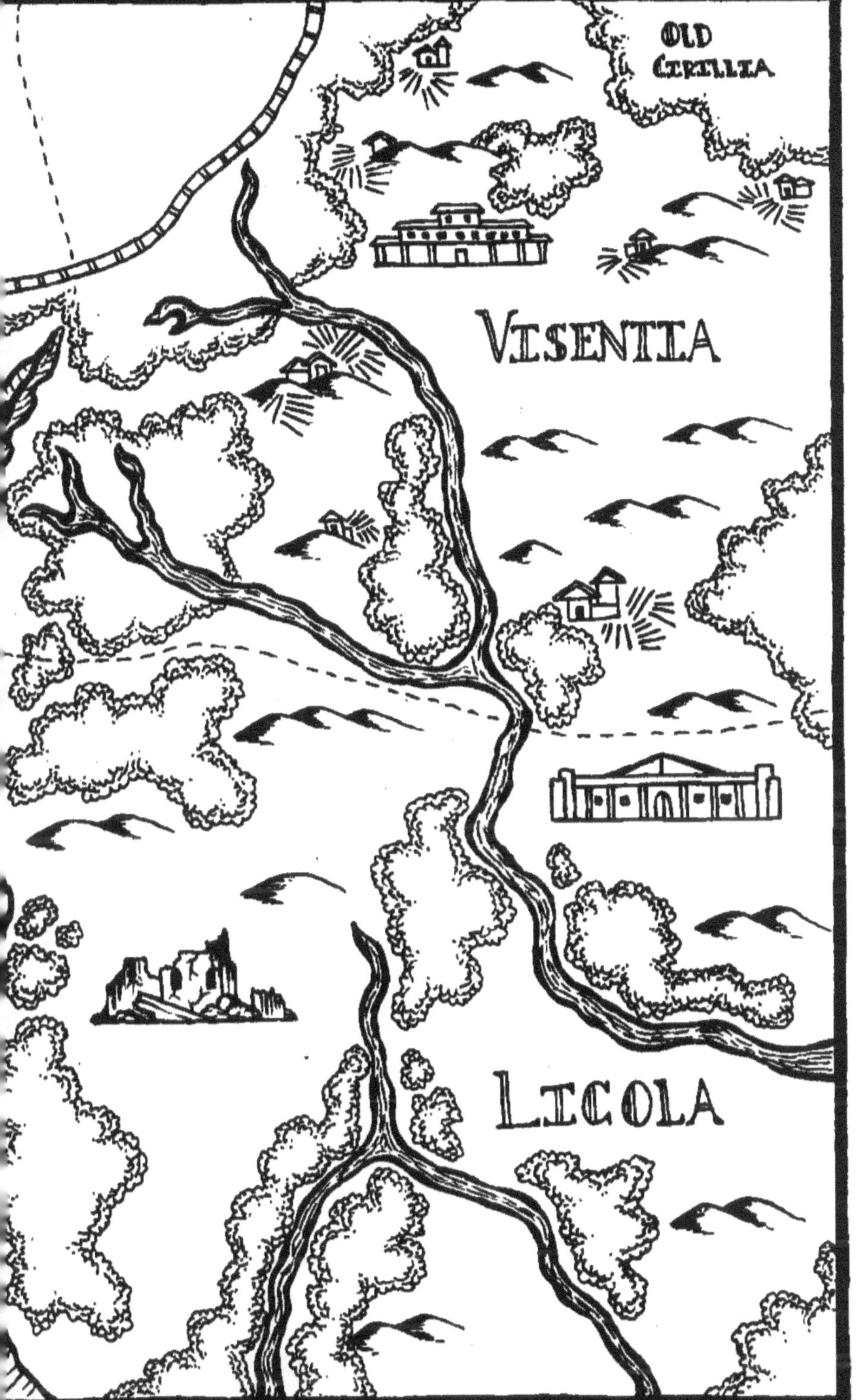

OLD CIRILLIA
VISENTIA
LICOLA

In the beginning, the Fates created the races of magic: the Torathar, the Dark, the Elvin, and the Light. After the Light, a fifth race was formed from the forbidden love of two Fates. The Gaern were a volatile blend of their Dark and Elvin heritage. Ruled by their emotions and fueled by an insatiable need for the Dark side of nature, they created chaos and havoc amidst the races.

It was decided that they, like the Torathar before them, should no longer walk the land, but the Mother Fate pleaded their case, swaying the others to let them live. They were instead banished from the lands that held the other races, exiled to a land beyond the realms of the immortals, their own immortality stripped as punishment, and their existence wiped from memory.

The Gaern vowed to forget the Fates and, over time, worshipped those they called the old gods, vowing with each generation that the immortal offspring of the cursed Fates be punished for the favor attributed them by the ones who had abandoned their people.

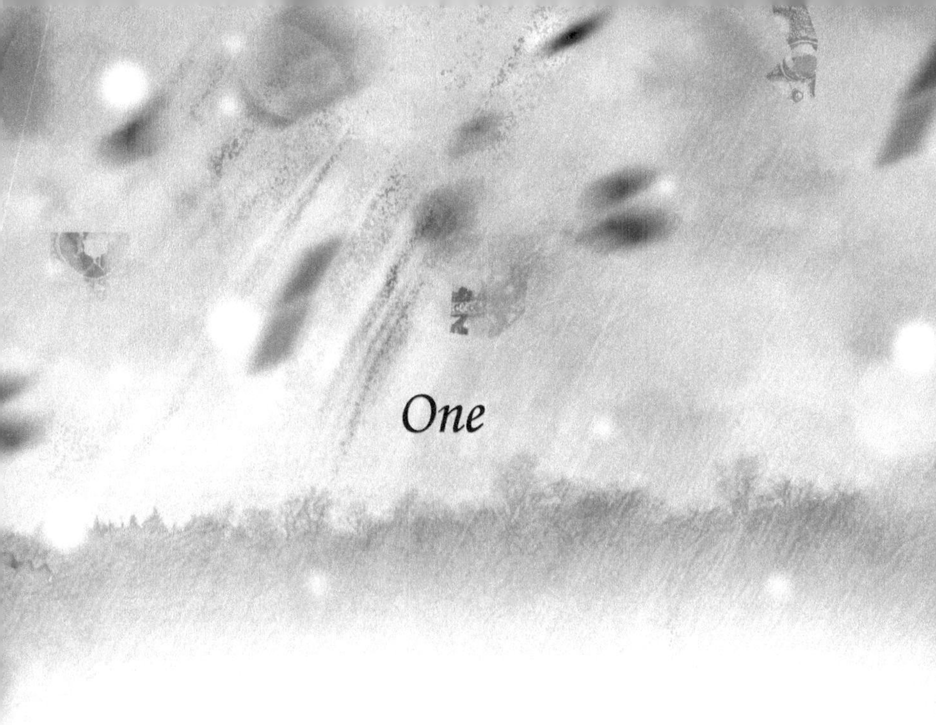

One

The room was alive with music and jovial conversation, but Xali had tuned it all out, her mind wandering as it often did.

"Xali," her brother Mendol said, nudging her arm.

She turned to him, his gray eyes gazing curiously at her.

"Where is it your mind wandered to this time?" he said playfully.

"Nowhere. What is it, Mendol?"

"Father has just toasted to his siblings. The dancing is about to begin."

As he said it, couples moved to the floor in the center of the room and began the opening dance of celebration.

"Xali," she heard from behind her.

Carnick's voice was deep and melodious, casting ripples across her skin. She turned to find his hand out-stretched to her, expecting that she would accompany him in the dance. Mendol rose, gave her a wink, and departed to find his betrothed, Fairenth.

As Carnick led her to the dance floor, he whispered, "I know your comfort lies in swords and the ways of battle, but I hope you don't mind if I challenge your agile skills to a dance."

She raised an eyebrow as they began the steps to the dance that had been performed at every family gathering since well before she'd been born.

"Are you implying that I cannot dance as well as the others here because I prefer the sword to the ballroom?"

"I've known you long enough to avoid answering that question honestly," he replied with a laugh.

He was right, she disliked events like this, preferring to be outdoors, wielding a weapon, honing her fighting skills, doing everything her female cousins disliked.

Xali was a second born. Expected to marry a chosen cousin and take her seat beside him to rule his province. Only first borns took the crown, and her brother had come first. Carnick was a first born, and so she'd been promised to him. Birth order was everything to the houses, regardless of sex, and she was a second born. Her brother had come a full ten years prior to her birth, leaving her the youngest of the cousins. For a time, it was thought that her mother would not bear a second born, something that had never happened since their ancestors had stepped foot on these lands, but finally Xali had come on the crest of the full moons.

Her mother often told her of how the moons had glowed a brilliant green that rivaled the emerald stones found on the shores of the Visentia province. They had thought it a blessing at first and then an omen as she had been born with no power. No one in their line had ever been born powerless. Eventually, it had come, like the trickle of a dammed stream, but she'd never gained the power her cousins or her brother had. She was weak. The strength of each house was marked by their magic, the matches of first to second born securing the family's place of rule in the realms.

Xali was a weak match, Carnick the strongest of all the cousins, but she'd been promised to him long before he'd had any say in the matter. She often wondered if her beauty hadn't rivaled that of the others, if he'd have broken tradition and stolen another's promised from them.

With her weak powers, she'd turned to the art of the sword, honing her fighting skills, strengthening her physical and mental muscles to make up for her lack of power. Her strength and agility, combined with her sharp mind, brought her to equal status to her cousins, at least in her mind.

"Do I bore you so much this eve that your mind would drift elsewhere?" Carnick asked, pulling her back from her thoughts.

"No, not at all. I was simply thinking of our impending union. Mendol will take Fairenth at the start of the warm season."

"Then I must wait another season to have you in my bed."

She rolled her eyes. "You have plenty of women warming your bed now, Carnick. I don't believe you're pining for me. Be thankful our parents agreed to break tradition and let us unite without waiting for me to reach the proper age. Otherwise, you'd be waiting much longer."

"This is true, but Xali—"

His words were cut short as a sharp crack broke through the music. Instinctively, her eyes were drawn upward. A line had formed vertically through the glass ceiling above, the stars and moons shining through, muted along its length.

"What in the gods' name is that from?" Carnick asked.

"All right, everyone, stay calm. Let's move away while we repair it," her father said, but as the words left his mouth, the crack widened.

A shattering sound filled the room as the ceiling caved down around them. Carnick pushed Xali behind him and raised his hand along with the others in the family, breaking the glass fragments into tiny soft grains of sand that fell across them like a quiet snow. Glass was something they could manipulate since it was organic, and they could strip it down to its original form. Anything from the ground, they could control. If it had been a wood ceiling, they would have had no control as trees and plants were a part of nature they had never mastered.

"Are you all right?" Carnick asked, brushing the fragments from her hair. It irritated her that he'd pushed her aside, assuming her power would be of no help. She wanted to complain but refrained, knowing he'd only been doing what he'd thought he needed to do, protecting her.

"I'm fine," she replied. "What do you suppose caused that?"

"No idea. That glass was thick. A fracture like that would have taken a major impact to form. Stay here."

He left her to join the others who were all gathering to discuss the matter, the first borns of her generation and those of her father's.

She caught her cousin Trevant's eyes, and he rolled them. She'd always wondered if being a second-born male stung more than it did for her as a female. Or perhaps it only stung to her, knowing she'd been the one born with faulty magic. Trevant was as powerful as his wife, Sartria. Xali was the only broken one in the family.

After a long discussion, the determination was made that perhaps the recent snowstorms had weakened the glass. No other reason could be found. She thought it doubtful, although they had been hit hard with storms this season. It was unusual to get more than a few light snows in this region. It was Carnick's mountainous province that tended to have the harsh winters. Regardless, the snow they had received didn't seem enough to break something that solid.

The festivities continued until the families all went their separate ways to be united again in the warm season for her brother's wedding to Fairenth.

As Xali lay down to sleep that evening, her thoughts weren't of Carnick or dancing or even the festivities. They were on the particles of glass scattered upon the floor. When sleep finally took her, her dreams were littered with those fragments, the shards of fractured glass, and a snow that cast down around her as she stared up toward the sky. The stars above seemed angry. Was that possible? Angry stars? As the thought floated through her conscious, the moons, full above her began to change, their color brightening to a gorgeous green that was reflected in the particles of glass below her feet.

Everything around her sparkled emerald until all she could see was a green hue that covered the landscape. She walked forward, unaware of the tiny particles of glass cutting her bare feet. The wall of the room faded, and she continued forward until grass lay below her. This time, she could feel it crunch with every footfall. The emerald faded, the moons casting a spotlight upon her so that when she looked down, she could see the green receding from the grass, leaving it brown and brittle. In time, the moonlight began to dissipate until she was left in total darkness.

A chill slid down her spine, and her chest tightened. Within seconds, the sense of awe turned to one of crushing weight that smothered the breath within her. She gasped for air as fear flooded her—that is, until a blue light trickled through the pitch black and reached out to her. As it touched her skin, her breathing calmed, the fear fleeing until all she felt was a sense of calm and warmth.

Xaliandri, a voice called her by her birth name.

She couldn't tell where it had come from, and she swiveled around to find it. As she turned, the green light returned, cutting another line through the ebony that had overcome her.

Xaliandri.

She kept turning, and as she did, the three colors seemed to wrap around each other, blending until they became a vibrant purple that blinded her with its power. She held her hand up to her eyes, but the brightness was too much to bear.

She cried out, sitting up in her bed, her heart pounding.

Immortals, her mind whispered.

But that couldn't be. The immortals were gone, defeated ten thousand years prior. Shakily, she pushed the bed coverings back and rose from her bed, walking across the room then out onto her balcony. The moons looked down upon her, their normal diamond light shining once again. A breeze touched her skin, her silver hair drifting before her with its touch. She closed her eyes to the feel of it, listening as the quiet of the night calmed her. She gave no thought to the cold of the air as she reached her hand out to the flakes of snow that had begun to fall.

Watching them, she let her mind drift back to her dream. The immortals. The magic in the dream had been magic from their time. But the immortals were long gone, destroyed by her fore-father, the great king of the kingdom of Gaernim. Why had she dreamt about them, about their power, and who had called her name? What did it mean?

"It means nothing, Xali," she said to herself, bringing her hand back down. "The immortals are gone. It's just your unchecked mind lost in fantasy again."

She turned from the balcony to walk back to her bed, but the breeze touched her again. Strands of her hair fluttered in the air before her morphing from silver to a brilliant white then curling like a snake slithering to the sun. The white faded, and the breeze abated. She ran to the mirror at the far end of her room, bringing her hand to her mouth as her eyes took in the loose curls that now embodied her once straight hair. Curls were never seen in their people—only in the lesser borns, the ones of Cirillian heritage. She backed away, her heel tripping on the loose throw covering the stone floor. Within seconds upon her head hitting the floor, blackness engulfed her.

Two

W"hat does it mean?" Xali's mother asked, staring at the curls that now tumbled through Xali's hair.

After Xali had woken on the floor and cleared her pounding head, she'd stared at the waves that now defined her completely from the rest of her family. As if she wasn't already different enough. Knowing she'd be expected to join her parents at the fast breaking, she put on a brave face and bore the reactions.

"It means nothing," her brother said in her defense.

"First, the length of time for her to arrive, then the powers, and now this?" her mother continued.

"Shalinia, calm yourself," Xali's father said. "I'm sure there's a reasonable explanation." Turning to Xali, he continued in an agitated tone, "Xaliandri, I want you to have the servants wash your hair until this nonsense is gone. Did you do this to challenge my patience? It's always something unusual with you. Now go."

She went to explain that she was responsible for none of it, but he waved her off. She knew better than to argue; her father was not one to be challenged. She did as he commanded, but no matter how many times it was washed in the scented water, the curl returned. By the fifth time, she smelled like a bed of flowers.

"You've been touched," Sianna the servant girl said.

"Touched?" Xali asked.

"Yes, by the Fates," she responded innocently.

"Do not let my father hear you say that, or you will be killed, Sianna."

The Fates were the heathen gods, buried with the remnants of the immortals. It was considered a slight against the gods to even whisper their name. The heathen gods. Punishment was death. Xali had not heard anyone ever mention their name other than in lessons.

"I'm sorry, my Lady. I don't know where that came from. Please forgive me." Fear had filled Sianna's eyes.

Xali studied the girl for a moment. She'd been in her service for a handful of seasons, but Xali had never truly looked at her. She was pretty, with auburn hair and blue eyes. It was that way with all the Cirillians, although their numbers were so sparse now that she truly only saw the slaves in the castle or the farmers in her cousin Sartria's province to the south. They were a weak-willed people, too kind to know better, easy prey for the Tenebrons who lived in the border villages of Carnick's province.

Xali thought them a sad people although she much preferred them to the unruly Tenebrons. Carnick's province as well as their cousin Ainia's fell in Old Tenebron. The people there, those not of her kind were hard and unmanageable. They challenged the crown, clinging to their old ways until they were almost extinct. They were lawbreakers. To this day, small uprisings would occasionally occur in those provinces. Their ways were cruel; she'd seen what they did to the Cirillians when they crossed the border. It was one reason her father and her aunt had begun protecting what Cirillian villages remained.

"My Lady?"

"Oh yes, you're fine. It will be our secret."

Relief filled the girl's face.

"Now go. I believe I am very late to lessons now, and Proctor Chenon will have my head."

"Yes, my Lady."

Xali made her way to the great library to find her brother already in discussion with the proctor. Her brother didn't have to attend lessons anymore, for he was well past the age of learning, but it didn't surprise her. He was a scholar at heart, nose always in a book, devouring everything new and obsessed with the history of their people. He'd make a good king one day.

"Xaliandri, nice of you to finally join us. I see your studies are your priority as usual."

"My apologies, Proctor Chenon."

He eyed her with disappointment then said, "Since you find your grasp of knowledge to be sufficient, tell me the history of your family back to the great war."

Again? She wanted to say but refrained.

"The great king Drakine waged war with the immortals, freeing our people and taking back our lands. He destroyed the immortals and reclaimed the lands as his, naming himself king of what was once Tenebron and Cirillia. He had two sons to whom he gave each half of the kingdom. They in turn had four children each. The lands were divided each in half to create the four provinces, Visentia, Licolca, Bortees, and Nobesn, that stand today. The youngest were then married to their cousins to ensure the line remained pure, their power undiluted. They in turn had two children each, one girl and one boy as it has continued since that time."

"Good, now Mendol, name the four houses and their originating rulers."

Xali's mind slipped back to the word immortals, her dream coming back to her.

"Proctor," she said, interrupting her brother, "how does one kill an immortal? Does the word not imply that they cannot be killed?"

He stared at her, as did her brother.

"What?" she asked. "Surely someone has asked that question before."

His face turned angry. "We do not question our history."

"I'm not questioning it. I am merely curious about how the great king killed several immortal beings on his own when he was clearly mortal."

The proctor slammed his hand on the table. "That will be enough! Now keep your mouth shut unless addressed, Xaliandri, or your father will be informed of these indiscretions."

Indiscretions? She'd merely asked a question. One she'd never thought to ask before, always taking their history at face value. His reaction gave her pause, but instead of stopping her curiosity, it spurred it. Her mind wandered through the rest of lessons, the proctor thankfully slighting her for her earlier behavior and addressing only her brother.

The wind whipped strands of Xali's hair free from her braid, but she continued to stare out into the forests below the guardian wall, her imagination filled with all sorts of adventures that lie far beyond her eye's sight. She'd come here to her favorite spot after lessons and remained for the past few hours. Sketching some then letting her hand rest, she stared out at the mysterious world below.

"What is your obsession with these heights, Xali?" her brother asked, carefully sitting next to her.

"How did you know I'd be here?"

"Because you're always here. You are lucky Father doesn't know you come here. How is it the guards have yet to tell him your secret?"

"I sneak them sweets from the kitchens," she said with a wink.

He laughed then looked out beyond to where her eyes had slipped.

"What lies beyond here, Mendol?"

"Xali, you ask too many questions of late. What has come over you?"

"I don't know, but my questions never seem to receive answers, do they?"

He sighed. "Nothing lies beyond here but wild animals and forests."

"Then why block it from the rest of our provinces and why guard it so heavily?"

"The ancient lands have always been behind this wall. It was erected by the great king to protect us from whatever lies beyond it."

It was the simplest answer and one she knew. The guardian wall had existed from the beginning of their family's reign. It ran from her father's province through Carnick's. No one ever crossed beyond it and to attempt so was death on sight. She'd come here since she was a child and her father had first shown it to her. There was a peace to this edge of their world; it was calming. Lately, however, it seemed to call to her. She'd begun coming every day, sitting in the very far corner of the structure, her mind drawn to the sounds below, the richness of the colors, the sweet lilac that drifted by her nose.

"What's going on, Xali?"

She sighed. "I don't know to be honest. I feel...restless. I'm not even sure that's the right word."

"It's all right, Xali. Things are getting ready to change. Fairenth and I will be joined soon and then you and Carnick. I'll be taking on more duties, and you'll be moved to Bortees with Carnick. It's easy to see why you're feeling that way."

She gave him a small smile. "I suppose."

The words fell flat, however, the mistruth audible to her ears. She wasn't certain those were the reasons, but she had no others to justify her recent state of mind.

"What are you drawing?" Mendol asked, picking up the sketch paper and coal she'd placed beside her.

"Nothing much, just something that came to mind."

Mendol looked at the picture, running his fingers over the figure. "Who is she?"

Xali looked down at the drawing, the figure of the beautiful woman with her flowing hair staring back at her.

"I honestly don't know. There was a voice in my dream last night, and when I thought of it, this is the image I drew."

"She's haunting, even with no color to her. Like a spirit."

Xali's eyes drifted back out to the untamed forest beyond them, the voice echoing through her head.

Mendol placed the sketch back down and patted her hand.

"Don't stay up here too long. The spirits of the forest may steal you away."

She laughed at the reference to the old children's story their mother would tell them.

"I won't. Besides, I've got plenty of protection up here."

Mendol left, but Xali remained, the image of the woman in her sketch and the sound of her voice too prominent in her head to ignore. She traced the features, wondering how she knew this was the woman. Why she felt so connected to her. Who was she, and what did she have to do with the immortals?

Xali's eyes drifted back out to the forests beyond, untamed, un-explored. She felt drawn to it, always had just as she felt drawn to the woman. Were the two connected? Something deep within her told her they were and that her own life was now intertwined with them. A shiver passed through her, a confirmation that all she knew was about to fracture just as the glass in the ballroom had.

Xali stepped into the hall of doorways. When the great king had taken the lands back, he'd created a doorway to the holy land that sat on the edge of what was known as Old Tenebron, that land now broken into the Bortees and Nobesn provinces. When his sons were born and the land divided, he'd then created a doorway so that they could easily pass to one another's provinces. He'd passed that knowledge to them, and they'd created doorways to the new provinces when the land was split one last time. The magic to create such a doorway had died with them; they had chosen not to pass on the knowledge, and since then, no one had mastered or even come close to mastering the ability. Within each castle sat four doorways connecting each province to one another and to the holy land. They were like glowing ovals that shimmered with sparks of gray and black.

As a child she'd been fascinated with them, sitting in the chamber staring into them, her eyes mesmerized by the magic and the flickering lights within. There were moments when random sparks of red would flicker through the constant gray and black, and she often wondered what the colors meant. When she'd finally been allowed to use the doorways alone, she had jumped through each so many times that her father had forbidden her to use them again until she was older. There was a feel to passing through them that exhilarated her. A warmth mixed with a feeling she couldn't name that traveled down her spine to her toes and left her craving more.

She stepped through the doorway to the holy land, closing her eyes as that familiar feeling washed over her.

Xaliandri.

The light of the sun burned behind her closed eyes as she stepped from the doorway. Squinting against it, she turned back to the doorway. She'd heard her name as clear as if someone had been there with her, yet no one emerged. Flickers of green flitted through the dark space, but there was nothing more there. Green…a new color to the doorways.

"You're losing your mind, Xali," she mumbled to herself, turning back to the holy land. She removed her slippers and let the sand slide through her toes as she walked. The holy land was completely different from the provinces. It had always seemed to her as if someone had picked it up from another place and dropped it on the shore of Old Tenebron. There was no other place in their world like it.

No vegetation grew. Instead, sand layered the land, the sun burning down upon it, causing heat to rise from below. Even in the cold seasons, it remained as if cursed to stay in this state. The lands had been home to their people before the great king had freed them from the binds of the immortals. He had erected a shrine to the gods after their victory and here it remained, the entrance to the land heavily guarded so that only royalty could visit, something she had always thought strange. Why build a shrine to the gods that the people could not access?

When she reached the shrine, she kneeled, sending her prayers to the gods, knowing they would be watching, expecting it from her. As always, however, her mind wandered past them, never truly feeling at one with them as the others did, her heart never fully into the prayers, a disconnect resonating.

She stepped onto the smooth stone floor, the shade from the rafters above providing relief from the sun's heat. It was a simple space, the sun shining through in streams between the wooden planks above, the wind rustling the white strands of silk that hung loosely down the side of them.

There were no statues of the gods; there had never been an instance where they had shown themselves to her people. However, the great king had insisted an etching be carved into the back of the shrine, likenesses of what he imagined them to be. She traced her fingers over the etchings, eight strong, intimidating males. As her fingers followed the jawline of the final one, a soft breeze pushed whisps of hair that had freed from her braid, tickling them against her face. She brought her hand away and moved the strands back, the breeze dancing along her fingers. She laughed, the feel of it familiar as it had been the night of her dream. Soft, feminine.

Her eyes moved back to the gods. Why were there no women? She tilted her head, studying them with what felt like freshly opened eyes. Who were these men? Imaginings from a long dead king's mind. That was really all they were.

Touched by the Fates, Sianna had said.

The breeze touched her skin in answer, as if confirming her thought.

"But that can't be. The Fates were heathen gods, fallen gods the lesser kind worshipped created by the immortals because they feared the true gods," she whispered.

The breeze stopped, and everything around her seemed to freeze before a wind whipped through the space, the silk hangings slapping at her skin, the rafters shaking, sand blasting her like pebbles. It was like a force of anger.

"Stop!" she screamed, and everything froze. The hangings stilled in midair, the sand in stasis all around her.

"Xali?" Carnick's voice called.

She turned to see him standing at the entrance, mouth agape at the frozen world around her. As she met his eyes, the sand fell, the hangings fluttering back to their original place.

He stared at her. "Please tell me that wasn't a lesser power you just wielded?"

She swallowed. The powers of the immortals were considered lesser powers, only the powers of their ruling family were considered dominant, and no one in their family was cursed with lesser powers.

Except Xali.

Three

They started a few years ago."

Xali had settled next to Carnick on a short wall leading into the shrine after his initial shock had worn off.

"Strange things like moving the water in the pond outside the castle, flowers tilting in my direction. Nothing noticeable until I got mad at Mendol, and storm clouds rose above us. I began watching the sky when my moods shifted, and it seemed to change with it."

Concern filled his eyes. "The snow storms?"

"I don't know, but I've been so anxious and out of sorts that I can't say for certain."

He pulled his eyes away and stared off.

"Carnick?"

"Does anyone else know?"

"I think Mendol suspects, but he hasn't said anything."

"Xali, you know they could have you killed for this?" Worry layered his voice.

The thought was horrifying. "My father—"

"Would have to follow tradition, law. Any reference to the heathen gods and the immortals…"

His eyes glanced toward the sky where the sun was now covered by rain clouds.

"You won't tell them, Carnick, will you?"

Her heart was racing, and her hold on her emotions slipped, a tear escaping. He held his hand out as a raindrop fell.

"Gods, Xali."

She wiped the tear away and pushed the fear back, the droplets of rain ceasing with the action.

"Is this why you bury yourself in sword practice and fighting skills? To hide this?"

"I don't know. I don't know what's going on or why any of this is happening to me."

He sat back down next to her, his eyes still filled with worry. He took his hand and fingered a loose strand of her hair, its slight curl evident.

"That's new," he said with a smile.

She laughed. "I'm a mess."

"Nothing we didn't already know."

"What will you do, Carnick?"

He sighed, and in that moment, he looked vulnerable, something she never saw in him.

"Xali, you are my betrothed—"

"A broken betrothed."

"A beautiful, strong, intelligent, independent, broken betrothed."

She laughed again.

"I knew you were a handful the moment I saw you, and as you've grown, you've continued to challenge everything we are, everything our family has always been."

"This isn't sounding good, Carnick."

"I'm not as smooth with words as your brother is. What I'm trying to say is that you're different from the other cousins, from all of us, and that's what makes you special. And it's why I love you, Xali." He took her hand. "Your secret is our secret."

"But, Carnick, your throne—"

"Is not in jeopardy. My mother would never let that happen. Now, do you have any more surprises I should know about?"

She thought about her dream but decided it was best to keep that to herself.

Smiling, she answered, "No."

"Then, why don't you come spend the day with me."

"I would like that."

She leaned up and kissed him, her heart swelling. They had been betrothed by the hands of others, but her heart had grown to love him as much more than her cousin.

"Carnick," she said, drawing away.

"Mmmm," he replied, pulling her back.

"Why are you here?"

He stopped and sighed. "You certainly could give me more than that one kiss, Xali, after all this time."

"You know the rules, Carnick."

"Rules that make no sense if you ask me."

His hand gently slid down her arm, and she could sense the longing.

He was right, the rules made no sense, a second born had to remain chaste, pure as a temple until the first born took her or him on the day of their joining. First borns were under no such constraints, and she knew Carnick enjoyed the flesh of others while he waited for her. It should have bothered her, but it didn't; the only thing that did bother her was that she did not enjoy the same freedom as he because of her birth rank.

"True, but we still must follow them. Besides, you have enough bedmates to keep you occupied."

"None of them are you," he replied, his gray eyes meeting hers. She was surprised by the honesty in his voice.

Giving him a half smile, she said, "It won't be long. And in the meantime, you can answer my question. Why are you here? It's not often I hear that you've visited the holy land when it's not a worship day."

He shrugged. "I don't know to be honest. I just had this feeling that I needed to come here. And so, I did."

It was a strange reply, and she wasn't sure how to respond.

"I suppose it's good since you were hiding a secret from me."

"One you swear on the gods you won't share."

He laughed. "I promise. The last thing I want is for my betrothed to be killed before I can be joined with her. Now, tell me why you're out here."

"I don't know." She looked back toward the temple, that feeling that it wasn't right gnawing at her again. "I…" she hesitated, not sure if this would push things too fast. "Did you ever wonder what made the heathen gods different than ours?"

He looked startled by her question. "Good gods, Xali, you really need to be careful."

She looked back at him. "Something doesn't feel right anymore. It's…it's as if I've awoken, and no one else has, so no one sees the things I see."

"You never see things the way others do, Xali, that's what makes you special and dangerous. You need to stop questioning, or you will be the first of our family to be sentenced to death for blasphemous crimes."

"And you will steal away another cousin to fill your bed?"

"There are no other second-born females, other than my sister, and as for the first borns, neither Sartria nor Ainia are my type."

She laughed.

"I'm serious, Xali. Don't let any of the elders hear you. I wouldn't even let the cousins hear those words. I don't want another to rule beside me. I only want you."

She studied his eyes, their gray turning stormy, his magic coming forth like it did any time he was emotional, sparkles of violet filling them.

"I love you, Carnick, but I won't stop asking questions. There's something wrong with our history. Something more to it." His face fell. "But I will be careful and keep my thoughts in check."

His smile returned, and he leaned down and kissed her again. It was gentle, filled with love.

"We should go," he said, dropping his head down to touch hers. "Did you skip lessons today?"

"Mendol covered for me."

"Why does he still attend lessons?"

"He says he loves to learn. I think he gets bored."

"He does love his books and studies, doesn't he?"

They began walking toward the doorways back to the provinces when something caught her eye in the distance. She stopped and studied it.

"What is it, Xali?"

"Did you ever notice that?"

"Notice what? All I see are guards and the shoreline."

She walked toward the shoreline, but he grabbed her arm.

"What are you doing, Xali?"

"Where this land meets the shoreline, the two don't just flow into each other like normal land would."

"Neither does the cliffside above. Why does it make a difference?"

"The cliffside is uniform. The shore is uniform until it meets the holy land."

She started walking again, and he followed. When they finally reached the shore, the guards bowed. This land was protected from all but the royal family and heavily guarded, both below and above the cliffside.

"What is it you're trying to find, Xali?" he whispered.

"This," she said, climbing the ridge that jutted up before the cliff began. "Why is it here?"

"Leave us," Carnick commanded the guards who drew away at his order.

She walked along the ridge then jumped down when it ended further along, her feet wincing at the rocky texture they met. The gentle sand ended at the ridgeline.

"Even the surfaces are different."

"What are you saying? That the land doesn't belong here?"

"Exactly. It's as if it were formed offshore—"

"And forced to connect to this part of the land," he finished.

"Yes."

"Gods, Xali, what has gotten into you?" he asked, rubbing his face.

"You see it, too, don't you, Carnick?"

"Yes," he snapped, "but it doesn't mean anything. It's just your wild imagination drawing me in."

"What lies beyond the temple?"

"Nothing but sand. It's unlivable, which is why the great king waged the war, to free our people from this wasteland where they'd been exiled."

"But if that land was somewhere else then who exiled them?"

"The immortals, Xali."

She looked at him, knowing her eyes were stormy, the same as his now were, the storm clouds floating through his rapidly. "If this land wasn't attached to the land of the immortals, if it were moved here with" she looked down at her hands, "with the power that runs through our blood—"

"Then that would make it an invasion and not a war of emancipation," he said, his tone heavy. "Those are treasonous words, Xali, and ones that could have us both killed. I would leave your thoughts here. Let them be. They'll cause nothing but trouble."

She met his eyes, which were full of concern, then nodded, swallowing back the bile that had filled her mouth. He took her hand.

"Let's go, come spend the day at my palace with me and forget all of this."

She nodded again and walked with him, her mind a whirlwind

as the world fell further from under her feet, the world built on lies that were slowly crumbling.

Their visit to Carnick's realm turned out to be just what Xali had needed. Carnick knew her well enough to know what would help take her mind from her treasonous thoughts. After they arrived, he took her down to the barracks.

"What are we doing here?" she asked, turning her hand over the hilt of a sword.

"We're going to burn off some of that reckless energy you have."

She raised her brow, but he'd walked through to the training grounds. It had been a while since she'd trained here. Carnick's province had the strongest army, his province having the most uprisings. Underground groups that called themselves the Scians, were prone to attack the castle in the name of the immortals, even after all this time. It was always a lost cause, as it was in the other province that sat in Old Tenebron. The people here were rough, stubborn, and even after so many millennia refused to admit their family ruled.

In her province, the lesser Cirillians lived peacefully with their people as it was in her cousin Sartria's province but not in this part of the kingdom.

"Well, well, look who's back to train with us," the captain of the guard said, bowing to her. "It's been a while, your highness."

"It's nice to see you, Captain. And yes, it has been a while."

She'd spent many a warm season here with Carnick, training and honing her skills.

"Let's see if your army is as tough on you as mine is," Carnick said with a wink.

"You mean your mother's?" she replied smartly while drawing her sword.

"Ouch, I hope your sword work is as swift as your tongue, my dear."

She laughed and faced her first opponent, cutting him down swiftly. She continued to defeat each soldier brought forth to fight her. She was a force when she held a sword, the feel of its weight in her hands, the dance of it as it met another sword, the distinct clash of metal to metal playing upon her ears. Something about the steel in her hands reached to her, a connection that funneled through to the ground below, the land strengthening her, urging her on. It was a trance of sorts, one she knew had to do with her magic, but as her magic was so weak, she had no real explanation.

"I can see you've been honing your skills, Princess. Either that or you lot need to work on yours," the captain said, eyeing his weary men.

She heard a sword exit its scabbard to her right and turned to see Carnick approaching her.

"My turn," he said with a wink.

"To have her crush you, sire?"

"Ha, if there's anyone I'd rather have crush me, it's the princess."

"So be it," she said with a smile as she moved her sword into position.

Carnick fought hard, and she wondered if he felt the same connection as she when he held the sword. Eventually, she disarmed him, drawing the tip to his neck. His eyes held hers, never flinching.

"Looks like you've been bested once again, son."

Xali lowered her sword and turned to see her aunt. Bowing, she gave her a warm smile.

"Xaliandri, you are quite something, aren't you? Impressive and I'm sure when you take Carnick's side, you'll be out here doing the captain's job. She defeated you all, did she not?"

There was a bit of awkward foot shuffling, and then the captain replied, "We'd be honored."

"I'm sure she's only as good as she is due to the warm seasons she spent under your instruction, captain."

Xali didn't like that her aunt was talking as if she weren't there, but it came with being a second born.

"Thank you, my queen."

"Now, carry on. Carnick, you and Xaliandri will join us for dinner before she returns home."

"Yes, Mother."

Her aunt walked away, and the power Xali had felt from the sparring faded with her every step as it had with her words. She knew her place, and no matter how many fights she won, her family would always see her as a second born whose power was subpar.

Carnick wrapped a sweaty arm around her and kissed her head.

"Don't let them bother you, Xali. Your rank means nothing," he whispered.

"It means everything."

"Only to them. Not to me."

She peeked up at him and curled her nose. "You need a bath."

He laughed. "As do you, my dear. Would you like to join me?"

She elbowed him and walked away.

"I'll use your sister's bath."

"Suit yourself, but mine's more exciting."

He ran off, leaving her to her thoughts. She knew her way around, as she did in every palace. As children, the cousins had spent much time together to fortify their bonds and allegiances to one another. They had been sent away to the other provinces for moons at a time to understand the differences between each province and their people.

Carnick's sister Fairenth helped her find clean clothes and let her bathe. Having been betrothed to Mendol, Fairenth and Xali were very close. She was also another second born, a bond that brought all the second born cousins closer, all knowing the lesser value they held in their family's eyes.

"What have you done to your hair, Xali?" Fairenth asked as she helped Xali with the dress's bindings.

"I've found it has a mind of its own of late. Please don't focus upon it or say anything," she said, trying to tame the wildness. She wondered if her aunt had noticed earlier. If so, she hadn't said anything. Would she have though? Perhaps not in front of the guards. Xali had no doubt that if she had, it would be a topic of heated discussion with her father shortly.

Sighing, she gave Fairenth a look that asked if she'd succeeded in making herself presentable. Fairenth shrugged then headed out of the room.

Dinner dragged as Xali made small talk with her aunt and uncle, her mind on the holy land the entire time. Although she'd fixed the loose strands of her hair, she still felt their eyes on it. Relief only came when they were finally excused, and her aunt told Carnick to see her to the doorways so she could return home.

As she and Carnick stood before the doorway that led back to her palace, he lifted her chin.

"Promise me you'll stop dwelling on this, Xali," he said. "It will only bring harm."

"I can't promise you that, Carnick. Can you truly say you're not curious now? That you don't want to know the truth?"

"It's not that simple, Xali. It's easy for you to question the truth, to buck the rules."

"Because I'm a second born," she said sourly.

"No, because it's in your nature. But as a first born, there is no place for me to do so. You have more freedom."

"Do I? You saw how your mother looked at me tonight. She saw the curls. She already thinks less of me because of my weak magic."

"Stop. My mother adores you; you know that." He sighed and moved his fingers through her hair, loosening her braid until her hair fell free. Then he let his fingers drift through it. "I wish you saw yourself the way I see you, Xali. There is nothing weak or less about you. There is only you."

He leaned down to kiss her head, and she closed her eyes to his touch.

"Go before your father worries that I've stolen you away."

She tilted her head and kissed him, letting her lips linger before she turned to leave.

"Promise me, Xali," he said as she stepped away. Turning back, she could read the worry in his eyes.

"I can't, Carnick," she replied before quickly going through the doorway.

She went straight to her room when she returned. The feel of Carnick's lips on hers remained as did her thoughts. Dropping to her bed, she stared at the blank ceiling.

What did any of it mean and what should she do with it? Nothing, Carnick would tell her. Mendol would say the same if she told him what she'd discovered. What had she discovered, really, and was there anything to substantiate it?

The stories weren't true; the great king hadn't reclaimed the land for his people. He'd invaded the land and used his magic to move the wasteland his people had lived on to become part of this kingdom. A kingdom stolen from the immortals. Was everything a lie? Were the immortals really the savage killers she'd been taught they were?

It was all too much, the thought that everything her life had been built upon might be false. Her eyes closed, and soon she drifted to sleep.

Xali, a voice called to her, the same voice from her dream. She opened her eyes and looked around. The room had grown dark.

Xaliandri, she heard again.

Rising, she walked to her balcony where the darkness continued, the moons obscured by some force. A breeze touched her, then everything seemed to fall away. She was in a forest, the black of night making it hard to get her bearings. She walked, seeking a way out. With each step, she felt her breath shorten, her chest tighten as if she couldn't breathe. The pressure sat within her even as she noticed a light through the forest's edge.

Stumbling, she followed it. As the pressure continued to build, she wanted to clear her chest to let the air in, but then her eyes noticed the source of the light. A shade of billowing white floated over a pile of rubble. Xali forgot about her inability to breathe, intrigued by the beautiful creature. It was the woman from her sketch. Her hair flowed in loose curls that met the billowing pieces of her dress. Her face was breathtaking as if she were one of the gods themselves. There was a kindness to her eyes and a slight shimmer of green. She was a glorious sight.

Xaliandri, her voice called in Xali's head.

Xali stepped forward in a peaceful trance.

Find me…listen to your magic, Xali. Own it, let it guide you.

"Who are you?"

You know the answer to that question, she said.

Before Xali could say more, the tightness increased in her chest, and the woman faded. Darkness surrounded her, but the pressure remained. Closing her eyes to the discomfort, she realized it was something deep inside of her, strangling her from the inside. Her eyes flew open as she brought her hands up to her neck, the pressure now filled with a burning from deep in the center of her stomach. Rays of green and black seemed to break through her skin, the same feeling inside her forcing her to give up, to give herself over to the need to pass out, to sleep. Finally, she succumbed, collapsing to the rubble below—the last thing her eyes saw was a chink of stone with the letters *Vi* on it.

Xali woke, gasping, her hands still around her neck.

"Xali!" Mendol broke through her door, his hands up ready to attack with his magic.

She was in her room, still on her bed. Dropping her hands, she coughed as her lungs tried to replace the air she'd lost.

"Are you all right?" he asked, coming to sit on the bed beside her. "You were screaming. Gods, Xali, your neck, you've scratched it raw."

Her body was still shaking as she continued to cough. When she could finally breathe, she stared at her lap.

"What is that?" Mendol asked.

Her fingers touched the shards of black and emerald that now lay on her lap. She had coughed them up.

"My power," she said hoarsely, the realization setting in.

"Xali?"

She met Mendol's eyes. "Can you get Carnick for me?"

"It's late, Xali. He'll be asleep by now."

"No, he won't." She heard.

Xali turned and found Carnick at the entrance to her room. He looked like she'd never seen him before, disheveled and frightened.

"What's going on?" she asked. "Why are you here, Carnick?"

Carnick closed the door. "I saw you in my dream, Xali." His eyes surveyed her throat. "Gods, it wasn't a dream, was it?"

"I don't know what it was."

"Would someone mind filling me in here?" Mendol asked, confused.

"I had a dream, and Xali was there. I don't know how, but it felt…it felt so real. I watched her, and I was helpless, something inside of me was…was taking hold, restraining me from helping her. I couldn't move, couldn't use my powers. She was choking on something, and then she fell as if she'd died."

"Did you feel it, Carnick?" Xali asked, exasperated. "The inability to breathe?"

"Yes, as if I would take my last breath, but I couldn't until I saw you collapse then something inside of me gave over to it, and I woke."

"Did you see her?"

"Who?"

"The shade. She was…glorious," her voice sounded gravely as she spoke.

"No, there was no one there but you."

"You two have me very confused," Mendol said, shaking his head. "I'll let you talk it out."

"No," she said, grabbing Mendol's hand. "I think you need to know."

"Xali, we don't know that this means anything," Carnick argued.

She picked up the shards from her dress and watched as they disintegrated from her touch, a black and green mist floating away.

"Those are remains of my power."

"That's ridiculous," Mendol said. "Our power does not reflect as black or green—it has a gray hue."

"Yours does but you know the truth about mine, Mendol."

"No, I don't and neither do you," he said defiantly.

"I know as well, Mendol," Carnick said.

Mendol's eyes grew concerned. He stood and drew closer to Carnick. Two future kings, she saw their power in that moment and noticed Carnick's aura was stronger.

"You won't report her, Carnick," Mendol said, fear edging his voice. "You know what they'll do to her."

"Of course, I won't, Mendol. I'm hurt that you would doubt my allegiance to your sister."

"Does your allegiance to family run deeper?"

"She is family, and her secret is safe with me." Turning to Xali, he asked, "Why do you think that stuff was your magic?"

"Because it was choking me. The immortals suffocated from the inside out. I think the great king killed them with their own magic."

"Why does that matter, Xali?" Mendol asked. "As disturbing as it sounds, he was killing his enemy."

"Because Xali doesn't think they were his enemy," Carnick said, meeting her eyes, "and neither do I."

"That's madness." Incredulity filled Mendol's voice. "That's treasonous."

"We invaded their land, Mendol," Xali said. "They never banished our people. They were innocent, and he murdered them, then stole their kingdom."

He stared at her. "Xali, they'll have you killed if anyone ever hears you say that. What proof do you have to support this insane theory?"

"Not anything substantial," Carnick answered for her. "Which is why I've asked her to keep quiet about it."

Mendol ran his hand down his face and sighed.

"You don't believe me," Xali whispered.

"I don't know what to believe. What you're suggesting rewrites everything we've ever known. It undoes our entire history and suggests that our kingdom was built on lies. If what you're saying is true, then we have destroyed a culture, a people…I don't know what to think right now." He walked to the door. "I suggest you go back to sleep and in the morn forget everything you've just said."

"Can you forget, cousin? I know I couldn't," Carnick said.

"I don't think we have a choice." Mendol walked out, the door softly closing behind him, Xali's heart dropping as it did.

She drew her eyes from the door and let them meet Carnick's. Once again, his were fraught with worry.

"What's going on with me, Carnick?"

He sat down on the bed beside her, drawing her into his arms. It felt safe there, as if none of the madness of her mind could get to her. He kissed her hair.

"I think it's more a matter of what's going on with us, Xali. I'm now drawn into this as much as you." He went silent for a moment. "When I saw you there, in my dream, your hair was a beautiful shade of gold with the moonbeams upon it. I was mesmerized, but then that turned to terror as you began to choke. Xali, I couldn't get to you, couldn't save you from whatever was harming you, and it tore me to pieces. Watching you collapse, it felt as if my entire existence had collapsed with you. I never realized my feelings were so deep until now. It was almost as if I weren't myself."

Lifting her head, she searched his gray eyes, the tiny sparkles of violet that once lie there were now replaced by black.

"We were both living their memories, Carnick." She pulled back as the reality of her words hit her. "We don't know anything about them. What if some of them were in love? Joined even."

"That would make some women. We've always been told they were men."

"No, the voice, the shade…she's female, and I think what you experienced was what her lover experienced."

He ran his hands through his hair. "Now you do sound mad, Xali."

"But you said yourself the feelings you felt for me were deeper than what you've ever known."

"Can't that simply mean I'm more in love with you than I realized?"

She smiled.

"I like that thought, and I'm sticking to it," he continued. "I was not persuaded by some long dead spirit of an immortal. That's wrong on so many levels."

"You were," she started to argue.

"That's enough, Xali. Now, I need to go. If your parents find me in here, it will be a scandal."

He rose, but she caught his hand.

"Stay with me, Carnick. I'm—"she hesitated, hating to admit any weakness,"—I'm afraid I'll have another dream."

He turned back to her. "It's against tradition."

"I seem quite good at going against tradition."

Laughing, he said, "That you are." He drew her into his arms. "You do know a night with you will be quite torturous." His hand drifted through her hair then his brow furrowed as he pulled one curl out, letting his finger drift along it.

She glanced at it, her breath catching. It was a bright golden, standing out against the silver of her locks.

"Yes," Carnick said, "I think it might be best if I stay."

Four

Xali woke the next morning to find Carnick gone, likely having snuck off in the early hours to avoid being found. She'd stayed in his arms until she'd drifted off, the feel of his presence easing her fears of another dream.

When she rose, she found no sign of her parents, her brother likely avoiding her. She tried to occupy her mind with some early sword practice until it was time for lessons. Even for lessons, Mendol didn't join her, and so she listened to Proctor Chenon drone on about the history of their people, knowing all the while it was a lie.

"Xaliandri!"

She jerked from her thoughts as he slammed his hand down.

"I know this part of lessons is boring, that you'd rather be out training your muscles or working on your magic, but our history is important. It's the foundation of our traditions and everything we stand for today."

"What history is there prior to the king?"

He looked befuddled for a moment. "The great king ruled ten thousand years ago. Is that not far enough back for you?"

"I'm curious as to how our people came to be enslaved. What was life like back then? How did we live?"

"I don't…there's…." He scratched his head then sighed. "You are a perplexing girl. I have no history before then. There is no written text and nothing that goes back that far."

"Huh. Strange," she replied, her mind putting more pieces together. "Then I'll be off to train my other muscles as you said. There's nothing more I need to learn here."

She walked out, leaving him staring at her with that baffled look. She knew why there was no history before the great king, she just had no way of proving that he'd erased it all. Stopping in the walk-through of the gardens, she looked down at her hands. She did need to train her powers, but ever since her magic had begun to change, she'd preferred to train by herself, far from the eyes of others.

She flexed her hands, noting how the blooms in the garden had turned in her direction as if reaching for her. Guiltily, she rubbed her palms on her legs, hoping they would turn away.

"Xali!" her brother called from the other end of the breezeway, causing her to jump. His eyes moved to the garden, and he hurriedly rushed to her, grabbing her arm and pulling her away from the flowers.

"Ouch, Mendol you're hurting me."

He pushed her against the wall, looking around suspiciously.

"Are you trying to get caught? What has gotten into you, Xali? This is not a game. You can't—"

"I didn't do anything, Mendol. It happens without my control. I can't make it stop."

"Well, you'd better find a way. I can't always protect you and neither can Carnick, even if he thinks he can. Let's go. Father has summoned you. He and Mother want to see you now."

Fear rushed through her. "They don't know, do they?"

"No, I don't believe so. It's something else."

She followed him silently to the throne room, which she found odd since it was such a formal place. Whatever it was they wanted to discuss with her had to be serious for them to call her here.

She walked in and gave a slight bow. Her father was seated on his throne, her mother next to him. Fear rippled through her; perhaps Mendol was wrong. This was the place her father sentenced people to death. It was a room for judgments.

"Xaliandri, come," he said, urging her forward.

"Father, Mother."

"Your mother and I have just returned from a morning in Bortees." That was Carnick's province. Gods had they found out he'd spent the evening with her? That would be the easier of her indiscretions to bear.

"I had a long discussion with my cousin, and it has been decided that given your recent *changes*—" The word was said with some hesitation.

"Changes?" she interrupted.

He gave her an irritated look. "The wave in your hair and this penchant you've gained of questioning your proctor."

So, the man had squealed on her about her questions regarding the immortals.

"In light of that, the decision has been made to join you with Carnick earlier than planned."

The floor seemed to fall below her feet, and she felt her knees weaken. "You can't do that—"

"It has been done. You will join when your brother joins with Fairenth."

"But that's in two moons. That's too soon. It goes against tradition."

Her father stood, his eyes turning stormy, the floor shaking.

"Everything about you goes against tradition, Xaliandri!" he boomed. "The decision has been made."

He turned and walked from the throne room.

Xali turned toward Mendol, but he dropped his head and left the room.

"Xaliandri," her mother said softly. She'd moved closer and now stood before Xali.

"Your father had a hard time with this decision, but we all feel it's for the best."

"The best for whom?"

"Do you not love Carnick?"

"Of course, I do."

"Then you should be happy to be joined with him."

"But it's too soon."

"Xali, your joining was always due to be early, your birth being so long after Carnick's. It already broke tradition."

"But…I'm not ready, Mother."

Her mother's eyes softened. "Oh, my sweet girl." She moved Xali's hair back from her shoulder, her eyes looking startled for a moment as she fingered a strand from below. The golden strand. Then they filled with sadness. "It is for the best, Xali. Carnick will be good to you."

She pushed the strand under the rest of her hair then met her eyes. "You are special, Xaliandri, different from the rest of us. But I fear those differences will mark you."

"They already have," Xali said.

She walked away, leaving her mother in the middle of the throne room, knowing there was nothing more to say.

Xali stormed through the halls, searching for Mendol until she found him entering the room of doorways.

"Mendol!" she yelled.

"I'm going to spend the day with Fairenth. Go occupy yourself,

Xali."

She grabbed his arm and spun him around. "This is your doing. You went to Father, didn't you? You told them."

"Hush," he said, taking her hand and leading her from the doorways out into the corridor. "Do you want someone to hear you?"

"Why does it matter? You've already told Father," she hissed.

"I didn't tell Father."

"It's your fault the joining has been moved. You couldn't keep your mouth shut."

He grabbed her shoulders. "I didn't tell them anything. I didn't move the joining, Xali."

"I did." She heard Carnick from behind them, having come through the doorway while they were arguing.

She looked at him, knowing her eyes held the disappointment she suddenly felt.

"I'll leave you two to talk this out," Mendol said, walking away, the hurt evident in his voice.

"You did this?"

"Yes."

Once again, the stone beneath her feet seemed to crumble.

"You told them?"

"No, now come away from here. There's too much chance someone may hear you."

He took her hand and pulled her through the hall until they came to an empty room. She let him lead her, too shocked to fight. He closed the door and turned to her. They were in a storage room, old furniture and random items gathering dust like a sleeping tomb.

"Xali, listen to me."

She backed away. "No, you told them and then you convinced them to change the joining. So desperate to have me in your bed, Carnick?"

His eyes darkened, black storm clouds filling them.

"I didn't tell them anything. There's already talk with your hair, and there's always been talk with who you are, Xali. And…do you truly think I would do something like that to have you in my bed?" His eyes, still dark, carried the hurt she'd given him.

"Then why else?"

"I did it to protect you, Xali. The sooner we join, the sooner you'll be under my protection. I thought you'd be happy."

"I don't need protection. I can protect myself."

"Can you? With your curious mind and powers that can barely move a stone?"

His words stung.

"You need my protection, Xali. Once we're wed, no one can hurt you. They wouldn't dare take you from me."

"Why? Because I'd be claimed by a first born?"

"Gods, Xali. Why do you have to twist my words around so?"

"Because you moved our joining. You're scared of who I'm becoming."

"I'm scared they'll take you from me, Xaliandri!"

Her anger dissipated slightly, the pain in his eyes too much to ignore.

"Then why didn't you talk to me about it first? Why blindside me?"

"You sound like you don't want to join with me. Are a few moons that hard to give up?"

"I do want to join with you, Carnick, but this should have been our decision not some fear driven one on your end."

His eyes deepened in color, a dark shade of gray that leaned on the edge of black.

"You have no idea what's going on around you, you don't care to look past your own selfish need to disrupt the norm. They've always watched you, always suspected that you might be a problem, might be one to disturb the traditions of this family. Your birth marked you, ten full years after Mendol's, ten years after mine, and under those massive green colored moons. I remember the talk, Xali, and the only reason the others didn't snatch you from your mother's breast is because I pleaded for your life. I've always protected you, Xali, but this time, if you refuse me, you'll go too far for even me to save."

"Maybe I don't need saving." She heard her voice crack. "Maybe you assume I need your protection when I never have." Her heart was wrenching as she said the words.

His face dropped, and he lowered his head before turning and walking from the room.

She stood there, not understanding what had happened but feeling as if it were something that couldn't be repaired. She dropped to the floor, the crushing emotions overcoming the strength in her legs. The damn broke, and the tears flowed, full of hurt, regret, and fear.

Five

Days went by, and Xali avoided her family, and Carnick avoided her. She spent most of her time sequestered in her room or losing her thoughts to the moves of her sword. Other times, she escaped to the solace of the guardian wall, her eyes staring off into the forests below, her hand sketching what her eyes could not see.

She'd come to the wall earlier that day and remained, her mind drifting. She'd dreamt of the woman's voice again the prior eve. It haunted her, as if it were calling her for something. This time the dream was filled with a sense of loss, a sadness that was palpable, a heartache that couldn't be fixed. When she'd woken, her pillow had been soaked with her tears. The dream had shaken her. She'd wondered at first if her feelings about the fight with Carnick had influenced it but then decided that was not the case. This emotion was deeper than any she'd ever felt, painful as if her heart had been torn to pieces. The feeling was too extreme to have been a reaction to Carnick. She loved him, but this was something else, something older, something indescribable.

"You know, Father will have your head if he ever finds you up here," she heard Mendol say as he sat down next to her. She'd been so lost in thought she hadn't heard him.

"Put it on my list of indiscretions."

"It's a growing one, isn't it?"

Xali remained silent.

"Are you going to avoid us until the joining?"

"Perhaps."

"I agree with Carnick, Xali." When she didn't respond, he continued, "The joining will protect you."

"I can protect myself."

"Not against our aunts and uncles, or even the cousins for that matter. Your magic is too weak, and swords hold nothing against them, you know that."

"I have this new magic—"

"Unpredictable, lesser magic. The immortals lost the battle for a reason, Xali. If you do have any of their lesser magic, it will not help you."

"Father—"

"Can't protect you if his cousins rise against you. If you're joined, then Carnick, Fairenth, and his parents will be obliged to stand with you. Then you have the protection of two houses."

She sighed. "I hate this…all of it. The politics of our family, this second born status"—she looked down at her hands—"being so different."

He drew her in to lean against his shoulder and kissed her head.

"That, little sister, is what makes you…well, you. I wouldn't want you any other way."

She peeked up at him. "Really? You wouldn't prefer me out of trouble and minding my curiosity?"

"Ha! I can't imagine you any other way."

They stayed like that for a time until Xali, her mind weighing heavily on recent events whispered, "What if all we are is nothing but a string of lies? What if none of it is true, Mendol, and this kingdom is a kingdom of lies? One our ancestor severed?"

"Then," he pulled away and looked at her, his eyes serious, "we need to pray to the gods that the string doesn't unravel."

"And if it does?"

"We lose everything that we are."

Xali made her way through the empty halls toward the dining room where she knew she'd find Carnick along with her aunt and uncle, and likely Fairenth since she wasn't with Mendol. She'd had Sianna put her hair up in the traditional style of their people. If the servant had noticed Xali's newly colored strand, she'd made no mention of it.

With her hair piled atop her head in ribbons and braids, she'd selected a traditional day gown, setting her typical attire of pantlings aside. The wispy material of the dress swished along the floor as she walked. Entering the room, she noted the shocked expression and sheer look of adoration that overtook Carnick's face as his eyes took her in.

"Xaliandri," her aunt said, resting her fork as Carnick stood to greet her. Xali raised a hand to stay him. She knew it went against her status as a second born to command a first born, but she needed to speak first, and as she'd been breaking so many rules, what was one more.

"Aunt Renia, Uncle," she started, using only her aunt's name as tradition dictated. Only the king or queen, the first born, was recognized. "I have come to apologize for my misconduct. You kindly agreed to move my joining with Carnick forward, and I foolishly disagreed with the decision. I regret that. Please accept my humble apologies and know that after much thought, I find that your wisdom is true as usual. I am blessed to have such a loving family to guide me."

She'd practiced the lines repeatedly, deciding after her talk with Mendol the prior day that the best choice for her was to stay in line and ignore her instincts until after the joining.

"Well, niece, I'm glad you've been swayed. It is not often we break tradition, and it seems each step in your journey to take your position at my son's side has tested that tradition," her aunt said.

Xali felt the sting in her words; they were as sharp as the steel eyes that stared back at her.

She nodded then bowed before turning to leave.

"Xali," Carnick said quickly. "Let me escort you back to the doorways."

He jumped from his seat and was by her side before she could refuse his offer. Silently, they walked from the room until they had moved past the main hall, and Carnick pulled her aside.

"What are you doing, Xali?" he asked, his fingers reaching to touch her caged hair.

"Playing my part. You were right. I need to stop tearing at the seams of my existence. I need to know my place."

"That is not the, Xali, I know."

"But it's the one you want."

His eyes turned a shade darker, storm clouds forming in them. She couldn't shake the feeling that their color was richer than before.

"I never said I wanted you to change. I want you safe."

"Which means I stop questioning and take my position by your side."

"Those are my mother's words; they are not, nor have they ever been mine. When will you realize that I love you because of who you are, Xali, what makes you different, not who you're expected to be?"

She chose to stay silent, knowing her face was pouty.

"I only moved the joining to help, Xali. I didn't realize you'd take it so hard."

That same hurt that had shown when they'd last spoken reflected in his eyes. Sighing, she brought her hand up to his face, feeling the strength below the slight growth of facial hair that had accumulated since she'd last seen him.

"I wasn't angry about the joining, Carnick. I was angry because you didn't discuss it with me first..." She paused, knowing her position gave her no right to say such a thing. "I'm angry that you and everyone else can make decisions for me, and I have no say."

"Xali, I would never—"

"I know, but as a first born, you can. Whether your intentions are admirable or not makes no difference. As a second born, I bear the weight of any decision you make for me."

His eyes, softer now, searched hers, his hand coming up to pull the ribbon holding her hair in place, sending her curls and braids tumbling.

"Tradition dictates we follow those norms, that I stand before you, that I make the rules, and that you obey. But I promise you, Xali, I will not let it dictate us or how I treat you when we are finally joined."

"But it will. When you finally take the throne, your position will be weakened if you do anything other than treat me as a second born."

He pulled her into his arms. "Damn them and their norms. You will rule by my side, Xali, and together, we will find the truth. Together, we will change history."

"No matter the price it extracts?"

He placed both hands on her face and said, "No matter the price," before kissing her passionately.

Later that evening, Xali sat quietly on the floor of her balcony, her back against the cold stone of the palace wall. She knew Carnick meant well, that at this point he believed everything he'd said, but she knew the truth, understood the politics of their family. Their rule was strict, their laws enforced, punishment swift. They were the higher borns of their people, the only ones gifted by the gods to rule. Their reign was inevitable and eternal. The great king had slayed the immortals, a feat that made his heirs terrifying to the people of these lands and worshipped by the people he'd freed.

But he didn't free them, her mind whispered. She forced the thought away. She couldn't afford to let her mind wander, couldn't let it redirect her path. She had to stay focused on the future, being joined with Carnick and eventually sitting by his side as queen.

Sighing, she let her head rest against the wall, her eyes staring out at the sky. Eventually, her eyes bound to the heaviness of their lids, and she succumbed to sleep's spell. She dreamed again, but this time her dream was fragmented. There were flickers of fabric, golden strands of hair, and the scent of lilac. Then, eyes as black as the vast emptiness that surrounded her, and a feeling that her heart would burst. The eyes faded, and panic filled her, flashes of color, blue, green, gray, black bombarding her sight while her panic grew. There was a moment when her eyes met another's in the distant smoke. These eyes were a striking violet, beautiful yet terrifying with their sheer power. Her heart filled again, but the violet faded, and pain tore at her heart. A field of mist and smoke lay before her as she felt the paralyzing suffocation once more and a sense of confusion.

How? The question floated through her consciousness.

Xaliandri, her name floated through the silence.

She looked around for the voice, the suffocation clearing, her breathing normal again. The mist lightened, and she found herself in a forest. There was something ancient about it, something magical. The gray of the night lifted, and the colors of the forest came to life. Xali's breath caught in her throat at the sheer beauty of it. The colors were vibrant shades that she'd never before seen. Calm and wonder wrapped around her. She bent to touch a crimson petal, and it reached toward her, climbing its way up her hand then up her arm. She watched as the petals fell but the vinelike roots remained, fading into her skin, leaving an imprint.

Her eyes were drawn away by a shimmering light, and she walked toward it.

You are home, Xaliandri, she heard the female voice whisper.

The woman stood across from her, a shining light of white that stung her eyes.

Claim your seat beside us, claim what is yours. The Fates have chosen you.

She faded, but her final words echoed through the now dark forest. *Find us.*

Xali woke with a start, her heart racing. She drew her legs in tight, her bare feet scraping against something colder than the stone should have been. In the light of the moons, she could see a layer of frost had developed on the floor below her. She stared at it then put her hand out to touch the small snowflakes that were falling.

She swallowed, knowing the flakes weren't natural; they were too close to the end of the cold season now. She was cursed, there was no way for her to turn away from her lesser powers, no way to ignore the calling of the strange woman, no way she could put on a brave face and follow the norms her family expected. The dreams would continue to haunt her, the strange abilities would continue to increase.

Resting her hand against the wall, she stared at the sky, wondering if it were the gods she needed to pray to or something completely unknown to her, the Fates.

Rising the next morning, Xali decided to continue her façade of the perfect second born. Sianna entered the room as she sat staring out to the snow-covered balcony.

"Morning, my Lady. Strange weather, so much snow this close to the warm season."

"Yes, it is, Sianna."

"Will you be needing training clothes today?" she asked, going to the massive wardrobe. Xali thought about the question. Part of her did want to train before lessons, lessons she wanted to avoid but knew she could not.

She shook her head. "No, I don't believe I will today but please find me something comfortable. I believe I may go riding after lessons."

"Yes, my Lady."

Xali played the dream over in her head as she waited for Sianna to bring her clothes. Sianna began going through the motions of helping her dress when she let out a small cry, standing back quickly.

"Fates," she said with a whisper. "You've been marked by the Fates."

"What did you say?" she asked, staring at Sianna who had brought a shaking hand to her mouth. She was staring at Xali's now bare arm.

Xali turned her head, her eyes widening, breath catching as her eyes took in the black lines that now lay on her upper arm, close to her shoulder. She brought her other hand up and traced the vinelike marks that lined her arm. It was as if the flower and vine from her dream had left an imprint.

She met Sianna's eyes.

"What's happening to me?" she whispered softly, feeling the tears build. Knowing the more she changed, the less she would be able to maintain appearances and the closer she came to certain death.

She swallowed the tears back, Sianna's blue eyes warming. "I don't know, but maybe you're meant to travel a different path than you expected." Her eyes carried hope, which Xali felt was strange. There was no hope in her own heart, so why would this girl believe the changes that were occurring were anything but a curse?

"Do not speak of this to anyone. Please, Sianna, I beg of you. They will kill me."

"But you are royalty, you are necessary for your line to continue."

"No, believe me, they would find another way for Carnick's line to continue. I am a second born, and tradition in my family is everything."

Sianna gave a nervous look around the room then stepped closer to Xali.

"Even if the values your family hold are based on falsehoods?"

Xali stared at her, feeling her mouth drop. She could have easily had Sianna put to death for the treasonous comment, but it was the same Xali had thought to herself.

"You shouldn't say such things. I can't protect you if someone hears you."

The girl's eyes, still filled with hope, shimmered with tears.

"I think you should search for answers, Princess. You know where to find them."

She went back to dressing Xali as if nothing had happened, making certain her arm was well covered. Finished, she bowed and moved toward the door.

"Sianna."

She stopped, turning back to Xali.

"Can you help me?"

She smiled. "When you are ready. You still have questions to discover."

She left, and Xali remained with her eyes to the door. Questions to discover. It seemed such a backward statement. One didn't find questions, they found answers.

As Xali went through the motions of the day, she couldn't keep her thoughts from Sianna's words. Her mind tumbled them around, trying to make sense of them.

"Xali, are you listening to me?" she heard her father say. They were supping, and her mind had drifted.

"Sorry, Father."

Her father gave her a stern look before speaking again.

"I said you will go to Licolca, to your cousin Sartria to spend the day within your aunt Katama's house."

"Oh? But I've spent plenty of time with Sartria seeing how their province differs from ours."

"Are you questioning me?"

"No, sir, of course not."

"When your day is over, you will spend the eve with her then journey to Nobesn. Carnick will join you. There is something you need to see in both provinces."

She wanted to question but thought better, knowing she'd only anger him.

"Yes, Father," she answered obediently.

As she looked away, she caught Fairenth's eyes. They glinted mischievously. Xali wondered what she knew. She'd spent the day with Mendol so that Xali had not been able to see her brother at all. She'd wanted to tell him about the dream, show him the marking, but had not been given the chance.

She never did have time alone with Mendol that eve, and early the next morn, she stepped through the doorway to the Licolca province to spend the day with Sartria. She'd slept peacefully, with no dreams to plague her and woken fully rested.

Sartria greeted her as she stepped through the doorway.

"Cousin," she said to Xali, kissing her on the cheek. "So, you've come to spend the day with me. I hear you've been vexing your father, but Mother wouldn't share what you've done this time."

"Done this time? Sartria, you make it seem as if I'm always vexing my father," she answered.

"Aren't you?"

Xali shot her a look, continuing to follow her out of the hall of doorways through the palace.

Sartria's palace was open like Xali's, but more so. Her mother's province sat to the south of Xali's, so even in the cold season, it remained warm. The land here was lush with fields, the few old Cirillian towns left intact, main sources of the food that sustained the province. Crops grew with ease in both provinces that fell within this part of the kingdom, and they were a source of trade with both Carnick's province and their uncle's to the south of his.

"Mother is awaiting your arrival and wishes to break fast with you," her cousin said, calling back Xali's wandering mind. She stopped walking and turned to Xali.

"I hear your joining has been moved forward."

"Yes," she answered, uncertain as to why no secrets could survive her family's quick tongue.

"What is it you've done, cousin? I don't believe tradition has ever been flaunted, and here you've managed to do so twice."

There was something in her voice that led Xali to believe she knew exactly why Xali had been sent to spend the day with her. "I didn't do anything, and I haven't broken tradition twice."

"No, I suppose it's thrice, is it not?"

Xali shot her an annoyed look. It was bad enough being a second born but being the youngest on top of it left her at even more of a disadvantage.

"First, your birth came so tediously late and poor cousin had to wait for you, then they set your joining early, no need to make him wait longer, and now they've moved it up once again? How do you manage to mock the very things that make our family whole?"

Her words stung, and Xali knew that's what she'd been going for. Sartria had always been jealous of her. She'd told her once when Xali was just a child that it was Carnick with whom she'd wanted to be joined but she'd been given Trevant instead; two first borns could never be joined, and that tradition was never broken.

"I don't know why you're so concerned with my joining, Sartria. Not still shamelessly craving my betrothed, are you? If you must know, Carnick requested our joining be early. He finds me too irresistible to wait upon for another season."

She walked past Sartria, knowing her way to the dining room as if this were her own palace.

"Shame he won't be satisfied with you, Xaliandri. He's had so many experienced women in his bed that having a *girl* like you might bring him cause to stray."

She stormed away, but the acidic tone in which she'd said the word *girl* had hit its mark, her words sewing a seed of doubt in Xali just as she'd known they would.

Six

Xali pulled her horse next to Sartria's. They'd gone further south than Xali had ever been. They had passed all the towns and journeyed half the day. She looked around, unsure of where she was then hopped from the horse and joined Sartria who was standing in front of a massive pile of rubble. A wave of familiarity, of something she couldn't quite identify swept through her.

"What is this?"

"This is what your father asked for you to be shown."

"My father asked you to bring me here?"

"Yes, to show you once and for all that there's nothing left of them."

Xali looked curiously at her.

"Are you really asking questions about the immortals, cousin?"

Xali turned back to the rubble. "This has something to do with the immortals?" she said in awe.

"You need to stop, Xali. As much as you annoy me, you are still my little cousin. You have the family in an uproar. You're raising questions that should be left buried with the dead."

"I thought you didn't know why my father had sent me to spend the day with you?"

"Of course, I did, but that doesn't mean I couldn't taunt you about it. I'm serious, Xali, you can't go poking around at our history. This is dangerous. Mother was furious when she told me."

"Why? Why the reaction to me questioning?"

"Because you ask questions that none of us should ask. We are given our history, and nothing differs from what we are told the great king did."

Xali looked at her for a moment. She was being groomed for the throne, just as Carnick was. How much did she know? More than she should?

"You've been there, haven't you? Beyond the guardian wall?" Xali asked, turning away and making her way into the rubble. She knew it was the right of each rising king or queen to be taken beyond the guardian wall to understand why it needed to be protected. Satria was the oldest of the cousins, her mother closest to stepping down. Had she shared the secret of the crown with her early?

"That is not what we're discussing."

"But you have. Even though you're not taking the throne yet, you've been there."

She hesitated for a moment before answering. "Yes."

"Tell me what's there. Why such secrecy?"

"It is not for you to know, Xali. Only the first borns are privy to it and for good reason. There is nothing there that you seek. Only ghosts."

"Ghosts don't always stay silent," she answered. "Sartria, why are we here? What importance does this rubble have? What lesson am I supposed to learn here?"

"These are the remnants of an immortal castle."

That surprised Xali, and she looked back at the rubble, only now seeing how extensive it was, how parts jutted up as if a wall or support had existed there at one time. Tiny fragments of shape lie throughout the field of stone, one that had once housed an elusive immortal.

"They lived here?" she mumbled as she walked further into the devastation.

"They are gone, Xali. Leave the past where it is and stop stirring up the dust that remains."

"Why? What do they not want me to know? Do you even know why we shouldn't question? Do you know anything more than I do about the immortals?"

"The immortals are gone, Xali. Whatever it is they don't want you to know doesn't matter. What matters is that our reign continue."

"The strength of the family always comes first." She repeated the words that had been ingrained in her from the time she could first remember. "What does it come before? At what cost?"

Knowing she would be given no answer, Xali walked back to her horse and pulled her drawing pages from her satchel.

"I'd like to stay and sketch for a while. Would you like to stay with me?"

"I don't think that was the point of this."

"No, I'm sure it wasn't."

"What is it you're expecting to find with your questions, Xali?"

"The truth."

"The truth is that the immortals have been dead for thousands of years and for reasons that we all know. The great king defeated them to free our people."

"Don't you ever question that story?" she braved.

"No."

"You should. Open your eyes, Sartria. How did one man, a mortal man with an army of mortals defeat multiple immortals?"

"We don't know how many—"

"No, we know nothing about them. Why is that? And even one immortal would have been a difficult victory."

"You question too much, cousin."

"And the rest of you don't question enough."

Sartria sighed. "Gods, I pray Carnick can marry you before your questions become a liability."

"And why would that be?" Xali asked, glad her cousin was finally opening up and hoping it would continue.

"There's already unrest in the Nobesn province. If people knew that one of us was talking like this, it would raise their own questions. That unrest could grow, and that's a problem."

"Is that you talking or your mother?"

"I love you, cousin, even if you are a thorn in my comfortable backside, but I won't be able to save you, none of us will." She climbed back on the horse. "You know your way back?"

Xali knew she'd be fine; she had an impressive sense of direction and a memory of land and paths that rivaled anyone's.

She nodded.

"Good. I don't like being down here, there's something unsettling about it. Be back by dark, the lesser folk from Uncle's province sometimes roam this area and with your weak powers, you might not be safe."

"So, you're leaving me anyway?"

"I think you'll be fine, Xali. You have a sword. Those were my mother's words not mine," she said with a wink before taking off.

Xali watched as Sartria rode away. They'd always had a relationship that ventured from love to hate. She had no double her cousin loved her, but her words cut at times, especially her comments about Carnick. Even as children, she would needle Xali about him, about how young she was, how he needed someone more experienced like herself, always hinting that she'd warm his bed until he was ready for Xali. She wondered sometimes if she had shared his bed before she and Trevant had been joined. Xali never asked, knowing Carnick had every right as a first born to take who he pleased until the joining. That didn't mean the thought of him with another didn't sting, regardless of how he told her he loved her. She wondered if Trevant knew of his wife's remaining lust for Carnick? Would it have mattered? He was a second born like Xali, given no voice to argue at the impropriety of coveting another's betrothed, especially when you shared a bed with your husband.

Xali pushed the thoughts away then peered over her shoulder toward the woods that sprawled in the distance. She'd forgotten her uncle's province still had a history of violence from their western neighbors. Xali's father kept their borders to Carnick's province fortified so it was no longer a worry for their people or the lesser Cirillians who remained. Sartria's mother, however, did not offer the same courtesy to the lesser ones who lived in her province, letting the violence in, a regular cleansing of sorts. It turned Xali's stomach, but she had no power to stop it. No power to do anything about the mistreatment of the lesser peoples who shared their lands with them.

She scanned the woods beyond, seeing no threat but instinctively touched the point of her sword. Something had told her to bring it and now that she'd been left alone, she was glad she had its company. Turning back to the ruins, she took in the sight before her. They spiraled across the open field, further than one would have thought. The castle that had once stood in its place must have been massive. There had always been a distinction made between the palaces her family resided in and the castles of the immortals, the castles said to have been nowhere near as grand as their palaces. She'd thought it an odd distinction to make. Now looking at the expanse of ruble before her, she saw that perhaps it was simply another twisted lie of the great king.

She placed her sketch paper and coal down, removing her sword in preparation to sit and take in the ruins. Then she stood before deciding to investigate a little first. Cautiously, she walked through the rubble, wondering why her family had left it after so many eons. Why had the great king left it? Their power lay in the elements of the ground, stone could easily be moved or crushed to dust. Why leave a reminder of the ones who had been here before them? Perhaps as a reminder of their strength? A reminder that their family had annihilated the immortals and were not to be questioned?

The further she walked into the rubble, the more excited she became. An immortal had lived here, had stood where she was standing. Possibly more than one, the images from her dreams clouded her mind. No, likely more than one. Who had they been? What had they been like? So many questions ran through her mind. She closed her eyes and quieted her thoughts, letting the sounds of the world around her in, the warmth of the southern sun sinking into her skin.

Xaliandri, she heard the soft whisper through her mind.

Her eyes flew open, and she swiveled around, the rubble no longer lay beneath her feet. Instead, she stood inside a glorious building, the stone floor a soft white, the ceilings seeming to go forever. Forcing herself to move, she came upon a staircase that reached to the stars it was so long. Voices filled the space as she touched the soft wood of the stair rail, voices filled with joy, with love, as if they belonged to a family. Men's voices and one distinct female voice, one that had become familiar to her.

The massive door behind her drifted open, the sun's light spilling in. She followed it through the doorway and out, her breath catching at the beauty before her. Flowers grew freely across the meadow, and upon their petals danced beautiful insect-like creatures with vibrant wings. She put her hand out to one, and it danced gently upon her fingers before taking flight once more.

Butterflies, the word drifted through her consciousness, but it was one she didn't know.

She continued to walk around the castle, marveling at its expanse and its mere presence. There was something calming about it, something good, that made one feel welcome and at home. As she made her way behind the structure, she came upon the most glorious garden she'd ever seen. The colors were like no other in their world, the blooms reaching up to her as she walked through.

She wasn't certain how she knew but somehow, she knew this was the female's garden. Xali could feel her presence, a gentle ease overtaking her. In that moment, she understood, the female was an immortal, this had been her home. A female immortal.

She turned back to the building, watching as it faded from her vision, the ancient rubble left in its absence. She reached up and wiped away the tears that had fallen. Her father had sent her here to subdue the talk of immortals and the history their family guarded, but he'd only succeeded in increasing her knowledge and her curiosity.

Something wanted her to question, to see what the others couldn't, to find the truth. She stared at the rubble, a slight sparkle of something nudging her forward, until she was close to it. Drawing her power, she focused on moving the stones, something that should have been easy for her, would have been easy for any of the others. Their power was grounded in the land's composition, so moving stone was like moving a dust fragment from the air—it was a miniscule task. After straining for some time and cursing her infuriating lack of power, she collapsed into the rubble, defeat encapsulating her. She would need to dig with her hands, she'd be mocked incessantly if anyone found out.

A soft wind tickled her neck, moving a loose strand of hair that had strayed from her braid. She preferred her hair loose but had wanted to avoid anyone noticing her new golden strand or the curls that now covered it. She put her hand up and let the breeze run through her fingers, her mind drifting back to the day in the holy lands.

What if the wind was trying to tell her something? Setting her fear aside, she tapped into the strange powers that had been growing within her lately, the lesser powers. She reached out for the wind and made the connection she'd been hoping for, before directing it forward toward the rubble. The top layer shifted slightly then she brought her hand up and guided the air, the pieces of stone beginning to move, drifting in a stream as the breeze carried them away.

Her heart raced in excitement. She was as strong as the others, just different. With no effort, she cleared the top layer from the space where she'd seen the flicker of light. She stared at her hands. She couldn't command the lifeless stones to move, but she could control the world around her. The things that were alive. All this time, they'd been training her as they would have trained any child, move the stones first, then move on to the land. She'd never gotten past the stones, her weak attempts frowned upon. But the land was alive. Could she move it? She held her hand out toward the field beyond the debris, but instead of forcing it to move as her family would have done, she reached out for it, to find a link to it as she had with the air. She cleared her mind and opened it, feeling the coolness of it, smelling the damp soil, imagining the feel of it between her fingers. When she felt the connection was complete, she opened herself to it, in a way, asking for permission to continue the new bond she'd formed with it. A peaceful wave swept through her, and she understood in that moment that this was who she was. This was her gift, and the strength she felt in this new alliance was not a lesser one by any means.

Opening her eyes, she brought her hand up, and the land grew to reach the level where her hand was raised. She stepped back in shock, stumbling slightly. Forgetting her search for a moment, she walked over to the newly formed hill, placing her hand upon it. The wildflowers spread out toward her face, reaching for her. Feeling no fear, she let them tangle in her hair until they pulled back, bloomless, having weaved their flowers through her braid.

Tears filled her eyes.

"This is how it's supposed to be, isn't it?"

Their powers were meant to bind them to the land, but her people had always used it destructively, as a weapon to maintain their rule. She thought back to the holy land and the way the land had looked as if it were forced together. She removed her hand and let the land return to its original shape. That was the key, it was a mutual relationship. She touched the flowers in her hair. Had their power ever extended to the plants like hers did? Was it meant to? Something in her told her this was unique to her. That she was a sort of bridge, but a bridge to what?

Her eyes drifted back to where she had cleared the rubble. There was nothing there. She moved closer, walking the distance until she was standing in the same spot. Stooping, she studied the space, but there was nothing but more broken white stone. Her hands reached out and started digging, an action they did on their own, her mind not instructing them. They dug, further and further, the sharp stone ripping into her fingers. Dropping to her knees, she continued in a frenzy until a small shimmer caught her eye. She froze, then slowly, gently, drew her sore fingers toward it. With a delicate move, she grasped the end of the golden hair that shimmered before her, pulling it until its length was completely free.

Xali stared at the golden hair with the slight curl to it. Then she pulled her braid forward looking at the golden strands that were tucked underneath to hide them from sight. They matched perfectly. Dropping the braid, she continued to stare at the strand, gently rolling it in her fingers. What did it mean? Had she been right?

The woman in her dream was an immortal. But why did it matter? Why did it matter who they had been if they were lost to the world? What difference did any of it make? Was any of it worth her life? Worth losing everything?

A raindrop splashed on the stone beside her, then another on the other side. She raised her head to the sky, noting only now the clouds that had rolled in to eclipse the sun. She brought her head back down, the strand continuing to shimmer in her fingers. Her heart hammered as she brought it closer to her, encasing it in her hand.

"What you're asking me to do will cost me everything," she whispered as a tear rolled down her cheek and landed on the strand.

Her hand warmed, the glowing golden color lifting from the strand, the length of it turning ebony like that of those from Old

Tenebron. Her heart raced as the golden mist seemed to dance in the air before her, within it sparkles of emerald and a blue of which she'd never seen the likes, shimmered. The ebony of the strand rose in a mist as well, the golden giving way to the emerald and blue, the remaining two hues dancing with the black, just as she'd seen in her dream.

"What are you trying to tell me?"

Tentatively, she reached her fingers toward the mist. She could feel the magic in each one. "Their source of magic," she muttered. "They had three lines of power. They weren't all the same as we are."

The black and green magic spread toward her, encapsulating her hand then teased her hair before making its way back down her other arm. She put her palm out and the two mists sat there before sinking into her skin then exiting to join the remaining blue mist still floating before her.

Her eyes widened. "I have two…I have two powers within me."

She sat back, too overwhelmed to remain on her knees. The mists began their dance around each other then blended to create a vibrant violet. The violet dove into the strand of hair, its color turning golden once again.

Xali brought the strand up, staring at it before rising.

What did it all mean? The immortals had lesser powers. But did they really? She thought of the feeling the two had given her, her own magic calling to it, rising within her. It didn't feel weak, lesser. She dropped her hands and stared at the sky, the rain was still flowing, but around her, it remained hanging mid-air in stasis. Frozen by magic. But where had the magic come from? Her or the mist? She touched a hanging drop and they all fell, the magic gone.

She didn't know what to do, so she remained with the rain pouring down around her. The immortals had been stronger; she knew it in her heart. There should have been no way the great king could have defeated them, but he had. She looked around at the ruins. He had taken everything from them.

"So, if I lose everything to find the truth, it will be the right thing to do."

She stood, sighing, knowing she had to continue, no matter the cost. She felt a tingling in her hand and looked down to see the strand had disintegrated, leaving only particles of silver that were washed away by the rain. As the last glimmer disappeared, the rain abated.

"Well, well. What do we have here?" She heard from behind her.

She turned to see a small group of five men, Tenebrons, approaching her, their brown eyes staring her down like she was prey for the hunting.

"A stray Gaern. Far from home, aren't you stray?"

"I could say the same to you, Tenebron," she replied. Carnick would have added a slur but given her recent revelations, she refrained.

"She's got a smart mouth, too. I thought all you Gaerns were prim and proper."

They were closing in, and she eyed her sword laying on the ground, a few feet from where she stood. The soaked drawing pages lay scattered around it. The men closed in. She'd heard tales of the Tenebrons, hard to tame, targeting their people until the royals stepped in and pushed them from the Gaernim towns to the outskirts of both Bortees and Nobesn. Now, they targeted the Cirillians, easy prey. Xali's people knew to stay in the confines of the safe zones, far from the wild unkempt lands of Old Tenebron. It amazed her that they hadn't all been eradicated by this point.

As they moved closer, she made her move, lunging in a graceful swing of her body to grasp the sword, pulling it swiftly from its scabbard and springing to her feet before they could reach her.

"Ah, we have a spry one."

"A fighter. This should be fun."

They drew their swords and attacked. She easily parried their blows, keeping her balance on the rough, slick surface as they continuously lost theirs.

As she disarmed the last of them, she swept her free arm out and threw them to the ground, rolling the stones up in one swift move, followed by the cresting of the meadow behind them, causing their moving bodies to slam into it.

Fear struck their eyes.

"She's a royal!" one yelled, scampering over the lowering mound of land.

"Run before she kills us!"

She laughed, the idea that they feared her magic more than her sword a humorous concept. She watched as they scattered, running back to the forests beyond and disappearing. Turning once more back to the ruins, she thought of her discovery, not quite knowing what to make of it or to do with this new knowledge. Nothing. There was nothing to do with it. All she could do was tuck it into the space where she held her other discoveries until the time came when she saw a clear path. Now was not that time.

When she returned to her aunt's palace, she spent the remains of the evening with them, the talk of both her confrontation with the Tenebrons and her use of magic as well as swordsmanship to protect herself, filling the time.

Lying in her guest quarters later that evening, she went through her experience at the ruins. Her head tilted to stare beyond the open balcony, the quiet of the night calming her nervous thoughts until she finally drifted off. Dreams alluded her, and she woke the next morn rested for what seemed the first time in days.

Seven

"Sweet morn," Carnick greeted her as she stepped through the doorway. Xali couldn't help but smile seeing him there, his face full of anticipation at her arrival. There were times she forgot his rank and power, seeing only the man she loved. The flecks of violet in his eyes sparkled in the torchlight.

She greeted him with a kiss.

"I hope you broke fast because we've got a journey ahead of us."

She arched her eyebrow as he guided her out of the room and through their uncle's palace.

"That sounds intriguing."

"You've no idea what your father has arranged for your final steps toward taking your place by my side."

She stopped, the tone of his voice and the meaning in the last few words giving her pause.

"Carnick, what's happened?"

His eyes grew worried, then darker, the flecks of violet disappearing beneath the storm clouds.

"There are whispers, Xali. I heard Mother arguing with our uncle last night." His voice was low as if he suspected he would be heard. They stood in the hall of doorways in that same uncle's palace. "He's against you, angry that the joining has been moved. I only heard a small amount before he stormed out and I had to hide. As he left, she threatened to step down early so that I could take the throne."

"Why would she do that?"

"No one would dare affront a reigning king's wife. He would be forced to withdraw his accusations, and it would be over."

"Your mother would do that for me?"

"No, but she would for me, and she knows what you mean to me."

She took his hand and kissed his cheek.

Sighing, he said, "If I am forced to take the throne sooner than expected…well, I'm not sure I'm ready for that."

Squeezing his hand, she said. "You're ready, Carnick, trust me. If it comes to that, you will make a fine king."

He reached his fingers out and touched the curls of the hair she'd worn down. "And I'll have you by my side?"

"Yes, of course."

There was a subtle shift in his eyes as he pulled one lock of hair from below the others, letting it slip slowly from his hand. She followed his eyes to see the golden lock falling to join the others then looked back up, meeting his eyes. She pushed her hair back, sweeping it around to the other side of her neck. Then she lowered the sleeve of her shirt to reveal the new markings on her shoulder. He furrowed his brow, his eyes growing a shade closer to black, sending a light chill down her spine. He traced the marking then met her eyes again.

"What does it mean?"

"I don't know."

He pulled her sleeve back up to cover it, looking around as if someone might have seen.

"But there's more," she said.

"More markings?"

"No, more changes."

He placed a finger on her lips. "Tell me about them on our journey. It's not safe here."

He glanced once more toward her shoulder then took her hand, his eyes growing softer.

"We've got quite a ride, so you'll have plenty of time."

They rode in silence, the rhythmic beat of the horse hoofs the only sound. Their cousin had not accompanied them on this trip, Carnick insisting he remembered how to get to the destination, wherever that might be. Xali noted that their uncle had not greeted them.

When they were well past the towns and villages, the open land around them, endless forests before them, Carnick drew his horse to a stop.

"Tell me. What else happened?"

She looked around. They were in the middle of nowhere.

"There's no one out here. Go ahead, Xali."

She proceeded to tell him everything, from the strand of hair to the men she'd defeated. The more she talked, the deeper the creases in his brow. It wasn't the confrontation with the men that was worrying him. He knew as well as anyone that she could best even the strongest of swordsmen, a few straggling, untrained Tenebrons were no threat to her.

"Show me," he said when she'd finished.

"Here?"

"As I said, there's no one this far east."

She hopped from her horse then closed her eyes, drawing on the feelings she'd had before. It was harder here, there was something else mixed with the touch of nature, something dark, mysterious.

She pushed it aside for the moment, then called the wind as she had, opening her eyes. *What if I don't need the wind?* she thought.

The trees far in the distance rustled their leaves as she released her hold on the wind. It drifted past her, raising the locks of hair she'd left loose. She focused on the ground below, not as she had been taught to dominate it, but as if she were equal to it, one with it. As her mind rose to the thought, so did the land, curving gently into the crest of a hill. She let the peace and oneness she felt with the land free and watched as the hill rolled wavelike across the open land, the trees in the distance raising their voices as if to call it to them.

The surrounding land curved and rolled in the same motion, and it felt as if she were floating in the ocean off the shores of her home like she'd done as child.

"Xali."

She heard Carnick's voice but was too lost in the sensation as the grass and wildflowers rose to touch her hands.

"Xali, stop." Worry shrouded his voice, so she turned to him.

His eyes widened in awe, and he took a step back. "Xali, please stop now," he said again, his voice shaking.

She released the connection and the land quieted, settling back to its original position.

Carnick stared at her, his eyes filled with emotion. She didn't know what to say, so she remained quiet. He wiped his hands over his face and then stared past her to the open land.

"Is that what you did?" he asked.

"Not quite. It's become stronger. I moved the ground, that's all."

"That's all," he mumbled, walking over to where the first hill had been, kneeling to feel the land.

"You didn't break the ground, Xali. It's as if nothing happened."

She understood his meaning. Their magic was forceful, it tore the ground asunder, ripping it at its foundation, leaving scars that never healed. There was a violence to their magic.

"There's not even a speck of dirt. It's as if nothing you did was real…but it was. If I hadn't seen it, I wouldn't believe it."

He stood and looked at her, his eyes filled with wonder.

"Your magic…it's—"

"Different," she said.

"Not just that."

"It's their magic, Carnick."

"Lesser magic but what you just did…it was by no means lesser."

He began to pace, running his hands through his shaggy silver hair.

"Do you know what this means?"

"I have the magic of the immortals. I know. I'm marked. I—"

"No, it's worse than that. What you did, Xali, that was not less than my power."

She was taken aback. "Are you afraid that I might be stronger than you?"

"Gods, Xali, with more practice you will be stronger than me." He took her hands. "That's not what frightens me. This means you were right. The immortals were stronger. Their magic wasn't weaker than ours. Xali, I have no doubt that if you understood your powers better, those trees would have picked up their roots and made their way to you."

"Don't be ridiculous."

"I saw them. They were leaning to you, watching. You have magic beyond what any of us have. You control the land, the air, the weather."

"I don't control the weather."

"Not yet, but you will. It responds to you."

"That's not true."

He gestured up to the sky where rich clouds were moving in.

"Right now, it responds to your emotions, but soon, very soon, you'll direct it. If you have the power of the immortals, then the lesser magic is ours not theirs."

He dropped her hands and walked to the horses.

"Does that scare you?"

He stopped and turned back to her, his eyes stormy, the worry overflowing.

"It terrifies me. Not because of your strength but because of what it means for your safety. If the family sees you as a threat not only to the lies they've built our lives around but to their power, even I can't protect you."

He turned back and mounted his horse. "Let's go. We still have a ways to ride before we get to our destination."

As they road, on a journey that seemed to have no end, neither discussed what had happened, silence dominating the mood. Half the day had passed when they finally broke through the forests. The midday sun bearing down upon them made Xali miss the cooler temperatures of her northern home.

"This isn't right," Carnick said as they came upon a cliff edge, pulling their horses to a stop. "We're too far east. I must have miscalculated." He scratched his head, an irritated look on his face.

Xali slipped from her horse and moved to the edge of the cliff, staring down on what looked as if it had once been a river. The ground far below dried up and dead, no vegetation to be seen.

"Xali, we're losing day quickly, let's go."

Still, she stared into the empty ravine, a strange familiarity filling her.

Xaliandri, she heard the voice that plagued her dreams.

"Did you hear that?" she whispered, knowing the answer but hoping for a different one.

"Hear what?"

"Nothing," she said. The voice had been for her and only her.

Her eyes drifted across the ravine.

"What is that land across the way?"

"The Licolca province. This ravine divides the lands down here until you get closer to our provinces where it stops."

She stared across, drawn to that spot, to whatever lie unseen across from her. The wind tickled her neck as it moved the strands of her hair, and at that moment, she felt it. A feeling so intense it pushed the air from her lungs.

"Xali?" Carnick said, his tone concerned. She ignored him and let herself own the feeling, drifting further into it as she closed her eyes. Her heart filled as if it would burst, a yearning swept through her, a sense of incompleteness, a knowledge that what lie on the other side of that ravine would fulfill that need and make her whole. As she thought her last thought, a rush of warmth crested within her, her breathing ragged from the intensity. Love.

Her eyes flew open as the sensation drifted away.

"They were in love," she said, bringing her fingers up to feel the moisture on her cheeks.

"Xali?"

She turned to meet Carnick's eyes, the worry evident within them.

"They were in love. The woman in my dream, she was in love with another immortal. Gods, Carnick, I felt it. It was like the world fell away and only that feeling between them existed. It was intense, deeper than any word could describe."

His eyes searched hers, and he brought his hand up to gently wipe a fresh tear.

"What did he do to them, Carnick? And for what? For land? For power? His ego?"

"I can't answer those questions, Xali."

"Whatever his reason, it was wrong. He was wrong." She looked back across the ravine, missing the intensity of emotion that had coursed through her, knowing no matter how much she and Carnick loved one another, they could never come close to that feeling.

He took her hand. "Come, we have more to see, although I don't believe this day or the one before has yielded the outcome your father had anticipated."

They rode south until they came upon a massive ruin of black stone that stretched two times the length the one in Sartria's province had. In the distance stood trees that enclosed the open space surrounding the ruins. A lone tree stood in the openness, its white bark stark against the black of the rubble to which it led. It seemed such a dichotomy, but then the ruins themselves were a striking contrast to the ones she'd seen the prior day.

Dismounting, she walked over to the rubble, squatting down to touch the black stone.

"Opposites," she stated.

"It would appear that way. It's always been a mystery as to why the ruins are opposing colors. No one knows why, and if they ever did, it's not documented anywhere."

She stood, brushing her hand on her pants.

"How do you know that?"

"My mother brought me to both sites when I was about your age. It's a rite, a passage for a first born, to see the fruits of the great king's fight and be reminded of where we come from."

She gave him a miffed look.

"I know, in light of what you seem to keep discovering, it no longer has the same meaning. It's more like the spoils of war now."

"So, my father wanted me to see what only first borns are shown to reinforce what?"

"To make you see that the immortals were weak and that our time, our rule was necessary."

"Do you believe that?"

"I did, but…let's just say, you've opened my eyes." He walked into the rubble. "A man once lived here—"

"No, a god once lived here."

Carnick turned swiftly. "That's blasphemous, Xaliandri. Even to my ears."

"They weren't ordinary men. These were men and…women who had extraordinary powers, immortals. The word in itself should bring some level of fear and respect."

"They were not our gods."

"I didn't say they were. In fact, I don't know who our gods are or if they actually exist."

She could see the anger in his expression; she'd pushed too far. The storm clouds in his eyes rose then did something strange. She watched as they turned black, filling his eyes with darkness, submerging the violet specks. She took a step back as the ruins behind him began to rise.

"You push, Xali, and there are some things I will not allow you to question." The sky had darkened, and thunder rumbled as her own powers responded. The very air around him seemed darker.

"What if their gods are our gods? What if they've been the same all this time?" she pushed. "What if it's the Fates we should have been calling them and their immortals were their children?"

As she said it, the sky opened above her, rain pounding against her skin.

"Even the gods are irritated with you now, Xali."

But then the rain grew softer, and streams of sunlight poked through the thunder clouds. The warmth of it tingled against her skin, and she raised her hand to one of the streams. The light sparkled, dancing upon her skin. Carnick sighed, and she felt the strange heaviness in the air dissipate. She looked up and met his eyes, seeing the gray return, the specks of violet resurfacing. He looked startled for a moment, and then his expression softened, and he moved toward her, bringing his fingers up to trace the corners of her eyes.

"Maybe you're right. Maybe we have it all wrong," he said softly, "and you've been chosen to open our eyes."

The power of his words struck her.

"I'm scared, Carnick," she whispered.

"I know. I am, too," he admitted. "Whatever is happening to you…whatever this is, I'll be right by your side."

A thought occurred to her, the seriousness of their situation apparent.

"What if they kill you for standing by me? What if—?"

"Shhh," he said, pulling her closer. "They won't. They'll kill you to punish me, as punishment to us both."

She snuggled into his chest, only somewhat relaxing within his hold, the gravity not eased by his statement.

"I won't let that happen, Xali. We'll keep this quiet, hide your new powers until after we join."

She pulled back. "It won't matter."

She realized the truth that he could not see.

"It will, they won't take my queen from me."

"But you won't be king yet, Carnick, not until your mother steps down. Even if she does so early, it may be too late. You won't be able to protect me. Maybe before you could have, but now…not when I'm questioning our very faith."

He kissed her head, then dropped his forehead to rest against her hair.

"Gods, Xali, why do you have to be the antithesis to everything we are, everything we know? You don't make things easy, do you?"

"I never have, why start now?" she said with a shrug.

He put his hands on her shoulders and pushed her back, the warmth of his body receding like a comforting blanket being pulled from her body.

"You tell no one what you told me, not even Mendol."

"But—"

"Not even Mendol. The more of us who know, the more the risk to you."

She swallowed, the thought of keeping her latest discoveries from her brother not setting well in her.

"Mendol would never—"

"No, he wouldn't, but someone might overhear you, or he might tell Fairenth. You cannot risk anyone hearing that you are questioning not only our history, the basis for our rule in this world, but the very gods we claim led our family to victory. Even as I say the words, it sounds false. If you hadn't…if your eyes hadn't—"

"Hadn't what?"

"They turned green, just as the sun was sparkling golden on your skin, your eyes for just a moment shimmered emerald."

"That's ridiculous. My eyes are the same as yours, they're gray."

"They're not the same as mine, they never have been. They shift. Where ours grow stormy with violet tones, yours grow stormy with green, slight shimmers of green that play among the clouds within your eyes. No one acknowledges it, no one tells you, but I've seen their reaction to it. Your eyes used to reflect the same violet as ours, but the green would speckle them at times. Now, it's completely replaced the violet, and just now…they were completely emerald."

She brought her fingers up to touch the corners of her eyes, then lowered them. She'd always felt different, always known she stood apart from her family, but she'd always looked like them, fit in outwardly. Now, the physical differences were setting her apart completely, putting more distance between the others and her, her hair, the marking on her arm, her eyes, and her magic.

"Hey," Carnick pulled her from her thoughts, lifting her chin so that she was forced to look at him.

"Do you know what I love most about you, Xaliandri?"

"My quirkiness?" she responded playfully.

"Well, that, too, but I love your differences. I love that you stand apart, that you see things differently, that your magic is unique. I'm even growing to adore these curls you've recently sprouted. You're challenging, Xali, and that's what makes you special."

"That's what will get me killed," she muttered.

"Well, that, too, but it sure does make this dull life exciting." He gave her a wink before glancing around. "Have you had enough of Old Tenebron?"

"I suppose."

"Then let's return. We'll supp with Uncle Crebant, then—"

"Then spend the evening together?"

He lifted an eyebrow.

"Not that way!" she responded with a laugh.

"Damn, only another moon cycle, and we can spend every evening that way."

She felt the blush climb her cheeks, his laugh making it deepen. She was about to bring her hand up to playfully hit his chest when something caught her eye behind him.

Her hand rested gently on his arm instead. "Carnick, look."

He turned to where she was looking. It took him a moment, but then he saw it as well. A section of the forests behind them was dying. The leaves were strikingly brown, those left on the dying limbs. Carnick looked back at her and then rushed to his horse, she doing the same. All worry of her situation left where they'd stood.

They rode the distance to the forest's edge, the south-eastern side of where they'd emerged when they'd come upon the ruins, their eyes drawn to the rubble and not what lie beyond.

Xali hopped from her horse, following Carnick into the dead forest, the brittle ground crunching beneath her feet.

"I wonder if Uncle knows of this."

"Do they come this far ever?"

"I don't think so, this area, as well as the ruins in Sartria's province are left untouched. Our people don't care for it, and the old people regard it with fear. It's removed far enough that no one likely knows. Patrols don't even bother with it."

"What does it mean?"

"I don't know."

They walked further into the forest, the sun streaming in through the empty branches above. As they came to the edge of the woods, having walked what seemed to her to have been miles, she saw they were at the ravine once more.

"The divide between the old lands," she mumbled, her mind catching on something from her dreams. "Different powers. If the immortals had different magic…"

She let the thought go, drifting closer to the edge of the cliff.

"Has the ravine always run dry?"

"I don't know to be honest. It ends before it gets to my province. What were you about to say, Xali?"

"The immortals had different powers."

"How do you know this?"

She wasn't certain how she knew, other than from the dream, the mists of color she'd seen, and her experiences at the ruins in Old Cirillia. But how did she explain that to Carnick or to anyone for that matter?

"Just trust me, they did."

She stooped and placed her hand on the browned grass below her, feeling the bitterness as it broke in her fingers.

"Something's changed." She thought about the powers she'd been gaining, lesser powers, the magic of the immortals…of one immortal. The female she'd seen and heard. "Her powers were tied to the land, like ours but different, deeper…on a grander scale."

She stood and looked at Carnick. "Her powers were like mine, but she wasn't merely connected to the land; it was connected to her." As she spoke the words, she knew them to be true. "Carnick, the land is dying because whatever magic she imbued in it is fading."

"That's insane, Xali. They've been gone for ages. Why would this happen now and not when the immortals died if that were the case? No one's magic is strong enough to last that long."

She chewed her finger. He was right. She was missing something, but what? What was she still blind to?

Everything, she thought.

They made their way back to their uncle's castle and supped with them. Xali felt her uncle's eyes as she ate, knew he was staring at the curls Carnick had insisted she leave loose. She'd wanted to pull her hair back so that it went unnoticed, but he had said it didn't matter. News in their family moved fast, and his mother had already spoken to their uncle.

She glanced up and caught her aunt's eye; she knew the sadness she saw was for her. The reality of her situation set upon her, and she pushed her plate away, her appetite fleeing. Had she sealed her fate with her actions or had the Fates sealed it for her? She thought it odd that the Fates now replaced the gods she'd been raised with, and with such ease. It was as if a part of her had always known them.

She went through the motions until it was time to leave. As they walked toward the hall of doorways, her cousin Herind came running to them.

"I don't have much time before they notice me missing," Herind said. "There's talk that Xali has broken tradition and law. Ainia's father wants punishment as does my mother. The only reason nothing's been done yet is because my sister has my mother's ear, and she's fond of you, Xali."

"What kind of punishment?" Carnick asked.

"I don't know, but I've heard the four heads speaking. Your father argued against it and walked out followed by your mother, Carnick. The provinces are divided on this."

"Divided?"

The provinces had never been divided on anything. The thought scared Xali.

"Whatever you're doing, Xali, you need to stop."

"I'm not doing anything, Herind."

"Your hair and this…" He grabbed her arm and pulled her sleeve down to reveal the marking. How had he known?

Carnick shoved him hard against the wall in defense as Xali quickly pushed it back up.

"Don't touch her, Herind."

He glared at Carnick. "I'm on your side, cousin, and you need as much of us on your side as you can. The heads know, your parents know. You've been marked, Xali, and none of them know by what. They see you as a threat, they see you as a lesser born, and they will treat you as so if you don't stop and let whatever it is you're doing go."

"I can't," she said softly.

Carnick released him.

"Then you will die," she heard Ainia, Herind's first born wife say.

Xali met her eyes, her heart racing, unsure of whether to see Ainia as a threat.

"Herind, you should not have come. I told you to leave it, and you disobeyed."

"Sorry, Ainia," he said, his head dropping. "I had to warn her. It's Xali, we always look out for her."

"And we've always protected her," she said to Carnick. "When she was born under those moons, and my father wanted her dead, we stood as cousins, the seven of us, and kept her alive."

It irritated Xali that she had spoken to Carnick as if Xali and Herind weren't there. The plight of the second born. But she refrained from saying anything, too fascinated by what she was hearing.

"And will you stand by her now?" Carnick asked. "Will you stand with me?"

"We have done what we can, Carnick. Xali needs to stop whatever this is or even your joining won't save her. Nothing will."

She turned her eyes to Xali. "Little cousin." She touched a curl of Xali's hair and then pushed her sleeve gently down, tracing the marking. "They say you've been marked with lesser magic. That the gods have cursed you. My father says you are an omen, a plight against us, that you will destroy us all. Is this true?"

"I only seek the truth."

"And what is that? Is it worth your life?"

She swallowed, pushing her sleeve back up and standing taller. "Yes, it is."

"We need to go," Carnick said.

"Please, Carnick," Ainia said, grabbing his arm. "Talk some sense into her."

He sighed, saying, "I can't," and then guided her to the doorway, leading her through.

Xali glanced back at her cousin in time to see her wipe away a falling tear.

Eight

This is bad, this is really bad, Xali."

Carnick was pacing her room, but she ignored him, instead staring out her balcony across toward where the guardian wall stood.

"If the family turns against her, even Father can't stop it," Mendol said.

They'd met him on the way to Xali's room and filled him in on all that he'd missed at their uncle's. They'd left some pieces out, particularly the new developments in her magic, but the rest they'd told him. Xali hated not telling him everything, but it was for his own good. The less he knew, the less he could be dragged into this mess with her. She wasn't certain they would ever punish a first born, but she didn't want to take a chance. Carnick was in deep enough; she didn't need to worry about Mendol as well.

"I need to get beyond the guardian wall," she said.

"What?" they answered in unison.

She turned to face them. "I need to see what lies beyond it. Whatever is going on with me is there. I know it."

"There's no way over it."

"My spot isn't guarded. I'm there all the time, and there's never a patrol on that end," she suggested.

"Even if that's true, there's no way down."

"You have magic, Mendol. Pull the land to meet us."

"It's too risky, Xali. The noise from the ground shifting would cause notice."

Carnick sighed. "Not if Xali does it."

"Xali can't move land, gods she can't even move a pebble without breaking a sweat."

Carnick met her eyes, then nodded.

"We may not have told you everything," Xali said.

Mendol crossed his arms. "Go on."

"I can move the land, my powers have grown, but they're different from everyone else's. Mine is more subtle. I can pull the land to us without anyone noticing."

"This, I have to see," he said.

"I still don't think this is a good idea," Carnick said. "What if we're seen? What if you're seen, Xali?"

"It's a risk I have to take. You two can stay here so you don't—"

"You think I'm letting you wander into that untamed land without me?" Carnick asked.

"I can protect myself."

"Highly unlikely against whatever is locked behind that wall," Mendol said.

"Then, it's settled, we all go," Carnick declared.

"A little late to be drawing in your corner, isn't it, Princess?" the guard greeted Xali as she ascended the last step. The wind whipped her hair around, and she cursed herself for not putting it back.

"My brother and the prince were annoying me, so I snuck out."

He laughed. "Well, your corner is open. It's a bit windy up here tonight, so be careful."

She smiled and nodded, then made her way to the end of the wall, sitting on her perch, feet dangling over the edge. The top of the wall was wide enough for multiple people to stand. In most places, a ledge could be found, ensuring no one accidently fell. Her spot, however, held no border; it lay wide open. She'd never thought about it, never wondered why this place had been left unfortified. She scooted over to the edge of where it stopped. There was enough room for two people to sit but not much more. Curious, she ran her fingers along the ending edge of it. It was ragged, as if it had been broken. Had someone fallen from this spot, breaking the ledge with the impact?

"It is said that when the wall was first erected, the day the immortals were defeated, the people rose up in rebellion. They were angered that they had been severed from the land that lay beyond. They attacked the wall, and some made it to the top. Several of them fell to their deaths," Mendol said, squatting next to her. "When father first brought me up here, he showed me this section as an example of how blind their people were to the truth, how devoted they were to their false gods and weak rulers. The land beyond was sacred to them, it was where they worshipped their gods. It was the reason the great king erected the wall, to break their attachment to the false deities."

"How many more were murdered for their beliefs that day?" she asked.

"How many since that day?" Carnick added, all of them realizing the gravity of the truth. False gods were not tolerated nor was talk of the immortals other than of their defeat. The penalty was death.

"You didn't wait long to find me," Xali said, changing the topic.

"Carnick here was too impatient."

She rolled her eyes, and Carnick shrugged. Continuing to finger the broken stone, she asked about the guards.

"We gave them a break. Since there are two first borns here, the wall is well guarded on this end."

"Hmmm," she mumbled, her mind on the fracture in the stone. It didn't feel right to support the theory Mendol had shared with her.

"It's broken toward us, not away."

"What are you mumbling about, Xali?"

"The fracture, it's directed in, not out. Someone broke it from the outside of the wall."

"That can't be," Carnick said, dropping down beside her.

"Feel." She pulled his hand, guiding his fingers over the stone.

"She's right. But no one lived beyond this border. It's always been a wild, untamed wilderness."

"One fortified so no one ever goes beyond or questions what lies on the other side. We need to see what's so special that the great king erected a wall to keep us out."

"Or to keep something in. Xali, there are wild creatures in those forests."

"Are you getting scared, Mendol? You can stay up here," she said, standing.

He shot her a dirty look. "You're annoying sometimes, little sister."

She felt for her connection, sending her senses out past the wind then felt for the ground below, calling it to her. Steadily, quietly it rose until it was close enough to hop onto.

"Gods, Xali," Mendol said, staring at her.

"Impressive, isn't she?" Carnick said with a hint of pride in his voice.

Xali jumped out onto the hill that now stood just below them, and then Carnick joined her. She looked up at her brother; she could tell he was nervous. He never broke the rules, never crossed the line or questioned anything. He was completely out of his element.

"Mendol, you stay here. Sit and wait for us, that way if a guard comes it will look like we're all still here, and they'll leave this corner be."

He looked relieved. "Are you sure, Xali?"

"I can protect her, Mendol. You stand guard. We'll be back soon."

With that, Xali directed the hill to lower, and they ran into the tree line, the black of night hiding them. Xali's eyes adjusted quickly, the light of the moons breaking through the tree cover enough to give them some sense of the terrain.

"Well, which way now?" Carnick asked.

She closed her eyes and listened, her senses guiding her.

"This way."

They ran, knowing they had limited time, and not knowing how much forest lie ahead of them. After about a mile, Carnick grabbed her arm.

"Xali, this is crazy. There's nothing out here. Nothing but trees."

"There's something here, Carnick. I can feel it."

He sighed. "I want to believe that, but you don't even know what you're looking for. If there is something, it could be a hundred miles from here. We can only see trees from the height of the wall, no open land."

"But the trees are higher than the wall in most parts, Carnick, they block our view."

"Xal…" He stopped, a noise in the forest drawing his attention.

They both listened, hearing it again. Something was coming toward them and rapidly. Xali pulled out her sword while Carnick drew his magic. They stood in the dark waiting as it approached. The noise grew until it was right upon them. Then the undergrowth parted and the biggest stallion they'd ever seen emerged, reeling back on its hind legs as it saw Xali's sword.

"What is that?" Carnick whispered.

It was standing, watching them, not moving.

"It looks like a horse."

"That's a beast, Xali. I've never seen something so big."

"I don't think it's here to hurt us," she said, lowering her sword and placing it back in its scabbard.

"Xali?"

Slowly, she walked closer to it, her hands shaking slightly. It lowered itself on its right knee and bowed its head as she approached.

"Gods, Xali, your hair…it's—"

She glanced down and saw that her hair had turned the golden color once more. Swallowing nervously, she looked at Carnick, seeing the fear in his eyes, feeling it in her heart.

"And your eyes…the specks of emerald are so bright."

He reached his hand out and touched a lock of her hair. The beast pawed the ground impatiently, and she turned away from Carnick and the changes he'd noticed. Tentatively, she brought her hand out to touch the massive horse. Its fur was softer than any she'd felt; it reminded her of a pelt that hung in the hall of doorways in the palace. It too was the midnight black that this beast was. Her heart dropped as she looked into its eyes.

"They hunted them," she said, thinking of how a pelt hung in each palace. "They hunted them down and skinned them." The horror of it was appalling. "I'm so sorry," she said to the beast.

Lowering its head, it nuzzled its nose against her face.

"Xali, we need to move, our time is limited."

The beast lowered its other leg and moved its head as if gesturing to its back.

"I think it's here to take us," she said, moving to climb on its back.

"Xali, wait."

The beast let out a low growl as Carnick grabbed her arm.

"This beast could be dangerous."

"No, he's not, and he's not a beast. I don't know what they're called, but he's not a beast."

"All right, let's just call it an overly large stallion, either way it just growled, and it looks as if it wants to eat me."

"Make friends with him, he's here to take us wherever it is we need to be."

"Make friends with him, she says," he mumbled as he moved closer to the stallion's face. "Since when is it a him?"

She ignored him and climbed onto its back, then after a few moments, the beast lowered its head again, and Carnick climbed on behind her. The stallion rose and began to move, quickly speeding its pace until she and Carnick were holding on for dear life. She'd never seen anything move so fast. It was exhilarating and terrifying at the same time. Carnick was holding her so close she could feel the quickening of his heartbeat.

Soon, the woods broke, and the stallion slowed its pace. Before them lay the ruins of what looked to have been a castle.

"Another castle?" Carnick asked. "No one's ever mentioned a third castle."

"No, but no one's ever said anything about what lies beyond the guardian wall."

The stallion slowly walked by the ruins.

"Why isn't it stopping?"

"I don't think this is what we're meant to see."

"But it slowed down."

"Yes. I think out of respect."

"You can't be serious, Xali."

"I am, look, he's passing it."

"Then we need to get off."

"No, trust me, Carnick, please."

He dropped his head on her shoulder just as the stallion picked up its pace, not to the original speed, however. She glanced back at the ruins as they rounded a corner of overgrown bushes.

"I wonder whose castle it was."

"Does it matter?"

"I think it does."

She felt them tilt and looked to see that they were taking a path downward. It wound for some distance, dropping them into a valley layered with more ruins.

"This is where we're meant to be."

The stallion stopped and lowered itself, allowing them to climb off, then wandered over to a patch of wildflowers and lay down to wait for them.

"Xali, your hair."

Carnick's eyes were wide in the moonlight as he reached over and picked up a lock of her hair.

"What's happening to me?"

"I don't know," he replied, his eyes still watching the glowing golden strands in his hands. They shone as bright as the sun, and she could feel the warmth within them. The moons above broke through the clouds, hitting the strands, causing them to shine brighter before morphing to her normal silver color, the brilliance of the moonlight still shimmering upon them.

Carnick dropped his hand and took a step back. Her hair was lighting the entire valley. She met his eyes, eyes filled with awe, and she didn't know what to make of it. She didn't know what to make of any of this.

"Let's find what it is you're here for," he said, his voice shaking slightly. "Somebody wants you here."

She nodded and felt the warmth flee from her body.

"Did it stop?" she asked.

He drew closer, this time bringing his fingers up to glide along the lock of hair that lie upon her cheek, tracing it from her scalp downward.

"All but this one."

He held it up, and she saw that it was a golden hue standing distinctly against the silver of her natural color, matching the one hidden behind her neck. This one, however, was directly against her face.

"There's no hiding that one," he said.

"No, there's not," she agreed, pulling it from his hand and

tucking it behind her ear. "Let's look around."

He gave her a look, his brow furrowed, but she walked away, feeling him pull his shields back up. She knew he hated how vulnerable they were right now. She looked around the valley before her, drawn to what appeared to be a dry riverbed, and stopped, touching the indent where the water had once been.

"Xali, this isn't just a valley," Carnick said.

She stood up and looked at him, her eyes then drifting past him, noticing the remnants of what must have been a massive structure at one time, the ruins still clinging to the cliffside as if it had been part of it at one time. Another castle.

"There was a city here," he continued.

Her eyes moved from it, taking in the remains of the former city, noticing the imprints leftover from smaller structures in different spots throughout the open space.

"Who lived here? And why hide this place from everyone?"

"I don't know, but I don't think these people were part of Old Tenebron or Old Cirillia."

"Who were they then?"

"I have no idea," he said.

She brought her hand up to her mouth, a thought occurring to her. "Did he annihilate an entire race?" she whispered, the horror of it too much to speak the words too loudly.

His eyes grew sad. "I don't know. Maybe, maybe not. We can't assume that, Xali. Perhaps this land was empty before the great king. Perhaps the immortals destroyed the people living here."

A breeze shifted her hair, loosening the now golden strand which tickled her cheek.

"I don't think so. I think whatever happened to their people, the great king was the reason."

She swallowed, not wanting to think on the brutality of the truth. Turning away, she began to look closer at the scattered remnants. She was drawn to a cluster of overgrown trees, the likes of which she'd never seen. They had long sweeping limbs that drooped down to cover the ground, leaving space below for one to walk. Their leaves were gone, only the dead limbs remaining, but she imagined they must have once been glorious.

Her foot hit something, and she stooped to find a pile of broken stone, grass, and wildflowers overgrown throughout it.

"It's just more debris, Xali, leave it."

The light of the moons faded as clouds covered them. In the remaining stream of moonlight, something caught her eye. She pushed the weeds and grass aside, pulling at the pieces of stone, feeling Carnick move closer, his curiosity likely piqued by her actions.

"There's something on the stone," she said.

She made a light, pulling the minerals from the ground and rock, imbuing them with her magic until they shone a bright green. It was the one use of her magic she'd mastered at a young age, the only one. The green shone across the stone, revealing letters etched into the broken pieces.

"Words?" he asked, kneeling next to her. She tucked her hair behind her ear and began digging through the pieces until her fingers wrapped upon one that felt right. She didn't know why, it just did.

"Vi," she said, tracing the letters. A memory from her dream returned, the same two letters shown to her. Digging more, she found another with *ssa* and then another with two more letters. She began trying to piece the fragments together and realized she was missing one. With a frenzy, she dug through the stone until she felt it.

Fitting it in with the others, she leaned back and looked at the finished product.

"Vi…o…lissa," Carnick slowly sounded out.

"No, I think it's pronounced Vi-o-leesa."

"That's not how it's spelled."

"Trust me," she said, her tone revealing her irritation.

"What does it mean?"

"Not a what, a who. Violissa, it's her, the woman from my

dream. She was an immortal."

He turned to her as her fingers traced the letters. "Violissa," she said once again, knowing she was right.

"Should I bother asking how you know?"

She laughed. "No, probably not."

His hand reached into the rubble, sifting through the fragments of letters.

"There's a dash," he said. "As if there's something after her name."

She looked at the last piece and saw he was correct, brushing her finger over it as he pulled a piece free from the rubble and stared at it. She glanced over his shoulder at the *Si* he held.

He met her eyes. "Did it feel as if someone else was driving your body?"

"Yes," she answered softly as he placed the newest letters against hers then reached back to the pile, sifting through the pieces. Finally, he came back with another piece.

Connecting it to the others, he said, "Sinow?"

The stone shifted slightly, then small fragments of the green light splintered away, dancing along the two names. They began to glow a brilliant green then the green changed to a blinding white, the pieces melding together. The light softened then dissipated, leaving only a silver sparkle in the names, the stone now fused as it must have been thousands of years before.

"They were real. They had names, they had families," Carnick said, his fingers reaching out to touch a line that extended below the two names.

"You didn't think they were real?"

"They never seemed real. More like ghosts. Ghosts of a past I didn't know. Ghosts not of men, and certainly not of women, but of monsters who deserved to die, cruel beasts, not men. Not men doing the same things we do, loving, having families, simply living their lives. That makes the great king seem…well, not so great."

Xali heard the sound of hooves behind her and felt the stallion's nose nuzzle against her arm. She continued to stare at the names. It pushed her arm again, nearly knocking her over, before Carnick caught her.

"I think it's time to go," he said, the stallion neighing in agreeance.

"We've seen what we were meant to see. Come, before we're discovered."

He rose, holding a hand out to help her up. Shaking the stiffness from her knees, she let him help her onto the great beast, leaning into him as he took position behind her. She watched as he extinguished her light, the names still shimmering silver in the dark of the now moonless night.

The stallion dropped them at the edge of the forest after the quick run from the ruins. Xali was still catching her balance, rubbing her neck from the force of the speed as she willed the land to rise and return them silently to the guardian wall. Mendol helped them up, the land sliding back to its original form.

They were standing, Mendol waiting for the details, Xali and Carnick still processing when the guard caught them unaware.

"Your highnesses? Everything all right?"

Mendol, always quick on his feet, replied, "Yes, my sister grew too close to the edge when she was rising. If not for Prince Carnick, she may have fallen."

"Princess, all the times I've warned you about that open space. I will put a request in with your father to have it repaired."

"Oh no! Really, I'm fine. There were too many bodies up here with me, and it threw my balance off. It was a one-time thing."

"Once is enough to lose you, Princess."

"But I can't draw if it's closed."

Carnick took her hand. "I don't think that's your biggest concern at this moment, Xali." She dropped her eyes. He was right, and the way things were proceeding, she doubted she'd have many more chances to sit quietly and sketch.

She nodded with a half-smile to the guard.

"Thank you for your concern. I'm sure my father will appreciate it."

They quickly left, remaining silent for the trip back to the palace. Xali couldn't get the name Violissa from her mind. Nor could she help but think their discovery was an important one. She prayed it wouldn't be one that secured her fate unless that fate was something other than the death sentence she anticipated.

Nine

Carnick watched as Xali paced the room, telling Mendol of their discoveries. The thick lock of golden hair was striking against her natural silver locks. He rubbed his face, unsure of how to feel about what they'd discovered, hidden in the forest behind the wall. It had left him with questions, too many questions.

"This is bad, Xali, all of it. And this," Mendol said, pointing to her hair, "what is this? There's no hiding that. Where does that even come from? No one has hair like that. First the curls, and now this?"

The door to the room opened before she could respond. Her father stood in the doorway, crossing his arms. He eyed Carnick then his children. If he noticed Xali's hair in the candlelight, he said nothing.

"It's late. Carnick, you should be in the guest quarters. Mendol, in your own quarters. And you, Xali, should know better than to have Carnick in your room this late."

Carnick saw the restraint as she held her tongue, dropping her head. If she'd been a first born, she could have had any man in her room with no question, but as a second born, she was required to stay chaste, obey, and not be heard. He knew it frustrated her. She hated her place as a second born.

He could have taken the blame, but it wouldn't have mattered, the blame was hers because of her birth order. Mendol walked from the room, nodding in respect to their father. Carnick followed, catching Xali's eyes as he walked by. She gave him a small smile then dropped her head again.

"Xaliandri."

"Yes, Father."

It seemed to Carnick that he wanted to say something more but gave a simple "good eve" to her as Carnick walked away.

"Good eve, Father." He heard her reply before her father closed the door.

"Carnick, will you be staying to break fast with us in the morn?"

"Yes, Uncle, if that is agreeable with you."

"Of course, it is. Good eve, Carnick, Mendol."

"Good eve," they both said.

Carnick found his way to the guest quarters having parted with Mendol. He lay in bed staring at the silk draping that decorated the corners of the canopy. A breeze from the open balcony moved the corners that draped down the frame like white ghosts.

He thought of Xali. She was stubborn headed and too independent. And he loved her for it. Everything she was challenged her position, the family, even her safety. She wasn't anything like them, especially not the female cousins. She was strong, fierce some would say. They saw her as reckless, but he saw her as driven. She pushed herself because they wanted an obedient second born. But she wasn't, he didn't think she could ever be. She was too independent and free spirited, questioning everything with eyes that were open, looking past the façade and seeing the truth of it all.

She was everything she shouldn't be, and he loved every bit of her. She wasn't the tamed, obedient, quiet flower they wanted her to be, but no matter how much he loved her for those qualities, it wouldn't be enough to save her if anyone found out how curious she really was or gods forbid, that she carried lesser powers.

He rubbed his hands over his head, then rose from the bed, knowing sleep was not likely to come. Dressing, he decided to stretch his legs. His uncle's palace was open, and in any season, it felt comfortable. Although it sat north in the province, it was always temperate, allowing the structure to remain open in many places. Stopping in an open vestibule, he leaned on the half wall that looked over a small pond, a blooming tree just opening its buds now that the unusually snowy cold season was departing.

It was a peaceful spot with flowers that lined both sides. Flowers. His mind slipped to Xali's lesser powers. Lesser. He wondered at the name. There seemed nothing less about anything he'd seen her do. She was just discovering her abilities and yet she could command the wind, move the trees, will the plants to grow, and he knew without a doubt the weather was influenced by her. There was nothing less about her magic; in fact, it was intimidating.

Was that why the great king had deemed the power of the immortals lesser? And why deem it a crime to have such powers if only the immortals had had them? What was it about their power that marked it as something wrong? Who would even have lesser powers? No one but the royal families had magical abilities. Why did it matter if one of them had been gifted with them? Unless... Was it possible? He looked at his hands. Were their powers somehow connected to those of the immortals? But that didn't make sense. No one had magic like Xali's, at least no one until Xali. What if her magic was simply a form of theirs? What if the great king had suspected that one day an anomaly would appear? To ensure the anomaly wouldn't infect the bloodline, he would have wanted it destroyed. He ran his hands through his hair, confused by his own thoughts, too lost in them to notice the other presence.

"Xali often came here as a child. I would find her here in the daytime, sketching the tree or in the eve, staring into the water. The flowers appeared some moons ago when only grass had grown for generations." His uncle stood quietly, looking into the water as if it would answer his many questions. "It is Xali's spirit that feeds them."

Carnick glanced quickly at his uncle who continued to stare ahead.

"Her mother and I have watched, praying to the gods that we were seeing more to it, that there was no connection. The curse of the emerald moons her mother says."

"And what do you say?" he braved.

"What you and Xaliandri have is special. I can see the love you hold for her. I've always seen it. The arranged marriages in our family never start with love. If we are lucky, it grows to more than the obligated love of cousins, but never does it run as deep as what I see in you and my daughter."

He hadn't answered the question, and Carnick wondered if he would.

"My daughter is special. Too special to keep hidden, and the gods apparently don't want her hidden."

"She's asking questions, Uncle."

"What kind of questions?"

"Ones for which I do not have the answers. Ones which cause me to question."

His uncle sighed. "There are some questions that should remain unasked."

He was tempted to push, but his uncle was hard to read, and he didn't want to cause Xali any further trouble.

"My cousin is becoming unsettled by the changes in her. He has always been wary of her. Now, he pushes for action. My cousin to the south follows his direction, I do not know why. They've always been close. Even my sister, as his wife, cannot seem to sway him."

"The unheard voice of the second born," Carnick muttered.

"You and my daughter are more alike than you suspect. That is why you must protect her. Only your mother and I stand against the other cousins. If somehow your mother is swayed—"

"She won't be."

"Even if she is not, it does not guarantee our cousins will not take action."

"And what would you have me do? How can I, who has no throne yet and who has yet to join with her protect her?"

"The second born are not always unheard, Carnick. Her mother thinks she serves a greater purpose. That she has been chosen by the gods."

"Not the gods," he said quietly, meeting his uncle's eyes.

His uncle didn't blink; there was no reaction.

"All the more reason to keep her quiet. If the others should rise against us, make her run. Xali is the type to fight, and she will not win."

"Is she right?"

"She must stop asking questions, reason with her."

"Is she right?" he demanded. "Is our kingdom a false one built upon lies?"

"You would be wise to stop questioning as well, nephew. There are things you will learn when you take the throne, things you will be sworn to protect and hold sacred. Until that time, you should remain silent and keep her silent."

He turned to walk away, but Carnick dared grab his arm to stay him. His uncle flashed him an angry look, and the ground below him rumbled.

"What lies beyond the wall?"

"Only ghosts lie beyond that wall, ghosts of a past that must remain buried. There is nothing else beyond that wall, Carnick." He removed Carnick's hand from his arm. "You should get some sleep. Will you still be joining us in the morn to break your fast?" he asked as if the prior conversation had never happened.

"Yes," Carnick said, bewildered by the sudden change.

"Good then I shall see you in the morn."

After he left, Carnick made his way back to his quarters. He still wasn't entirely certain what had happened or what his uncle knew. Whatever it was, he wanted Carnick to keep Xali quiet, to keep her under control. He didn't think he wanted to, no matter that it was seen as his responsibility as a first born to remind her of her status. He'd never believed in the second born tradition. Being second born made one no less than a first born. Birth order did not dictate abilities or intelligence. Xali was no less than he nor was his sister, yet they were looked upon as if they were. It angered Carnick, it always had, but he was outnumbered and outpowered. There was no way to change the status quo, at least not until he took the throne. Perhaps then things could change. His mind was still going when he lay down to sleep but eventually, he drifted off.

The next morn he went directly to Xali's room. She sat on her bed, her legs crossed, the morning sun's rays reaching through the balcony across the room to light the emerald specks in her eyes. Her hair was piled atop her head, in a useless attempt to hide her new lock of gold. It hadn't worked, the golden roots shone brightly in contrast to the silver that surrounded it. He watched as the lock made its way out of its binds and fell loosely against her face. She gave it a frustrated blow of her breath then looked back at him in defeat.

"I don't think it wants to be wrangled," he said as he approached her. She looked breathtaking in the morning light, her eyes filled with vulnerability.

"Carnick, what am I to do? I've tried everything, and it always breaks free."

"I suppose we'll simply have to lock you away where they can't see it," he teased as he drew closer and kissed her. Reaching up, he untied the rest of her hair, watching as it tumbled down around her.

She narrowed her eyes in irritation.

"Do you have any idea how long that took me?"

"Isn't that what your handmaids are for?"

He kissed her again before she could reply. The vulnerability was gone, replaced by the fierceness he loved in her. She pushed him away, glaring at him.

"I should make you put it back up."

"No need, I'll just take it back down again."

He pushed her down on the bed and climbed atop her.

"Carnick—"

"Shhh," he said, stopping her words with his mouth. He wanted to hold her before the day became wrought with politics and whatever else was waiting for them. She returned his kiss, her lips soft and full. His hand brushed through her hair as his other hand pulled her closer. He desired her but knew he had to wait; she had enough strikes against her. If he took her purity before they joined, he would seal her fate.

He pulled back then kissed her forehead, taking in the lush green specks in her eyes, the gray stormy as expected. He kissed the bridge of her nose, and she giggled, the specks turning emerald once more.

"Join with me early, Xali," he said.

Xali heard the desperation in his voice. "But it has already been moved forward."

"Let's move it even closer. Let's do it today, Xali. Join with me today."

She moved herself to her elbows. "Carnick, what's wrong?" Concern filled her eyes.

"Nothing, I just don't want to wait any longer, I need you in my bed."

"You've always wanted me in your bed. What's happened?"

He dropped his forehead down to touch hers. "I fear what will happen if we do not."

"It won't be long, Carnick. The warm season is upon us, and when the moons reach their fullness, it will be so."

Drawing his head up, he took her in, the beauty of her, the

delicate features that held the strength below.

"We're going to make it," she said, hopeful.

"What if it's not enough?" He ran his fingers through the golden lock. "What if they still take you from me?"

"Then I will fight."

"If you fight, they will surely kill you without hesitation."

"If I do not fight, they will kill me."

"Xali, you must not."

"I will and…I might even win."

Her eyes sparkled, the clouds growing thicker within them. Could she win? Her magic was vastly different from his, from the rest of the family's. But was it enough?

"You can't beat them with wind and flowers, Xali. You barely know how to use what you have. It's not a fight you or I want."

Her eyes dropped, growing lighter, the disappointment reflected in them.

"And what would you have me do?"

"Stop searching, stop questioning until our joining at least."

"And if I don't?"

"I don't know that any of us can protect you."

She pushed him away and rose from the bed.

"You think I can stop what's happening to me? Do you think I want this?"

She pulled the sleeve of her shirt down, the swell of her breast exposed but he took no notice, his eyes drawn to the marking that now spread down half her arm.

"I don't want this, Carnick. I'm scared, too. I never liked being a second born, but I certainly would accept that curse in a moment's time if all of this would go away."

She pulled her sleeve back and walked away, moving out to her balcony. Joining her, he put his arms around her, bringing her back to his chest and resting his head close to hers.

"I'm sorry. You're right. You have to follow your destiny, and if this is it, then I'll be right by your side, even if they kill me alongside you. You have a purpose, Xaliandri. Whatever that purpose is, you have to discover it."

He felt her relax as her body leaned into his.

"That was a quick change of heart," she said softly.

"I wasn't speaking only for myself. Your father met me in the eve when I couldn't sleep."

She turned, her eyes searching his.

"My father?"

"Yes, he's concerned for you. He confirmed what Herind told us. Our uncle grows restless as does our aunt. My mother and your father are the only things keeping them at bay. I'm guessing that's why your father insisted you see the ruins in their realms, to appease them. To make them see that he was trying to rein you in, to tamper down your curiosity."

"Even though it didn't work. I told Aunt Katama about discovering my powers at the ruins in Old Cirillia. What if she suspects I only told part of the truth? What if she suspects they're lesser powers?"

"Why would she?"

"I don't know. Just paranoia I suppose."

"Then put it aside, there's no way she knows unless someone saw you, and if they had, she would have brought the witness forth." He kissed her nose. "Now, I'm famished, let's put all this aside and break our fast."

Xali was restless. Carnick had returned to his province that morn, and she'd spent the remainder of her day locked away in lessons with Proctor Chenon. Two days had passed since, and she was growing anxious. She'd tried going to her favorite spot but had been told for the first time that she was forbidden.

"I'm sorry, Princess," the guard said. "When your father found out you'd been up here, he gave strict orders that you were not to be allowed here again. It's too dangerous."

"What about another spot?"

"No, the guardian wall is now off limits to you."

"But—"

"I'm sorry, king's orders on threat of execution if anyone disobeys."

She had raised an eyebrow. "Execution? That seems a high cost."

"Those are the orders."

She had walked away, knowing there was no swaying him. King's orders trumped hers, and she didn't want to see any of them punished for her selfishness. She'd spent the rest of the day training and doing her best to keep her mind from everything.

Now, another morn was upon her.

A servant girl entered her room, intent on helping her dress.

"I'm fine," she said, quickly obscuring her golden lock.

"Are you certain, my Lady?"

"Yes…but where is Sianna? I haven't seen her in quite a few days." Xali wondered if she'd been caught using the word Fates by someone not as forgiving as she.

"She is home tending to her father who has fallen ill. She will return soon, but her mother needed help."

"Oh, I'm sorry to hear that."

The girl started to close the door to leave when Xali said, "Do you know where she lives?"

The servant gave her a strange look. "In the lesser town outside the town of Ceinton. It is where I live as well."

"And if I were to send her family something…how would I find them?"

A look of surprise crossed her face.

"You would ask for the Maeson family. They are known in town, a family whose roots go back to…" *the time of the immortals,* Xali thought as the girl paused, "…before the great king."

"Thank you, that is all."

She bowed and left. Xali dropped back to her bed. It had been on impulse that she'd asked. Sianna had used the word Fates as if she were accustomed to saying it. There was a chance she had the answers Xali sought. It was a long shot, but as tension was growing between the provinces, it was one she would risk taking.

She rose and after dressing, then fighting to secure the damned lock of hair, she headed to break her fast. As she came upon the dining room, she heard her parents. Drawing closer, she could tell they were arguing.

"You have to do something more," her mother pleaded.

"I'm doing everything in my power. Your brother has always been an unsatisfied man, you know that. He resents me for being born to rule this province. He's always been jealous and has never been satisfied with his own land."

"It's the same land our line has ruled for thousands of years."

"And he wants to change that. Xaliandri is his way in," her father said.

"But she is a second born. Mendol will take this throne."

"Yes, but he thinks Xaliandri will stain us all. He's always thought of her as a curse to the family. He will use that excuse to take down our entire house and with ours, Renia's."

"Do you think that's possible?"

"Carnick loves her, he will fight against Crebant as will his mother if Crebant dares turn against Carnick."

"Then we have a stale mate, the two northern provinces against the southern ones. They would not dare move without persuading Renia, and she will not turn against Carnick."

"For now."

Xali backed away. It was worse than she had thought.

"Xaliandri," she heard her father who must have seen her movement. She quickly regained her composure, then entered the room acting as if she hadn't heard anything.

"Good morn, Father, Mother."

They both eyed her, looking for any sign she might have been privy to their conversation.

She grabbed a piece of sweet bread and said, "I've been looking for Mendol, have you seen him?"

"He's with Fairenth in Bortees."

"Oh, then I'll join him. I can spend time with Carnick."

"No," her father commanded.

"But—"

"No, you are not to leave this province. In fact, you are not to leave this palace."

"I don't understand."

"Things are tense, Xaliandri. You need to stay safe."

She paused a moment before saying, "They mistrust me?"

"It has grown dangerous for you."

"I can protect myself."

"With your sword? Against one of our family? Your sword is nothing but a toy against our magic, you know that."

"Carnick can keep me safe."

"I said no. You will remain here, under my protection. That is an order."

She bit her tongue as he stormed from the room. Her mother gave her a sad look, rose, and then kissed her on the cheek before leaving her alone.

She'd suddenly become a prisoner.

Ten

With no way to leave the palace, Xali remained restless. Her father had placed a guard in the hall of doorways so she couldn't even sneak through one. She spent the day stewing, avoiding her father until night fell. Then, she made her move. She stole from her room, her navy cape concealing her from sight. Ducking into the kitchen, she found a Cirillian cape and exchanged it for hers. The people had different colored capes to signify their station. Royalty wore deep blue almost black as night, the Gaerns, their people, wore a light gray, the Cirillians a forest green, and Tenebrons a ruby red. Both stood out if in a mix of Gaerns, which was rare unless they were passing through the higher towns to get to the palace for work. Of course, there were no Tenebrons, at least not in her province. The Cirillians obeyed the law of wearing their identifying cape but from what she'd heard from her cousins, the Tenebrons weren't as obedient. She'd been with her cousin

Ainia when one was caught without it; the consequence was swift and deadly. The rankings were to be obeyed.

Donning the green cape and tucking her strands of hair so they wouldn't show, she slipped from the palace. She headed for the stables, hiding behind the building as a set of guards made their rounds. Then she made her way to her horse. Standing before the stall, she realized this part of her plan might not work as well as she'd thought. Starfall was a gray mare, her hide too light to go unnoticed.

"Damn, sorry, girl. I'll need to take Mendol's horse." She gave her a pat and nuzzled her nose before moving to the next stall where Mendol's horse eyed her suspiciously.

Grabbing his bridle and bit, she readied him for the excursion. His black fur would blend into the night better than Starfall's. Just as she was getting ready to saddle the horse, she realized her biggest mistake. It was fine for a royal or even one of her people to have a horse, but the Cirillians had no horses. If they were lucky enough to have one for farming, they were distinctly marked and never allowed beyond their village boundaries.

"Dammit," she muttered, knowing she shouldn't have been so impulsive. She removed the harness and patted him.

"Guess I'm on my own, boy."

She snuck back through the stable doors and ran through her options. It was a few miles no matter which way she went. If she walked too long the entire village would be asleep before she reached it. She'd have to run the distance. For ease, she removed the cape, tucking it in a roll under her arm. Then she ran. She avoided the main streets of town, wrapping through the outskirts to avoid being seen. Her hair would give her up immediately, and she'd have to explain why she was running through town with a Cirillian cape tucked under her arm.

As she approached the end of town, the main street widened, the houses fading. Soon, she was alone, the dark of the forests surrounding her on both sides. She stayed off the road in case there were any late-night travelers, running until she finally reached the end of the road, the dirt changing to grass with a small walking path, treaded from the many footfalls. She slowed her run and donned the cape, remaining off the path until she finally reached the first Cirillian town.

There were many scattered through the province just as there were a few Gaern villages past the main town that lie just outside the palace. This village fed the palace with servants and workers. The village was quiet, most having turned in, the journey to the palace requiring an early morn rise, likely before sunrise. Xali had never thought about it, always taking for granted that things ran their course in the palace. She could always count on food to break her fast, a servant to help her dress, the halls to be clean. What was it like for them to make that trek every morn and every eve?

There were some who stayed in the servants' quarters for a cut in their rations, but those were the older, more tenured of the servants, and they were small in number.

"Miss?" A man's voice interrupted her thoughts. "You shouldn't be about this late."

He had come from the direction of what looked like a tavern, the warm light streaming out of a partially closed door that released the sounds of laughter.

"I…I'm looking for the Maeson house," she stuttered, trying her best to hide her Gaern accent.

He eyed her for a moment then smiled, saying, "Ah, then you need to go down another ten houses, make a left then look for the home with the flowers adorning the windowsills, about four houses after the turn. And hurry along. If the guard catches you out here past curfew, you'll be whipped."

"Curfew?" she wondered aloud.

"Where are you from?"

"Thank you, kind sir," she said quickly and hurried along as he'd instructed.

She counted the houses, although the term houses seemed a bit off considering how small and cramped the buildings looked. The next street was the same, and as she approached the door of the house with the white flowers, just budding in the warming weather, she hesitated. What if this wasn't the right one? The lights were out; they were likely all asleep. What if they were? What if this had all been for naught?

Her hand hung in the air until finally she brought it down in a quiet knock.

There was no answer, so she knocked again, this time a bit harder. She heard rustling then a light appeared through the window, the door opening a crack.

"Hello, how can we help you at this late hour?"

"I'm looking for Sianna."

"It's awfully late, dear."

"It's very important."

The woman eyed her then opened the door.

"Well, come in, you don't want the guard catching you out here."

"Mother? Who is it?" She heard Sianna ask.

"Someone for you, dear," she said as Xali entered the home, closing the door behind her.

She'd never been in any home other than the palace. She was surprised to find that although it was small, without many things, it felt warm as if it made up for the lack of physical items with the love that filled it.

"Do I know you?" Sianna asked.

"I…" Xali was at a loss for words. She'd come this distance for answers but hadn't thought about what she'd say. "I…I…" She sighed and pushed her hood back slightly to show her face. "I need your help."

Both women dropped to the floor.

"Your highness," Sianna's mother said.

"Please rise, there's no time for formalities."

"Princess, what are you doing here? Are you by yourself?"

"I am, I need help, and I think you might be the one to help me.

Do you remember how you said I'd been touched by the Fates?"

"Sianna!" her mother cried.

"It's all right, she's not in trouble. In fact," Xali said, lowering her hood to expose her golden lock among the curls. "I think she might be right."

Both women couldn't hide their shock. "It was only curls before," Sianna whispered.

"I need answers, and I think you might have them. I need you to tell me everything you know about the immortals."

"We don't talk about them, my Lady. To do so is a crime."

"Please, I have nowhere else to go. I need to know the truth, I need to know who they were and the truth of what really happened in the great war. Something is happening to me, and I believe it has to do with them."

The women exchanged glances.

"We cannot tell you what happened."

Xali's face dropped along with her hope.

"But we can tell you who they were if you truly do seek the truth."

"I do." She removed her cape and brushing her hair back, lowered her sleeve to expose the markings. "I think I've been chosen. I keep dreaming of a woman, hearing her voice call my name."

Sianna's mother ran her finger down the black vines, her expression serious.

"Come, we will teach you our past." She walked to the hearth of the fireplace and bent down, moving the stone that lie in front of it, Sianna helping her. Then, she pulled a large slab of stone to the side exposing a small opening.

"Come." She disappeared down the opening followed by Sianna.

Xali swallowed, touching the knife she had stowed in her waistband, then followed them. A dirt slope led her down to another room, wood beams covered her head, the walls and floors made from the ground itself. The lighting was dimmer, the smell of the hearth overpowering, the space larger than she'd expected.

She used her power to draw out the minerals in the ground to further light the room, giving it a greenish hue.

"Incredible," Sianna's mother said.

"It's one of the only abilities I share with my family. The rest… well the rest I think I share with them."

"With whom?"

"The immortals."

They gaped at her.

"My family calls them lesser powers but so far they are anything but."

"The magic of the immortals was endless. But to know them, one must know their history."

There was a small table which Sianna's mother quickly dusted off with her hand while Sianna ran to the other corner of the small room. Xali watched as she dug something from the ground then brought it over and placed it on the table. It was wrapped in a dirty cloth, aged with time and soiled with dirt.

"Go ahead," Sianna said, nodding to Xali.

Xali pushed the cloth back to reveal a thick book. It was worn with use and age.

"This is our history; it is all we have left. I imagine there are others like it throughout what's left of our people and likely in Tenebron, but this one is ours. You see, your people destroyed the physical reminders of our past, they silenced us, but they could not keep us from remembering what once was."

Xali gently ran her fingers over the cover and then opened the first page. There were sketches and etchings she imagined must have been carried through the book. The first page was dedicated to the Fates.

"Tell me about them."

"Are you sure you want to know the truth?"

"Yes, I know what it will cost me."

Sianna's mother reached her hand over and placed it on top of Xali's. She looked up at the woman who smiled lovingly at her.

"Then so you will learn."

"In the beginning of time, the Fates created the world. Using the magic of Light, Dark, and nature, they made the world, Cirillia, Tenebron, and the Elvin lands. There is some debate about who came first, but we think that the Elvin were created first, then the Tenebrons, and finally the Cirillians. For each people, the Fates gifted one ruler to whom they granted power and immortality. To the Tenebrons, they gave Dark magic as these people were made in the likeness of the Dark magic wielding Fates. To the Cirillian ruler, Light power from the Light wielding Fates. Only one Fate held nature gifts, the Mother Fate. She was different from the other Fates and stripped the immortality from the ruling Elvin; their lives would be long but not cursed with the same weight of immortality she'd been handed.

"She also gave the Elvin a female ruler, their ruling line would be led by whomever was born to the ruling family first. This was not the case of the Light and Dark who gave power only to the males. These immortals, as you call them, would bear only one child each generation, and they would return their spirits to the Fates upon the ascension of each new king. So, you see they were immortal, but their lifespans in physical form were still dictated by the Fates.

"Light and Dark were also given advisors, ten to each who held, lesser, yet still extensive, power and immortality. There were the Councils, Darkbearers serving the Dark king, Lightbearers, the Light king.

"The Fates were a combustible group, their power often at odds with each other, and so it was with the peoples they had created. Light and Dark are in essence opposites, and the Dark kings were particularly prone to madness. The realms fought constantly and so the Fates, driven by the Mother Fate, created a prophecy to one day bring peace to the realms."

Sianna flipped the pages of the book further back, Xali's eyes taking in names of kings and their stories, sketches of some. She saw a sketch of the castle she'd seen in her vision and stopped her. "That's the castle in Old Cirillia, the ruins."

"Yes."

It was just as she'd pictured but even more glorious.

"How many castles were there?"

Sianna's eyes grew large. "Many and they were said to rival any of the four province palaces."

She flipped the pages back to show a dark and terrifying castle that fascinated her.

"Wait, Sianna. You go too far before the story arrives there. First, you must know the immortals who ruled when your people came."

She flipped the pages back until she came to a page with a sketch on each. Xali's heart raced. "That's her. It's the woman from my dream," she whispered, her fingers tracing the features of the beautiful face.

"That cannot be."

"But it is, and I'm sure it's her voice that calls me. Who is she?"

"This is our queen. Queen Violissa. She was said to be the image of the Mother Fate herself. Her beauty rivaled no other."

Sianna's hand reached over to touch Xali's golden lock. "And her hair was the golden color of sun beams."

"It is she," Xali said. "Tell me more about her."

"She was the daughter of the Light king and an Elvin princess. She had hair of honey and eyes of emerald. Her power matched no other but that of her husband. Her kindness and gentle spirit are what fills our people to this day. Legend says she would spend most of her days with her people, she loved them beyond anything but her husband."

"This is her husband?"

She pointed to the sketch on the opposite page. She'd never seen such a striking man. His hair was darkened in by the artist, his eyes left with no distinction between the iris and the pupil.

"Yes, this was King Sinow. He was king of Tenebron, a Dark

king. It is said he was so terrifying that to look upon him was death. Only the guilty ever gazed upon his face or his Council's."

"The guilty?"

"Legend says armies were not needed in those days; the king was the law. If you broke it, you forfeited your life or suffered a cruel punishment from his Council."

"Sounds barbaric."

"Aye, it does, but in those times, there was no crime, no one dared cross the king's law."

Xali stared at the picture. Sianna's mother had used the names she and Carnick had discovered behind the guardian wall, the drawings bringing the two immortals to life. She brought her fingers up to touch the eyes of the king. There was something in them that reminded her of the recent hues in Carnick's eyes.

"His Dark powers turned his eyes black when he used his magic. It is said it was terrifying just to be in his presence, even when he was cloaked. To dare look at him was instant death," Sianna said with a whisper.

A shiver slipped down Xali's spine. "Dark power, and she held Light magic?"

"And nature from her Elvin side. Their union brought peace to our world. The prophecy fulfilled."

"Prophecy? The one from the Fates that you mentioned?"

"Oh yes, they were part of the most sacred prophecy our people know. The Fates created it at the beginning of our world. It joined the queen and king, prophesizing her birth as the first ever Light queen. The details have faded with time, but it is said their love was unlike any other, that it withstood the tests that were given them, that it grew so that in time they were inseparable. A love story like no other." Sianna had a glazed look to her eyes as if she wished for the unattainable love for herself.

Xali turned the page, glancing at the pictures, trying to find answers but still not certain she had any. She turned back to the line of kings, staring at the queen and then the Dark king. Something

Sianna's mother had said gave her pause.

"If it was death to look upon him, how is there a sketch of him?"

Sianna's mother flipped the pages forward and stopped on the sketch of a man who looked just like the Dark king but with lighter eyes.

"They had a child?"

"Yes, Prince Drostiren."

"His eyes were like hers?"

"No, he held the blue of our ancestors, the cerulean of the Light kings. The queen was the only one with the green of her Elvin heritage. He would have been king; his ascension was close."

"Ascension?"

"The day the Fates blessed a king with his full power. The prior king would step down, returning himself to the Fates and the new king would take the throne."

"But I thought they lived forever?" Xali's head was starting to hurt.

Sianna's mother shrugged. "It was always that way. They lived lives that were long, ten thousand years, sometimes longer. I suppose one would grow weary after all those millennia."

"So, he would have been king," she said softly.

"Yes, with his wife Paige by his side. She is the one who chronicled their history, who made the sketches. This book was hers, hidden from your great king, and protected by our family through each generation."

"He had a wife…" Xali said, backing away, the information swirling in her head. These had been real people, caring people, a family. Why had they been such a threat?

"Where do my people come in to all this? Why are we not even in the story of the world's creation?"

"No one knows. No one knows where your people came from. You're not mentioned in our history until the end of ours. All it mentions is the invaders from the sea."

"From the sea." She thought about the strange shape of the land near the holy lands. So, it was true. This land had never been theirs. Had they ever even set foot on these shores before the great king? Perhaps the great king was a fraud, stealing a crown that should have belonged to the son. Taking what was never his.

"But how?" she said aloud. "How did he defeat them?"

"No one has that answer. It happened suddenly, our history ends at that line, the rest became your history."

"But they were immortals…" Her mind drifted back to the dream. The choking feeling, the shards she'd coughed up. Was her theory correct? Had he turned on them so quickly that even their people hadn't known how they'd been defeated? Murdered? She looked back to Sianna and her mother.

"Thank you both. I understand the risk you took in sharing this with me. I swear to you that I will keep it safe and never reveal where I discovered it. I must go now before it becomes light."

"Your highness," Sianna's mother said, stepping to her. "The Fates have chosen you; you have been touched by them just as she was. Whatever the reason, do not turn a deaf ear to them. Hear them, follow their signs. Queen Violissa turned her back on them at one point and although that history is lost, it was said to have been a journey that tested them both, one that took thousands of years to resolve itself."

"I do not have that luxury of time."

"Then hear them no matter how arduous the path. They must be followed." She kissed Xali's cheek. "May the Fates bless you."

"Thank you. Thank you both." She ascended from the lower room and slipped away from the house, the subtle pink glow on the horizon pressing her for time, the thoughts in her mind pressing her for action.

Carnick paced his room. It had been three days since he'd seen

Xali, told by his mother that she was under lockdown, her father permitting her to go nowhere beyond the palace walls. He'd tried to go to her but had been stopped when he'd walked through her hall of doorways. Guards had been posted and ordered to bar anyone from entry.

It had grown serious if her father was that worried. Concern nagged him. He'd tried talking to Mendol, but Mendol knew nothing more than Xali. He'd gone back to Fairenth, waving Carnick's concern off, but Carnick wasn't so sure there was nothing to worry about. Xali was being purposely separated from him, from everyone. Held prisoner. Was it for her own good? To stop her meddling or to stop the rising threat? But Mendol had been sent home early this morn, before the breaking of fast, rushed off to his own province.

A knock on his door tore his thoughts away.

"Your highness," one of the guards greeted him as he entered, bowing. "Your mother has commanded your presence."

Commanded was an unusual choice of words, and Carnick eyed the guard. He remained silent, waiting for Carnick to vacate the room. Sighing, he walked out, the guard joined by another, the two flanking him.

"Am I being summoned or led to my sentencing?" he mumbled.

Neither replied, and the silence ensued until they arrived at the meeting hall. Only the heads were ever allowed in a meeting hall, each palace having its own. They were used rarely, only the most serious of situations requiring it.

He pushed through the great doors to find the four heads staring back at him, grim faces on all except Xali's father who looked shaken. Fairenth entered the room behind him, a nervous look to her eyes.

"Carnick, come forth," his mother said. "It is time you tell us the truth about your betrothed."

Xali was able to sneak back to the palace undetected, or so she thought. She made it past the kitchen staff unnoticed, switching capes quickly while they were occupied. Then she ran to her quarters hastily, leaning on the door, her heart pounding. She dropped the cape and eyed her bed. It looked tempting, and she was exhausted. As she debated the consequence of missing the usual breaking of fast with her family, her mother stepped from her balcony. Xali jumped in fright, her nerves already on edge.

"Your father has been called to Renia's province."

Gaining her composure, she responded, "Really? This early?"

"Where have you been, Xaliandri?"

"I went for an early morning walk."

Her mother eyed her, clearly not believing her.

"What have you done, Xaliandri? Why could you not leave things alone? Why could you not—"

"Because it's not in my nature. I have done nothing wrong, Mother."

Her mother came closer, picking up the golden strands. Her eyes held a sadness Xali had never seen in them.

"Some things are best left as they are."

"Even when those things are lies?"

Her mother looked taken aback for a moment.

"We all must come to terms with who we are at some point, Xali. We always have."

"So, you know?"

"The heads must know what is needed for our world to continue. We second borns accept it just as they swear to protect it."

"But, Mother…" Xali had a feeling her mother knew more, that what she was referring to was even greater than what Xali had pieced together.

"That will be enough, Xaliandri. You will clean up and break your fast with me and your brother."

"Mendol's home?"

"Yes, your aunt sent him home this morning when she summoned your father."

"Mother, what is it I don't know?"

"I do not know what you have discovered, Xaliandri, but you would be best to put it aside if it's not too late."

She kissed Xali's forehead then left the room. Xali collapsed on the bed, staring at the silk that hung loose above her. She didn't know what to think. Her father had been summoned, the heads were meeting, and her mother was warning her. There was no doubt in her mind they were discussing her, but why? No one knew what was going on with her but Carnick and Mendol. What could they possibly know except that she'd been inquisitive?

They broke their fast in silence. Mendol seemed nervous, barely touching his food. He grabbed Xali's arm as she made her way back to her room, the idea of resting her tired mind for a while, very appealing.

"Xali, wait."

She turned and saw the fear in his eyes.

"Mendol, what's happened?"

"I don't know, but it's serious. Aunt Renia called the heads at sunrise and sent me to summon Father. When she called me to speak with her, she was in the meeting hall. The captain of her guard was speaking with her."

"Why is that strange?"

"Because no one but family steps foot in the meeting hall, Xali. It's a strict rule that is never broken."

She swallowed; he was right. It was rare that even second borns were privy to what happened in that room, crown affairs only. It was only used in times of serious duress.

"You think they're discussing me."

"Yes, I fear our aunt has somehow been swayed to the side of the other houses."

"But how can that be? No one knows anything but you and Carnick."

"Where were you last night, Xali?"

"I…I was here."

"No, when I arrived, I came straight to wake you after I gave Father the message. You were not here, your bed had been untouched."

She thought about Sianna and her mother, the risk they'd taken to share their history with her, then thought it best to keep that to herself.

"Nowhere, I couldn't sleep."

She could tell Mendol didn't believe her.

"Did anyone see you?"

"No, I was very discreet."

"And you won't tell me?"

"It's best I don't, not yet."

He nodded. "Well, then, come with me. There's nothing we can do but keep our minds from wandering. I haven't trained my sword skills lately, and I'm sure you wouldn't be opposed to whipping my butt another time."

She laughed. "No, I wouldn't."

They trained, not on Xali's level but on a level where Mendol was comfortable. With his strength having always lain in his magic, he'd never needed to be proficient in sword skills like Xali. He only practiced with her to appease her.

They were laughing at yet another chance he'd missed to best her when the captain of their guard entered the courtyard, accompanied by the captains of the three other houses and a handful of soldiers.

"Princess," he said.

"No," her mother yelled as she came running past them to her children.

"My queen, I have orders."

"You will not take my daughter."

Xali felt her draw her powers, knowing she could slay all of them easily.

"Please, your highness, the orders come from all four heads.

You are all summoned to the Bortees province. We are to take the princess into custody."

Xali could see that he didn't want to do as commanded, he had known Xali since she'd held her first weapon, training directly with her, teaching her the ways of battle. He adored her, and she knew this was breaking his heart. Xali dropped her sword and placed her hand on her mother's shoulder.

"It's all right, Mother, I'll go with them."

"Xali, no," Mendol said.

"It's time to face them, face my fate."

A gentle wind stirred as she said the word, the whisps of hair that had escaped her braid drifting around her face. She walked past them and over to the guards.

"Thank you, Captain," she said before leading the way to the hall of doorways.

She walked, head held high, through the halls of her aunt's castle then into the meeting room, the guards escorting her in. Her aunts and uncle, and her father were all seated, the second borns all standing behind them, the cousins with them. This was serious for everyone to have been called. She looked at the heads defiantly, her eyes glancing toward Carnick who stood behind his mother. He avoided her gaze, his eyes downcast, and her heart dropped. Why wasn't he looking at her?

"Thank you, Captain. Shalinia, Mendol please go stand with your house. Xaliandri, come forward," her aunt instructed.

She moved into the semicircle as her mother and Mendol did as directed, pushing aside her nerves and keeping her head held high.

"It has come to our attention that you have been practicing lesser magic," her aunt said.

She had to keep her jaw from dropping. She'd expected her inquisitions to garnish disapproval but hadn't expected them to know about her magic. How? She looked to Carnick, his eyes still downcast, and her heart broke.

"What do you have to say to these charges?"

"I…I…" She couldn't talk, stung from the betrayal, her mind tumbling with her heart.

"Answer the question," her uncle demanded, slamming his hand on the table and startling her. "I always knew you were a bad omen on this family," he said when she didn't answer.

"Crebant!" her father scolded.

"You have no say, cousin. She is your spawn. She's been nothing but strange since her birth, and now she's brought ill upon this family."

He had stood in his anger, her father standing to argue back.

"Enough!" her aunt yelled.

"Xaliandri, how do you answer the charge?" her other aunt asked.

Swallowing her fear, she answered, "Yes, but I can't help it. That's all I have, and they're not lesser. They never were. The immortals were strong. They—"

The room erupted, everyone talking at once, the sound overpowering her. They continued, each trying to overtake the other, the room a cacophony of voices. As it grew so did Xali's feeling of being out of control. It had to end. She put her hand over her ears, the noise, the vitriol of the words too much to take.

"Stop," she whispered. "Please, just stop."

She felt the tingling magic grow with each plea until it was as loud as the room. The ground shook, the windows rattled as the glass tried to escape, pieces of the ceiling beginning to crumble.

"Stop!" she screamed, throwing her arms out and her head back. Roots exploded through the stone floor, vines plunged through the windows that lined the room, glass pelting them, the wind adding force to it as everyone ducked and crouched. As her eyes met Carnick's, she read the sadness and the guilt they carried.

She let out a cry, and rain tore through the room, the ground rising on all sides of her as her family, the elders fought back. It enclosed her, suffocating her, and something reached into her, an attempt to suffocate the power within her. *Just as it did to the immortals,* her mind screamed. She spotted her uncle who was chanting and knew he was the one. So that was how it had been done. He was shaking, and she could tell he didn't understand how to use the spell, not like the great king must have. She called to a vine that shot from behind him and entangled him, pulling him to the ground. The feeling fled, and she relaxed, letting the magic reach the torn ground that encased her, calming it, taking control of it. She willed it to lower, removing her family's control from it and stepped out as it returned to its place. They all stared at her, their hands still raised to the ground that no longer heeded their call.

"They are not lesser powers!" she screamed. "The immortals were stronger, their powers greater, they were not the guilty ones, we are. We invaded their land; we stole what the Fates had given them. We built a kingdom on lies that all of you have upheld since the great king committed his atrocities. It is time we find the truth. It is time we stopped living in the shadow of a man who was nothing more than a liar, a murderer."

"Blasphemy!" her aunt yelled. "You have sealed your own fate, Xaliandri."

"I know," she said then thought of going far from all of this. She was tired of the lies, tired of hiding, scared for her life. In that moment, she thought of the peace she'd had in the land behind the guardian wall.

"Seize her!"

The magic of her family attacked again, and she sent her anger out toward it, the rising stones exploding as she thought desperately of leaving. Then everything went black, her breath was knocked from her, and she felt a warmth that encased her before she felt something solid against her feet. She blinked, the darkness gone, her feet now standing in a grassy area. She tumbled, a wave of dizziness hitting her as she tried to grasp her surroundings. The sun streamed on the ruins of the land behind the guardian wall. She had somehow escaped, somehow transported herself to where she'd wanted to be. She stared down at the stone pieces that held the names *Violissa* and *Sinow*, then bent down, running her hand across the ancient stone. In her heart, she knew this was exactly where she was supposed to be.

Eleven

The room broke out in a blare of voices, but Carnick ignored them. Instead, he continued to stare at the space where Xali had been. The look of hurt in her eyes had shredded his heart. She blamed him, she hated him, and now, she was alone somewhere. Where had she gone? And how? It was as if she had stepped through a doorway—she'd simply disappeared.

"Carnick," his mother said, breaking his trance, "where did she go?"

The room had grown silent, and they were all staring at him. He had his suspicions, but he wouldn't tell them. She needed to stay safe, and for the moment, she was safe from them.

"I don't know. I don't even know how she did that."

"Don't protect her, son."

"I'm not, and she can clearly protect herself." He'd had enough. "You all turned on her as if she were a lesser kind. She's one of us, she's family."

"She's a traitor," his uncle said.

"Why? Because she asked questions? Questions many of us should ask. Questions that should have been addressed long before now."

His uncle's eyes grew stormy. "The traditions of this family are what keep us in power. We obey the laws of the great king, our forefathers, no matter the cost."

Carnick knew he was on tenuous ground, but he was a first born and the strongest of his cousins. "What keeps us in power is hiding, distorting the truth—"

"Enough, Carnick," Xali's father said. "When you are king, the answers will be provided. They are not for a second born to know or understand. It is your duty as a first born to accept them when you take the throne. Now, if you'll all excuse me, I need to find my daughter."

His other uncle started to complain, but his mother raised her hand to silence him. As he left with Xali's mother, the others filtered out, whispers of finding her on their tongues.

Once the heads had left, Carnick looked around, noticing Mendol and Fairenth were no longer with them, and he stormed out to find them.

"Carnick!" he heard Ainia call. He stopped and turned toward her. As a first born, she would one day rule the Nobesn province; it was her father who had turned on Xali.

"What is it, Ainia?"

She pulled him to the side where a doorway stood leading to the gardens. They were tucked where the others could no longer see them.

"Is it true?"

"Is what true?"

"Everything that Xali said?"

He eyed her suspiciously. "Leave me be, Ainia. It is your father who wanted this."

He moved to walk away, but she grabbed his arm. "I am not my father. Xali is my cousin, too. Do not think I want her harmed."

"Why should I tell you anything?"

"Because there are more of us who have questions. We simply refrain from asking them. Please, Carnick."

"Yes, it's true, but this is not a safe place to discuss anything."

"Then tell me where and when."

"Fine, meet me in…" He thought about where to go, where no one would be scouting for Xali or find it suspicious that cousins were together if discovered. "Meet me in the holy land when the moons are at their peak."

She nodded and hurried off. He then headed for his sister's room.

Carnick stormed through Fairenth's door, slamming it shut with a force that rocked the walls.

"How dare you," he said, going straight to her and grabbing her arms tightly.

"Carnick, I had no choice," she cried.

"You had no choice but to sell her out? Why? To protect your precious standing with Mother?"

"Carnick, that's enough!" Mendol yelled, pulling him from her.

"And you!" He punched Mendol.

"Couldn't keep your mouth shut? She's your sister for gods' sakes. And you tell Fairenth of all people? She who can't keep anything to herself. Are you an idiot?"

Mendol straightened, rubbing his cheek, his eyes stormy, just as Carnick knew his own were. Carnick stepped back, running his hand through his hair, trying to catch hold of his temper. His blood felt as if it were on fire.

Fairenth was crying. "I didn't know this would happen."

"Are you serious?" he asked. "You didn't think they would turn on her if you validated their suspicions? Dammit, Fairenth, you told them she had lesser powers, that she was using them. That's a death sentence. Mother was the only one keeping her safe, and you forced her hand."

"I had no choice, Carnick. It was an accident, I slipped, and she caught it. I was forced to tell her all I knew."

"Which you wouldn't have known if Mendol had kept his mouth shut. If anything happens to her, I hold both of you responsible."

"She's my sister. You don't think I'm concerned?"

"Not concerned enough to hold your tongue."

Carnick stormed from the room, the desire to bring great harm to Mendol too high to contain if he stayed longer.

Carnick paced the stone walkway that led to the shrine of the gods. He'd come early, his mind racing too rapidly to remain in the palace. The look in Xali's eyes still haunted him. She blamed him, he'd taken the blame, not fighting the accusation her eyes had held, the disappointment, the hurt. It had killed him.

Now, she was out there somewhere alone, likely frightened, thinking that he'd betrayed her. Damn Fairenth and her loose tongue. Curse Mendol for telling her in the first place. He rubbed his face, stopping before the shrine, facing the carvings of the gods. Was she right? Were they false idols? Was everything she was fighting to reveal worth it?

"If you truly are the Fates, if all of this is a lie, please protect her. She's seeking the truth, she shouldn't have to die for it, for you."

He stared at the mantle, the mural that stood above it. From their stone, he pulled minerals to light the area, their twinkling a delicate mix of hues that lent a peaceful feel to the space, a dichotomy to the feeling of angst that filled the moment.

"Carnick," he heard Ainia's voice.

He turned to see her with the other cousins, all but Mendol and his sister.

"I thought it was just us, Ainia?"

"We all deserve to know the truth."

"Even second borns?" He cringed as the word left his mouth, knowing the hurt they would have brought Xali.

"It is clear being second no longer makes us lesser born. Xali overwhelmed them all, she's stronger," Trevant said.

He nodded. "And why should I risk telling any of you what I know, what she's discovered?"

"Because she's not the only one who questions. She's simply the only one brave enough to seek the answers."

He wasn't sure what to say. It had never occurred to him that any of the others were suspicious of their history.

"They'll kill her if any of you—"

"She's already dead if they find her. There will be no trial, she just showed them all that she's guilty," Ainia said.

"They won't really kill her, right? She's family," Herind said.

"It's never happened before."

"Yes, it has," he heard Mendol say.

Carnick looked to see him walking up to them.

"What are you doing here?" Carnick growled.

"I'm here to help my sister. Fairenth doesn't know. I didn't realize she was so weak willed, Carnick. Do you really think I want to see my sister hurt? That I want to lose her?" He was sincere, his eyes filled with regret. "I only want her safe, and I'll do whatever it takes to ensure she is."

Carnick sighed, relaxing some. "Tell us why you think there's been killing in the past."

"I found it when I was researching our history. It was early on after we settled these lands. A few generations after the great king, a second born exhibited lesser powers. She tried to hide it but was discovered. They executed her."

"But the houses...how did they replace her?"

"They didn't. Another second born was split between the two houses. She stayed with the king in the Visentia province until she birthed two children then was sent to the Bortees province where she remained with that king until his two children were birthed. It's the only history of anyone producing more than two heirs."

"Those are our provinces, mine and Xali's," Carnick said, astonished at the story.

No one seemed to know what to say. To treat a second born like a birthing vessel was beyond cruel even to their standards. The truly appalling part, the mere thought that one cousin had taken his own sister in order to continue their line. The vileness of it left it best unspoken.

"Why are lesser powers so bad?" Trevant asked. "It's still magic."

"Because they're unknown, and we fear the unknown. And because lesser powers are thought to have been those of the immortals. We can't have any thought that the immortals had stronger magic than our own. It would crush the lies our kingdom has been built upon."

"They're still powers and only a member of our family has them whether they are shared by the ancient immortals or not," Herind said.

"But that begs a question. How are they shared? If Xali is right, and the great king invaded this land, why is there a connection between rare members of our family and the immortals?" Mendol asked.

"Who said anything about invasion? Are you saying that's what Xali thinks?"

Carnick proceeded to share everything he and Xali had discovered, Mendol's question still in the back of his mind, all of them trying to grasp what he'd told them.

There was a long silence, and he gave them the time.

"What do we do now?" Sartria finally asked.

"We wait for Xali's next move."

"And you think she has one? Do you even know where she is?"

He suspected, but he wasn't about to share, not entirely certain he trusted all of them.

"No. Whatever this is, whatever is awakening in her, there's a reason. There are simply too many questions she's brought to light. I think this is her path, to bring about change, whether the family likes it or not, so we wait for her."

"It's a lot to take in, Carnick."

"I know."

"And so we sit on it and wait?"

He nodded.

"Then that's what we'll do."

Twelve

Xali stared at the stone, her fingers tracing the names as the rain began to fall. She'd been frozen in shock and fear, unable to move as the sun had set and the moons had taken its place. She was behind the guardian wall but for what reason? She wasn't even sure how she'd gotten here. One moment she'd been fighting for her life, the next she'd been in the peaceful quiet of the ruins she and Carnick had discovered.

"Why am I here?" she asked, turning to face the sky. "Why are you doing this to me?"

No answer came, and so she pulled her knees into her chest, the rain soaking her clothes, droplets running from her hair across her eyes.

"I don't know what you want me to do," she whispered.

"The Fates do not always clearly reveal our path, child."

Xali turned quickly toward the voice. A woman stood across

from her, her hair shielded from the rain with a pale green cloak, her sage eyes friendly.

"Who are you? No one lives beyond the guardian wall."

"There are things that remain hidden from eyes that are not fully open to the truth. Come." She offered Xali a hand.

Xali waited for a moment before accepting it. She felt no threat from the woman. In fact, she felt a connection of sorts. Her wise eyes waited patiently, non-judgmental. Xali took her hand and rose from the ground. She followed the woman as she made her way across the ruins and on to the towering remnants of what could only have been a castle at one time. She remembered seeing the shadow of it the night she'd been here with Carnick, but now she saw the sheer magnitude of it. It was unlike any structure she'd ever seen. Fragments hung in the cliffside that overlooked the area, as if it had once been part of the land, built from it.

"There are no castles beyond the guardian wall, only wild animals lie here."

"Then why is it sealed from your people, from your knowledge?" the woman asked.

Xali continued to follow her, marveling at the structure which even in its dilapidated state spoke of its former glory. On they walked, deep into its bones until they came upon a massive tree root. Xali followed it with her eyes, seeing how it flowed in and out of the structure's remains.

"The tree once stood proud as the center of the castle, the heart of it. I'm told it was a sight that inspired all who witnessed it. With the fall of the immortals, as you call them, our people were left defenseless, the invaders ripping through what had been present since the creation of the races. Our people fell that day, lost with all that defined our world."

Xali turned to the woman. "Who are you and who are your people?"

She brought her hood down to reveal long, straight golden hair, her sage eyes soft.

"We are the Elvin. There are few of us left, our ancestors hiding beneath the tree's protection, the Mother Fate guiding them to safety. Here we have remained, hidden from all when that monstrosity was built to hide our land and its secrets from the rest of the realms."

Xali reached her fingers up and pulled her golden lock free from her braid. Even soaked with water, the curl remained. As her fingers touched it, a golden shimmer rose from it, the strand drying to reveal color that mirrored the woman's.

"You have been chosen," she said, eyeing the curl. "Our queen calls you. It is time for them to return, and you will guide their way."

She turned abruptly, placing her hand on the root which to Xali's amazement drew back to reveal an entranceway. The woman walked in, leaving Xali still frozen by her words and the tree's movement.

"Follow closely, the tree does not like to linger."

Xali woke from her shock and caught up with the woman.

"What is your name, child?" she asked as darkness engulfed them, the sound of the tree's root echoing around her. Xali placed a hand on the wall of the tunnel, calling forth the elements within it until the corridor sparkled with shimmers of green, blue, and silver.

The woman turned and studied her.

She shrugged. "One of the only abilities I share with my family."

An awkward silence followed as the woman's eyes remained fixed.

"Chosen, indeed. Now what do they call you?"

"My name is Xali."

"Xaliandri," the woman responded, her eyes wide with realization. "We have heard the echoes of her voice in our dreams, she calls you."

"You, you hear her, too?" Xali couldn't hide her surprise.

She didn't answer, instead saying, "I am Tialiav."

She turned and began walking again, the corridor never seeming to end until finally she reached another tree root that pulled back, light filtering through. Xali followed Tialiav, her eyes widening in wonder as she entered a massive room, rays of moonlight filtering down from unseen spaces high above them. Xali turned, taking in the beauty of it. Tree roots and vines wrapped the white marble like etchings that told a story of time and knowledge. The moonlight streams shimmered on the stone from below her feet, it's texture smooth, no imperfections to be seen. From the great hall, tunnels spanned out to places unseen, twists of vines and flowers outlining each.

"Where are we?" Xali asked in wonder.

"You are deep in the Elvin home of our royal family."

"The castle?" She thought back to the ruins. "But it was destroyed, we walked through the remains of it." She was befuddled; it was as if she'd crossed through a doorway to another realm.

"Our people have endured many hardships. This castle has existed since the beginning of our creation. As strife increasingly threatened our people during the great war, the Light king assisted us in building this sanctuary, hidden far behind the original castle, a safe haven if the Dark kings ever breeched our borders."

Xali stared at her, not comprehending.

"The great war? That's what they call it, what the great king did?"

Tialiav's face contorted to disgust. "Your great king drove us here, nearly wiping my people from existence. He was no great king, he was a pretender, a usurper, a scourge to this world." She spat on the ground as if doing so would rid a rancid taste from her mouth.

"You will have to forgive us. We are not fond of the one your people call the great king," a golden-haired man said, emerging from one of the tunnels. His green eyes shimmered as he walked through a moonbeam.

"There were many great kings that ruled these lands before

your ancestor stole them. There were also many terrifying kings, Dark magic kings to be truly feared, your family's magic no match for theirs."

Xali straightened, the insult not missed. "And yet my family rules these lands."

He studied her, the green of his eyes changing to a rich sage. "You have been raised on lies, ones I believe you have questioned; otherwise, you would not be standing here. That will be all, Tialiav," he said to Xali's guide.

She nodded and scurried off.

"You're their king?" she asked, the realization dawning on her.

"I am Narilen, and yes, what remains of the Elvin are my people. I am the last king of the Elvin."

Xali was taken aback, all of it overwhelming her. Too much had happened this day for her to comprehend any more. As if sensing this, Narilen took her arm and guided her across the open space then down one of the corridors.

"Come, you're tired. Rest and we'll talk in the morn."

She stopped, pulling her arm away. "Why have we never seen your people? The term Elvin is mentioned rarely and only from the tongues of Cirillians. You're a myth, something told of in backwards towns and in murmurings."

"Your great king, as you call him, hunted my people down, slaying our royal family, all but one small child who was whisked away to the safety of this shelter. It is said our guards fought a battle that distracted his gaze and allowed for our few survivors to shield themselves and the princess from his eyes. We have hidden here since, living in obscurity, venturing out only when necessary beyond that monstrosity that enclosed our lands from the other realms. It is not the first time my people have been hunted, not the first time we've lived hidden from those who hunt us."

"He thought he killed you all and left it from our history."

"As he did most things that cast doubt on his legitimacy."

"How do you know that?"

"As I said, we venture beyond to the towns. We have scouts, trained to stay hidden, to move in the shadows or risk exposing us to the cruelty of your family."

"How do you know they are my family?"

"The storm clouds in your eyes belie your magic. Although the emerald specks tell me there is more to you than I have surmised."

"Much more." She thought about the green flecks in her eyes and the emerald in his.

"Your people have magic?"

"Some might call it magic, but it is only a connection to the land. We ask, and the land answers. It protects us here, feeds us. It responds to our call. That connection runs through the blood of all our people. The royal family once had magic that moved the wind, summoned storms, breathed renewal into failing plants, some even changing the seasons themselves. As time passed, the magic has lessened. The princess who had been saved, was young, still untrained, her magic in its infancy. The longer we live confined to experience the sun's presence only through the beams that are directed into this sanctuary, the less power our royal line holds. The magic was lost, severed when the kingdoms were severed, when our tie to the high queen was severed."

"The high queen?"

"Queen Violissa. Now that is enough talk for today." He turned and left her lost in her thoughts. She ran to catch up with him, her mind busy making sense of everything. The name confirming her suspicions. The same name she'd found in the stones, the same Sianna had given her when Xali had gone to her home.

He stopped in front of a door that opened with the twist of a vine. A slim stream of moonlight drifted down, only allowing a small amount of the room to be seen.

"You will sleep here. Tialiav will fetch you in the morn. We will talk more and begin your training."

"Training?"

"You hold the magic of our people, untapped, uncontrolled.

It is time you understand that with which you have been blessed."

The door closed, and Xali was left alone, the darkness of the room engulfing her as she stood in the moon's soft glow. In that moment, she felt small and afraid. Alone in a world that was larger than it had ever felt. Alone in a world where she didn't belong, no matter which part of it she stepped into.

Finding her way to the bed, she rested her head on a pillow that smelled as if it were filled with flower petals. Her dreams were touched with images of Carnick and feelings of betrayal, loss, and an endless sadness. They were empty of the woman and her calming voice, something Xali would have welcomed to stave off the pain that otherwise drowned her.

Xali woke, the feel of the unfamiliar bed below her causing her to rise faster than her usual casual start. A stream of sunlight highlighted the marble floor, fanning out to encompass the bottom of what looked like a wardrobe. The light cast enough of its ray to leave most of the room in gray, leaving only the corners hidden from her sight. The events of the prior night returned to her, the weight of all that had happened flooding back. She wiped the sleep from her eyes and eventually found her way out of the room, following the dark corridor, the way she remembered from the prior evening.

Sunlight shone in her path, and she stepped out into the great hall where she'd met the Elvin king that night. She took it in, the beauty of it striking as if she'd not seen it before. It was like nothing she'd seen, the stream of sunbeams giving it the feel she experienced when she visited the holy land, an ephemeral reverence, ancient in the impression it lent. She held her hand out to the sunbeam, feeling warmth where there should have been none. The source was not direct, one that she still could not fathom.

Movement caught her eye, and she was drawn to a light fabric that blew gently in a breeze she could not feel as she pushed the material aside and continued forward. She stepped into a garden that encapsulated the space before her. A fountain of stone sat in the center, water flowing from it onto small pathways that ran through the room, disappearing to where Xali could not see. Running water? Flowers that bloomed with no sun?

She leaned over and fingered a mauve petal on a plant with which she was unfamiliar. It leaned into her hand, rising as she drew her fingers back.

"The flowers favor you." She heard Narilen's voice behind her.

Startled, she turned quickly. She hadn't heard him enter the room. His green eyes evaluated her, making her strangely self-conscious. She looked away, her eyes drifting to a ray of light that flickered against the water.

"How is it they grow here? The light isn't from the sun. Where does it come from?"

"You ask many questions. I suppose it's something for which we should all be grateful. Your questioning will be our saving grace."

He had walked toward the fountain, his eyes turning up to the light. "As I said, our people have been hunted in the past. The Dark king Theonelle was especially vicious. During the great war, our people fled to this vale, our king trading favor with the Light king Viliren. Viliren and his Lightbearers helped build this sanctuary, his magic still remains in the light. It pulls from unseen places to keep us healthy, to keep our plants alive. It is in the water that flows through it, the air that we breathe. In turn, the Light king made his home in our sun castle while our royal family took to the moon castle. The two kings left their mark on our kind, forever changing us all as Theonelle raged like the wind in an unstoppable storm."

Xali had no idea who any of these people were. Her knowledge of the great war was when the great king had taken their lands back. But Narilen wasn't speaking of that time. These men were ones lost to a history that had been submerged in lies.

"The sun castle," she said, her mind wandering to the ruins she and Carnick had passed the night they'd ventured beyond the guardian wall. "It stood atop the valley?"

"Aye, it had been our family seat since the beginning of time, the moon castle only reserved for the extended family of the king until we gifted the sun castle to Viliren. The Light king resided in the sun castle until the day Theonelle forced the first steps in the prophecy. But that is a story for another day. Come, we have work to do."

"No, wait. There's a history to this world that I don't know. Please. Who or what is a Light king? And what do the Elvin have to do with all of this? Why aren't you dead like the other immortals? Are there more alive?"

He laughed. "Questions. So many questions. I am not immortal, our line was never blessed as the Light and Dark races were. Elvin magic is the lesser of the three magics. We are but limbs bowing to the force of their power. Our magic has been split and fractured through the ages. It lives in all our people to some extent, our royal family diluting its power with birth, as each child is born so the power splits. Our kings fragmented it with multiple children, none ever sealing its force within one. Although some say it was the Mother Fate who chose that path for us."

"Our family has two children in each province. It's always been that way."

"Hah, so your great king wanted you to believe. When he waged his actions against the immortals, as your people call them, the Fates cursed him. His power was fractured, two sons he was given, and then two heirs each to them as it would remain. Upon his death, his high power was diluted, weakened by his own pride and greed, none of his heirs to ever hold the same power he held. That is until you."

"I don't understand. So, the Elvin and our people were cursed?"

"The Elvin chose to spread their magic; the Mother Fate had already shared it among all her Elvin children. It wasn't meant to be housed in one ruler as it was with the other races. Dark magic and Light magic are too potent for more than one bearer. There has only been one time an exception was ever made to that rule and that was with purpose."

Xali was more confused than she'd ever been.

"Your ancestor cursed your line to live as lesser-powered, their full potential never met because of his recklessness."

Although she'd only just woken, Xali was suddenly exhausted, overwhelmed with the thought that a vast history existed, one that clearly left her people weaker than those who had existed before them.

"Enough questions. There is no time for history lessons. That is something you will need to discover on your own."

"But if we were once a higher power, why was the great…my ancestor not immortal?"

"And yet you continue to ask. I will indulge this final one. He was not meant to be as the Elvin were not. Dark and Light balance the world. It is a balance that has always existed, and without the balance, the world suffers. Those carrying Dark and Light magic were blessed with immortality because their power required it. To carry the magic of the Fates, one must be as close as possible to them. Immortality is the vessel that allowed those powers to be present in our world and to maintain the balance."

"Our world is not out of balance."

"Is it not? Does strife not run through the people? Do not the moon and sun cycles flow erratically? Do the seasons not change inconsistently?"

She thought about his words. He was right, but those things had always been there, winter came when the change of leaves should have happened, the warm seasons sometime lasted two cycles. The moons rose at inconsistent times. All of it part of life. But perhaps it had been different once.

"They held that kind of power? How is that possible?"

"Their power was endless, child. They were children of the

Fates."

She went to ask him another question, but he stopped her.

"That is enough, the rest you will have to learn on your own. You are not here to understand our history, you are here to discover your potential, to understand the magic you hold within you. We have a finite amount of time, so let us begin."

"A finite amount of time before what?"

"Before she calls you again."

He walked off, leaving her staring at the space where he'd been, too stunned by all the revelations to move.

"Follow or you will remain lost."

His words woke her, and she ran to catch up, the true meaning of those words clear to her. She felt lost, in a forest of infinite stories, ones that defined the land she stood upon and destroyed the very world she'd been raised upon.

Xali sat back against the column, the cool of the marble refreshing. She hadn't worked this hard since she'd first taken up the sword. Drops of sweat rolled down her nose and rested on her lip. She wiped them away with the back of her hand. Why was magic so difficult to master?

"You worked hard today, Xali, just as you have each day since you arrived," Narilen said, coming to stand over her.

"It's not helping. Why can't I just raise the land, listening to the wind, as I did before. Why fight my instincts, why harness what wants to be released?"

"Your magic is more than what you know from the way your family uses it. To truly master the connection you have to the land, you must master the delicate side of your power. That is what your family has lost and what you have found."

"Delicate? It was always non-existent," she grumbled.

"No. It was always there, it simply waited for you to discover it. You are special, Xaliandri. It is easy to call forth the land with force and destruction. It is a difficult task to convince it to come forth, to open to your call, to heed your desires willingly. You have mastered that; you have learned what you can from me."

He extended his hand.

"But I haven't mastered anything. I break a sweat just restraining the magic, I—"

"You are ready. I can only teach you so much. There are two sides to your magic, Xali. The other is for you to discover on your own, to learn on the next part of your journey."

"Two sides?" She thought about Carnick for the first time in days, having pushed him from her mind, thoughts of him only dredging up the hurt. She thought of how dark his eyes had become lately, the violet disappearing to an ebony that swirled among the storm clouds.

"Dark." She looked at Narilen. "We have both Elvin and Dark power? Both run through our veins? But how? I don't understand."

"It is not my place to explain. You will find out, but not here. It is time for you to step forward to the next path, Xali."

She took his hand and let him pull her up.

"I'm leaving, aren't I?"

"Yes, there is much for you to discover, and I am only a part of it. Your future awaits outside this sanctuary."

"They'll kill me. My family has sentenced me to death, they will kill me."

His emerald eyes grew sad. "Perhaps, but I believe the Fates have other plans for you, Xaliandri. You will be the salvation of us all."

Thirteen

Carnick had no idea how long the wait for Xali would be. Strife encompassed the western provinces, sending repercussions throughout Old Tenebron and discontent in the provinces that covered Old Cirillia. The lesser people had heard a rumor, and it had spread like wildfire. The immortals were on their minds; someone with their powers was said to have emerged. No one knew how the rumor had started or if they really did know about Xali, but it took over the mindset, and the fragile calm in the provinces within Old Tenebron crumbled.

Fighting had broken out as uprisings began, the Gaern towns were put on high guard, Carnick and his parents forced to create borders to keep the lesser kind out, drawing the land up to encase their towns. Carnick had never seen anything like it.

Weeks passed, the joining of Mendol and Fairenth was postponed, and, of course, his joining with Xali was canceled—to be dealt with at a later time. Carnick wondered if it would ever come, if she'd even return, and if she did, would they take him from her and kill her for being who she was. He missed her greatly, and each day that passed only increased his desire to find her. She was the key to stopping this. He didn't know how, but he knew she was. Since she hadn't returned, he'd set out to find her himself. He had an idea of where she was, a suspicion he couldn't explain other than with instinct. Sneaking from the palace, he readied his horse and rode toward her, determined to find her no matter the cost, knowing this move would be seen as treason, and he would be marked for death along with her, regardless of his first born status.

He rode his horse hard to the guardian wall where it met the border of his mother's province. Dismounting, he looked around to see if he'd been noticed. He'd stayed in the shadows, but with the guards on high alert, there was still a good chance he could have been seen. He slapped his horse, setting it free then sent a quick prayer to the gods before bringing his hand up and willing the stone of the wall to move, forcing it from its long slumber and wrenching it so that it crumbled enough so that he could climb through an opening. He then forced the stone to reform. It wasn't a perfect replica of how it had been, but it was close enough. He ran into the forest, praying he could find his way back to the ruins where he knew Xali had gone, praying he found her before the rest of the family did.

The woods were dark, and he lost his bearings. He knew he had to go east; they'd journeyed into the forest from Xali's province. If he was too far west, he risked accidently stumbling over the cliffs that had stood above the ruins. A noise caused him to halt. Were the rumors of wild animals in these woods true? Would he be eaten before he found her? The noise grew, and he drew his power right before the green eyes of the strange stallion appeared from the darkness. Carnick hesitated, unsure if the beast would be friendly without Xali. It came closer then leaned so that he could mount it.

"I'll be damned," he muttered, before climbing atop the massive beast. "Take me to her," he whispered then held tight as it took off.

Xali gathered her things, Narilen's words running through her head. She changed back into the clothes she'd arrived in then left the room that had been her safe haven for the past few weeks. Standing in the great hall, a small bag of supplies in her hand, she said her goodbyes to the Elvin, leaving Narilen in the gardens. With a deep breath, she turned to the tree root, willing it to allow her passage, and walked the corridor, the minerals in the walls lighting her way with no effort on her part. They shimmered brightly as if bidding her farewell. As she exited the tunnel, the root closed behind her. She didn't look back. Narilen was right; she was on a new path, one from which she couldn't stray. With a new determination, she made her way out of the exterior castle ruins, following the edge of the valley.

Movement caught her eye, and she stepped back into the shadows, her heart racing. In the center of the vale stood Carnick. He was searching for something, a frantic look in his eyes, his usual kempt appearance now disheveled.

Slowly, she walked closer until she was near enough to hear him whisper, "Where are you, Xali?" His voice was set with worry. Part of her wanted to flee, to turn her back on him and disappear, remaining in the shadows where he would never find her. The other part of her longed for his touch, to see the violet specks in his eyes light up when he saw her. She'd missed him, more than she'd allowed herself to acknowledge, and it hurt to admit it. The sting of his betrayal still lingered, regardless of the pull of her heart.

He turned so that the moonlight lit his silver hair, and there were the violet specks glowing in the night sky, awakening her pained heart. Reluctantly, she stepped out into the moonlight, and his head turned to her immediately, relief filling his face.

"Xali, you're safe."

She wanted to run to him, she'd lost count of how long she'd been away. She had missed him, but she refrained, still angry at his betrayal.

"How did you find me, Carnick?" she asked, the bitterness evident in her tone.

"Xali, I…it just seemed like a place you would go." He appeared as if he were going to say something different, and she sensed hesitation in his voice. "How did you get here? You disappeared, as if a doorway had taken you."

"I don't know to be honest. I thought about escaping, and then I was here."

He looked at her, his eyes sad, and she wondered if it were regret she was seeing.

It doesn't matter, she told herself. *He betrayed me. I can no longer be his.* "Leave, Carnick."

He looked surprised. "Xali, I came to help."

"Help? You're the reason I'm abandoned here, the reason they all turned against me."

"They were already against you."

He hadn't denied his involvement, and it stung. She walked closer so that she was directly in front of him.

"Did you ever love me or was it all a lie?"

"You can't be serious. I've done everything for you, risked everything. How can you even ask me that?"

"You told them everything, Carnick. You're the only one who knew other than my brother. You turned on me, fed me to the wolves, and didn't have the nerve to even look at me."

Her anger overcame her, the weeks of pent-up rage and emotion spilling out with a hard slap across his cheek. He didn't flinch, his eyes full of pain.

"I loved you, and you threw that away," she said, backing away from him.

"Xali, stop, you don't know what you're saying."

The ground rumbled, her new powers swelling within her and the land responding.

"I know exactly what I'm saying."

She heard the land creak as a wave of power crested through it. It shook with a force that was beyond her control.

"Xali, stop. We can talk this through."

Before she could respond, there was a loud crack and the ground collapsed below her feet. She screamed as she fell, Carnick's face a mirror to her fear.

He should have told her the truth. Should have told her Fairenth was the one, but he hadn't. Instead Carnick stayed quiet, taking the blame to protect his sister, praying Xali would forgive him one day. He rubbed his cheek where she had slapped him, biting back the pain in his chest as the words tumbled from her mouth. He wanted to grab her, to kiss her, to fix the rift that his sister had caused but he couldn't. She was so hurt that the ground was quaking below them, her magic seeping from her. The grass had grown to reach her waist, vines thickened around the pile of ruins, but she didn't seem to notice. Then, the ground ripped open, and she fell, the collapsing land falling around her.

He ran to her but was too late. He yelled her name as her scream disappeared with her.

"Xali!" he called, peering over the edge of the cavern that now lay below him. She was pulling herself up on her elbow and rubbing her head.

"I'm all right," she called to him.

"I'm coming down to help you."

"No, I'm fine."

He ignored her, using his power to pull the debris into a swollen mound that reached close enough for him to jump onto, then he let it bring him down to her level. She was bleeding on her temple where debris had hit her as she'd fallen. He stooped down next to her, bringing his fingers to touch the blood.

"You're wounded," he said, but she pushed his hand away and scooted back. Sighing, he stood and held a hand out to her. "Are you able to stand?"

She gave his hand an irritated look but took it, letting him pull her up.

"Yes, I'm fine." But she swayed as she stood and couldn't hide the wince of pain.

"You're hurt, we should get you back and have someone look at your injuries."

"Why bother? They'll just kill me anyway. Is that why you're here?"

"Of course not!" he bit back, his irritance at her stubbornness too great to hide.

She turned from him and gingerly walked over the debris, taking in her surroundings.

"What is this place?"

He shrugged, saying, "Probably a pocket of air in the land."

"No, pockets of air don't have stone walls or…what is that?"

She was right, this was no defect in the land, it had been a room, he could see sconces in the moonlight and, where she was pointing, what looked like an entranceway that had been sealed.

"I don't know."

He walked closer, trying to keep his balance. The entranceway was massive with no way in. The only way he knew there was something beyond was the indent between the wall and the stone sealing it; otherwise, one might think it one solid piece of stone.

"We need to get in there," she said.

"Do we?"

"You don't have to stay. Crawl back to your mother for all I care. I'm getting through this doorway."

"That stings, Xali. I'm not crawling back to my mother. I'm staying right here by your side. "

She gave him a side-glance, her brow furrowed. He knew she didn't understand, her mind still set that he'd betrayed her, but he wasn't about to leave her alone.

"How do you suppose we get this open?"

"We break through," he answered.

He put his hand on the stone out of some need to feel it, the cold of it seeking the warmth of his skin. Below his hand, the stone began to warm, and he felt something within him being called, a tug on his power but not his usual powers, that deeper, darker magic he'd been experiencing lately. It frightened him, the feeling still foreign to him, but he ignored the fear and let his guard down, the magic answering the call. He was aware of Xali stepping back as she inhaled sharply, but he couldn't take his eyes from the stone which was turning black. A crack split the silence and ripped through the stone, splitting it into hundreds of fractures before the door collapsed altogether.

He didn't move, his hand still hanging midair. The call to that part of his magic that he could only name as dark was overwhelming. It drew something from deep within him, unsealing it, and as it freed itself, it intertwined with his existing magic. His hand dropped, and a feeling of completeness came over him.

"Carnick?"

He turned to her, and a look of surprise reflected upon her face.

"Your eyes. They're…they're filled with black. Stormy clouds of black where you usually have violet."

He didn't know how to respond, something far within him had changed, and with it, his magic was now different.

He turned back to the opening that now stood before them.

"Something is down there. Do you feel it?"

"Yes."

He stepped into the darkness, drawn to continue. The further they went, the more engulfed in black they became, the path slanting downward into an unseen abyss.

"I can't see, Carnick."

"I know, I can't pull any light from whatever these walls are made of."

"Here." He felt her draw her magic, and suddenly, the path before them was filled with light.

A ball of white light floated in the air behind her.

"What is that?"

"They call it a light sphere. It's how the immortals lit the night."

He stared at her for a moment, waiting for more on how she'd learned this trick and garnered that knowledge.

She shrugged. "I've been studying while I've been away."

She walked past him, the sphere following her. Down they continued, the sloped tunnel never seeming to end until finally, they reached an opening that led into a small room.

"This has to be a mile below the other room," she said. "What would the Elvin need to hide this far below ground?"

"Elvin?"

"They were the people who once inhabited this land, the Elvin Enclave. Their power was nature driven."

"But the Elvin are a myth, a story told to frighten children."

"Just trust me."

There was a certainty to the way she said the words, and he wondered what she'd been doing in the time she'd been missing. Knowing now wasn't the moment to broach that subject, he instead looked around the room, an odd sensation overcoming him, a familiarity to the magic he could feel against his skin. "I don't think this was the work of your mythical Elvin," he said.

"No, it wasn't," she whispered, her voice full of fear. She brought her hand up and pointed. "Why is that here?"

He followed the direction of her finger. A doorway matching the one from their palaces stood in the corner, its magic pulsing a deep ebony. Tendrils of black were climbing from it. His eyes followed the vinelike streams to their source, a long stone box with intricate engraving on it. It looked like a bed for the dead. Xali started toward it, but Carnick grabbed her arm.

She shot him a nasty look.

"We don't know what's in there. Someone went to great lengths to ensure whatever it is stays hidden."

"Then I think it's time we reveal it."

She pulled her arm away and moved to the box, Carnick following. Then she drew a shaky breath. Peering in to see what she'd found, his knees almost gave way.

"It's a man," he said, his voice unsteady.

"An immortal," she said softly.

"No, the immortals are dead."

"Carnick, he's an immortal…king of them all. He's the immortal Dark king."

"Sinow." The name from the broken stone came back to him. "But how do you know?"

"The same way you know that was his name. And…there was a sketch. It looks just like him."

"A sketch?"

"I was right, Carnick, about all of it. He was just a man, with a family. A wife he adored, a son they both loved. All of them were a family doing what was right for their people when we invaded them."

"If you are right, then he's not a man, Xali. He's a very dangerous, powerful immortal. We need to get out of here."

"No, we don't. We need to do what's right and wake him."

"What makes you think he's not dead?"

"Are you trying to remain blind to the truth, Carnick? Go home then. I can do this myself."

Carnick poked at the man. His hair was blacker than night, his face chiseled and strong. He was large, the largest man Carnick had ever seen, even in this state, his muscles made him appear larger than life. He was intimidating, and he was breathing. Carnick watched the slight rise and fall of his chest.

"I'm staying by your side."

"Why bother? You didn't before," she said nonchalantly as she eyed the room. Her comment stung, but he made no rebuttal.

"How do you suppose we wake him?"

"I don't know." She was staring at the doorway. "Why is that here?"

"It looks like those black lines lead to him, is it keeping him alive?"

"I don't think so." She moved, following the streams. "I think he's feeding it. This is his magic, somehow being siphoned out to the doorway."

"That's why there is a set amount. Why no one's been able to make more. Gods, Xali, the doorways we have are being fed by him."

"And I think the others." She turned to him. "The great king didn't kill them, he couldn't. They were immortal. Instead, he…" She brought her hand to her throat. "I was right, he somehow used their power against them, trapping it within them. The force incapacitating them, suffocating them, and finally rendering them unconscious to sleep an eternal sleep so he could then bleed their power from them for his own use."

Carnick swallowed, the thought of what she was saying, revolting. He looked back to the case. "Let's wake him and find out."

They moved closer.

"How do we do that?"

"We don't." His mind went to the dream where he'd watched Xali choking. She'd brought her hands to her neck moments ago as if she were remembering the dream. "We're connected to them, you to her and me to him. That's why I was in your dream. I wasn't watching you. He was watching her. Unable to save her, to reach her. I'm the one to wake him and you—"

"To wake her," she said, meeting his eyes. The green flecks were glowing a brilliant emerald, the golden lock of hair shining in the light of her magic.

He nodded then stepped to the stone enclosure. He wasn't entirely sure how he knew he was the one to wake the man, but he did, he felt it deep within him, it was something to do with the strange darkness that had settled within him.

There were words written all along the outside of the case. He circled it, reading them first in his mind, memorizing them. Then, once he had returned to the front, he kneeled and placed his hand on the side where the first words began. He closed his eyes and reached down to the new darkness he felt, letting it wash over him. He could sense it coming through his body, ready for release. As he began to speak the words, he let go of the hold he'd had on it, opening his eyes as it poured into the stone. The writing glowed to a brilliant white then faded to a deep ebony as the room began to shake. He couldn't remove his hand, a force pulling his power forth until none of the dark feeling remained.

The stone began to crack, tiny fractures reaching like cobwebs across it then a massive force threw him backward. His heart hammered as the light faded, a cloud of ebony cascading through the room and with it a sense of terror that permeated his senses.

What had they released?

Fourteen

As Carnick spoke the words, Xali couldn't draw her eyes from him. It seemed as if a cloud of black had encased him, and his eyes…his eyes were the shade of endless night. A shiver went through her. When the last word was spoken, she tried to keep her balance, the room shaking as if it were angry at what they'd done. Doubt filled her head. What if she was wrong? What if this man was everything their history said he was, and they were releasing him into the unsuspecting world?

As she thought it, the stone crumbled, and a force hit her, throwing her across the room where she collapsed from the impact. All light was extinguished, and, in its place, fear like she'd never experienced arose. It gripped her, holding her breath hostage, increasing her heartbeat, and forcing quivers through her body. She tried to breathe but couldn't, and she wondered if this was how death felt.

The darkness abated, drawing from the far reaches of the room, lifting from the light sphere and gathering where he stood, a Dark immortal, the Dark king as Sianna had called him.

The air returned to her lungs, but she didn't move, her body too gripped with fear. He flexed his hands and rolled his neck, and when he opened his eyes, Xali didn't think light could exist. They were a deeper black than endless night, a void that could take your soul and hold it hostage for eternity. He looked around before setting his eyes on her and Carnick. Then he stepped forward.

"Where is my wife?" he demanded, his voice one you didn't refuse an answer.

She continued to stare at him; he had to have been the most beautiful man she'd ever seen, a stark contrast to the power that encased him. She heard a groan from Carnick and turned to see him being drawn into the air.

"I said where is my wife?" Each word was emphasized as he said it.

Xali woke from her trance, realizing he held Carnick in his power. Gods, if this was what the great king thought of as lesser magic, he had to have been mad. He hadn't even moved a muscle, yet Carnick was in his grip, struggling to free himself.

"We don't know where she is," he grunted. "We didn't even know you were here."

The man moved his other hand, and the light sphere drew closer to Xali and Carnick. He studied them both, his expression growing more agitated.

"You are one of his. Where is Drakine?"

The name, why did she know that name? His hold on Carnick tightened, and Carnick gasped for breath. Then it dawned on her, it was a name they rarely used, deferring instead to his royal title.

"The great king?" she said quickly.

He jerked his eyes to Xali, and a shiver ran through her, his grasp never loosening on Carnick.

"Great king? Is that what he's calling himself. Trickster, liar, deceiver, usurper, all are a better fit. Now, tell me where he is or this one dies."

"He's dead."

His grip loosened, surprise filling his eyes for just a split second before he covered it.

"Did Violissa kill him? She's saved?"

"Violissa…your wife?" she asked, remembering the name from the stone.

"Yes. Where is she?"

"I don't know where she is. The great…Drakine died ten thousand years ago of old age."

He stared at her, dropping Carnick who began coughing as he hit the ground with a thud. The Dark king came close to Xali, and she stayed the desire to step back, knowing instinctively that this man loathed any sign of weakness.

"Ten thousand years?"

"Yes. We…well, we thought you were dead, all of you. He said he'd killed you all, at least that's what our history says."

He let out a booming laugh. "Killed us? We're immortal and he a mere mortal man."

He brought his hand to his throat, his expression tensing, eyes turning closer to brown. "No, he didn't kill us, he poisoned us. Violissa, she couldn't breathe. Nor could I…our power."

He stopped, apparently lost in the memory. She'd been right about how Drakine had defeated them.

"He did turn your power against you, within you. Gods, that's what he did."

Her mind was reeling from the thought. It had only been a theory, but now that it was true, it was inconceivable. How had it even been possible? What spell held such power? She thought of her uncle, how he'd been chanting as they'd attacked her. The feeling so similar to what she'd experienced in the dream. A spell to render all opponents helpless. How had he known such a spell? Did her father know it as well or was her uncle keeping secrets, plotting more than she'd suspected, than any of them had suspected?

For a moment, she forgot where she was as the questions bounded through her head, until the Dark king said, "We trusted him, and he turned on us…well, Violissa trusted him. I despised him, but foolishly never saw him as a threat."

He looked over at Carnick then back at her, his eyes darkening. "Ten thousand years. You both look an awful lot like him."

She swallowed, trying her best not to look away.

"And you can meet my eyes, which tells me you are royalty. Otherwise, you'd be dead already. If I can't punish him, I can punish his heirs."

The air expelled from her lungs as his power grabbed her, crushing her. She gasped for breath, the force overwhelming.

"Please no!" Carnick yelled, his voice still rough from being held. "Please don't hurt her!"

The Dark king put his hand up, and Carnick was thrown. He landed on his feet, still determined to save her. Xali watched, her vision growing blurry as Carnick pulled the ground from below the Dark king. It crumbled instantly, his grip never loosening from Xali's neck. A section of the wall freed, and Carnick sent it at the king who easily blocked it.

"Your powers are meek, they are lesser powers not blessed by the Fates. Why are you so determined to save her?"

"She's my betrothed. Please—"

"You love her?"

"With all of my heart."

"Are you willing to die for her?"

"Yes," he answered with no hesitation.

Xali's heart swelled, but still she struggled to breathe.

"Then defend her. Why should I spare your lives, her life?"

"Because she is the only reason you are awake. She risked her life to defend you and your kind."

"My kind?"

"The immortals. That's what we call you. Everyone thought you were dead, everyone thought you deserved it, that you were invaders who needed to be destroyed. Xali is the only one fighting against that, fighting to show that Drakine was the enemy, not you."

His grip loosened, and Xali fell to the floor, gasping in large breaths.

"We were not the invaders," he gritted. "He came by sea, he and his forces, and then that land mass appeared, moving closer and closer until he turned on us."

He paced the room, running his hand through his hair. "One man, one mortal man. Ten thousand years we've been gone? Ten thousand? Do you have any idea what he's done? What he did? He changed it all, changed our future—"

For a moment, he looked defeated. Then he turned to them. "Who are you? It's clear you're one of his, and you…you have power. Who are you and why should I believe you'll help me?"

Carnick reached a hand out to help Xali up. She took it, his words still going through her mind.

"Tell him," he said.

She turned to face the Dark king.

"I am Xaliandri, second born of the Visentia province, and this is Carnick first born of the Bortees province."

"First born? Second born?"

"It's a rank system for who takes the throne and gets privilege in our family."

He raised his brow but didn't question. "And Xaliandri…"

"Xali is fine."

She thought she caught a glimmer of a smile.

"Xali, you woke me?"

"No, Carnick woke you. I found you. I think we're connected to you both somehow."

"Both?"

"Yes. Carnick to you and me to your wife."

"Vi." There was such pain when he said it. "You can find her? I can't sense her. I can't sense any of them."

"I think so. She's been calling me."

"How so?"

"In different ways. I hear her voice calling my name. I see her in my dreams, I feel her in the wind. I need to find her."

"As do I."

"There are a few things you need to know first—" Carnick started but was interrupted when they heard voices.

"Xaliandri?"

"Xaliandri? Carnick?"

The corridor that led to the room widened, the walls morphing, the magic of her family ripping it open. They'd found her. They must have trailed Carnick. The thought of his carelessness angered her, but then she felt the king draw his power.

"Gods, what have you done?" her father asked upon seeing them.

All of her aunts and uncles were there, first and second born, as were her parents.

"Xaliandri," her mother called, moving to rush to her, but her father stopped her.

"What have you done, you foolish child?" her uncle spat.

"Gods, is that…is that an immortal?" her mother asked, drawing her hand to her mouth.

"Are these the ones who've kept me asleep?" the Dark king asked.

"It's complicated. This is our family, and I think we need a moment."

"A moment? I have little patience, and after ten thousand years, a moment is a lot of you to ask."

"Please," she pleaded. "I can help you find her, but please let me talk to them first."

He glared at her and crossed his arms, taking a step back, his power still thick in the air. She knew he'd granted her a privilege not often extended.

"Do you have any idea what you've done, you fool?" her uncle asked immediately.

"I'm not a fool. I'm correcting the wrongs we've covered, the past you and everyone before you chose to bury."

"And we will bury it once more. You have compromised the family, our rule, and for that you will pay. You are sentenced to execution for your crimes, Xaliandri."

Carnick stepped in front of her. "You touch her, and you'll have me to reckon with."

"Carnick," his mother said, "come stand by me. Leave her to her fate. We will find you another to join with."

"Are you mad? All of you? Do you not see the immortal ready to punish everyone in this room? And you worry about who I'll join with?"

"Carnick, go to your mother now."

"No, Uncle. If Xali dies, I die with her."

"Then so be it. We will let another rule in your place."

"Crebant? What are you doing? You can't kill my son."

"Hasty to kill my daughter, but when the tables are turned, you hesitate," Xali's mother said. Her heart swelled; her mother had found her voice.

"Mind your place, Shalinia, you are not part of this."

"No, but I am," her father said.

"Berant, this immortal cannot be freed. It will cost us everything."

"Will it, Uncle?" Xali asked. "And what did it cost them? Their people? This land was never ours to take. And now it is dying."

"Enough!" the king bellowed, all of them jumping. "What do you mean the land is dying?"

"The land near your castle ruins is dying."

"Ruins? The land…Vi. I've had enough of this nonsense. I will see what you have done to my world, and then you will find my wife and the rest of my family, or I will kill you all."

He disappeared, and there was silence as they all realized that was exactly how Xali had disappeared from the sentencing. Xali and Carnick stood, the two of them against the eight elders, no one moving until her father stepped forward. He looked defeated and worn. Xali had never known him as anything but a strong force in her life, but she had brought him to this point. She looked at her uncle and aunts, noticing that all of them looked less than they had always been.

"Xali, there is more danger here than you realize. You have woken an immortal."

"He is nothing, Berant," Xali's uncle said. "The immortals had lesser powers just as Xali does. There is nothing to fear. We will put him back to sleep. Then we will kill the traitor daughter of yours like we should have."

Her father turned to her uncle, a look of pure hatred in his eyes, but Carnick spoke up first. "It's a lie, Uncle. We were the ones with lesser powers. The great king—"

"The great king defeated the immortals, and he was one man. We are many."

"With weaker powers. She has…we have started something you cannot undo."

"Their powers were never less. He tricked them, poisoned them somehow," Xali said, drawing on her own power. Gracefully, she willed the ground above to move, the dirt gently shifting, parting until the sky opened far above them, revealing the full light of the moons. Vines and grass weaved down the walls as they stared at her.

"The powers I hold are the same as hers. They deserve to be awakened."

"And what happens when you do that, Xaliandri?" Carnick's mother asked. "What will become of us?"

"You were quick to give up my place in this world, yet when yours is threatened—" She was interrupted, the ground shaking as the king returned, appearing with a thunderous crash. Everyone around her scattered but Carnick.

"What have you done to my world?" he growled.

Xali held her breath as her chest tightened, the room filling with a black mist that poured from him.

No one moved, no one spoke.

"I asked a question."

"We have done nothing but take back what was rightfully ours," her uncle stated. He had taken a defensive stance, the other heads doing the same, including her father. They thought they could fight him, that they had the upper hand, but they didn't. "It's time you go back to sleep."

Her uncle attacked, the ground erupting around them. She saw her aunt pull pieces of the wall out, directing them toward the king.

"Stop!" she screamed, but it was too late. The attack had started. Within seconds, it was over. The king disintegrated the pieces of stone, the erupting land shattering, sending fragments of dirt and stone everywhere. Carnick grabbed her and used himself to shield her from the debris.

The king roared, pinning all four of them to the ground. She heard the crack of bones as they hit.

"Stop, please!" Xali yelled, pulling herself from Carnick whose arms and back were riddled with tears from the debris. She felt the air drain from her lungs as the king gripped her with his magic. He turned to her, his eyes so black no pupil could be discerned.

"Let her go!" Carnick demanded, the violet disappearing from his eyes.

The king eyed him. "There is Darkness within you," he mumbled.

He released Xali and turned back to the heads. The second borns were standing over them, their power drawn. As Xali recovered, she saw her mother draw her power. It was the first time she'd seen her mother look so strong.

"We won't stand down," her mother said.

"Then you will all die."

"No! Please let them be!" Xali yelled as her mother rose in the air in his grip.

Xali felt her own power course through her in response. It

seemed to burn from her every cell, and she aimed it at him. The ground below erupted, the sides of the room exploding as roots broke free. Magic poured from her hands, a river of green that caused him to drop her mother, his body thrown back into the roots, which dragged him into the wall until he disappeared.

Xali dropped her hands, shaking from the adrenaline. They all gaped at her. The king's magic broken, the heads quickly rose, their eyes wide with disbelief.

"I don't think that will hold him long," she said. "You all need to go, now."

"You don't command us, young lady," her uncle said, but the force was gone from his voice as if he no longer believed his own words.

She glanced down at her hands as Carnick stepped next to her. "I believe she does. Now go, before he returns."

As he finished speaking, the wall erupted. Xali ducked as huge chunks of land flew past her, the wall behind her crumbling. He stepped out, a swirl of black surrounding him, tendrils of ebony flowing from his body. She swallowed, fear sweeping through her. His black eyes glared at her, evaluating her.

He came closer, and she knew this was her death.

"Your power, it comes from the Elvin?" he asked, surprising her.

"I think so," she answered shakily.

"My wife used that move. Frustrated me every time we'd spar. Damned Elvin blood." He took another step forward. "And you… you hold Dark power."

He was looking at Carnick. "I, I don't know."

"It's like a darkness that eats at your soul, a need to punish, to hurt that you can't shake."

"Yes, that's exactly it."

"What are the Fates up to this time?" He looked over at the others. "But you only have Drakine's power. Weak, useful, but nothing like our power."

Her uncle started to object, but her father stopped him.

"Correct," her father said. "It would appear that everything we've known is wrong."

The king nodded then turned back to Xali and Carnick. "Has your magic always been like this?"

"No," Carnick replied. "In fact, Xali had no magic until recently."

"And you said Violissa has been calling to you?"

Xali pushed her hair back, pulling her sleeve down to expose the vines that ran up her arm then picked up the golden strand of hair.

"I'd say it's true."

"I'll be damned. What is she up to? All of you out. I'll determine your punishment in due time. You two will help me find my wife and the rest of our family."

A chunk of wall behind her fell, having loosened earlier. Xali turned as the king's eyes went to it. Another room stood behind them, and deep within it sat a second death bed.

Black mist covered the ground as it had when they'd found the king. He stooped and ran his hand through it.

"Drostiren. That is my son's magic."

He moved across the room.

"Xali." Her father grabbed her arm. "Don't go any further. Don't wake another."

"They deserve to be woken."

"Their power connects the doorways."

The king stopped. "What doorways?"

"They are connections to the provinces so we can move instantly between them," she answered for her father. "Let me guess, there's one that connects here?"

Her father nodded.

"Shifting? You can't shift so you've been draining our powers from us to give you the ability?" the king asked.

Xali lifted an eyebrow. "Shifting?"

"It's how all of us move from place to place. All immortals, as you call us, can shift. Drakine knew this and found a way to channel it from us while we slept."

"Only three of you," her aunt said.

"Mother? You knew this? Knew they were here? Alive?" Carnick asked.

"It's revealed when you take the throne, you must swear to uphold the family secrets or…or stand aside for another to take your throne."

"And you couldn't do that? None of you could?" Carnick asked angrily.

"You don't understand, son, you forfeit your crown, your life, and that of your heir. I couldn't let them take you."

"I thought my family had problems," the king said. He put his hand up, and all but Xali and Carnick were thrown back.

Her father rose and ran forward only to be stopped by an invisible shield. He pounded on it, trying to break through.

"You two will help me wake my son."

"She said the three of you," Xali said. "There's someone else down here."

He aimed his power at the far wall, and it crumpled. Carnick sent his magic out to keep the ceiling from caving in on them.

A shiver went through her, a frightening foul sensation washing over her. Whoever was in the next room was someone she wasn't certain she wanted to be woken.

"Tynan," he said, drawing the deep black mist to him. "Help me wake my son first, then we wake my brother."

"Are there any more here?" Xali said, turning back to her family. She hoped they could hear her through the barrier.

"These are the only ones of whom we know the whereabouts," her father answered, shaking his head.

"But do you know where the rest are?"

"No, the only other one we even know is alive is his wife."

"Vi. She is alive?" the king said hastily, hope in his voice.

"Berant, stop. You should not be telling him anything more," her uncle said, pulling at her father's arm.

Her father shrugged his hand off. "Yes, but asleep as you were. He kept her to feed the land."

Xali couldn't keep her mouth from dropping. She could feel the rise in the king's power.

"Feed the land?" he growled.

"That's all I know. It's all any of us knows. He never told anyone where he placed her. Only you three because you fed the doorways."

The king roared, a force that shook the room. Pieces of stone and ground fell from above them but sprinkled like sand as Carnick disintegrated them.

"Be careful! We're not immortal like you. Kill us in your anger and you have no hope of finding her!" he yelled at the king.

Carnick flew against the barrier.

"You forget who you speak to, ancestor to a usurper. This is my world and my law. You are lucky I choose to keep you, any of you alive. The only reason you still breathe is because you serve a purpose. Just as my family, my wife served Drakine's purpose."

He flung Carnick toward the case.

"Now free my son!"

Xali ran to Carnick and helped him stand. He met her eyes and the question lingered there…was it worth it.

Was it?

She looked back at her family. Would he let them live? Had they let his people live? Those who had challenged their rule? Who had dared say the immortals were the true rulers?

No, they hadn't. She turned back to the case, looking in to view the son. He was sleeping in the same peaceful slumber. He could have been mistaken for his father, they looked so much alike. The only difference, the softness to his face. She'd truly never seen such beautiful men. She wondered if they all looked like this and if the queen was just as stunning in real life.

"Xali?" Carnick brought her from her thoughts. "All right let's see if it will work again."

Carnick rested his hand on the side and spoke the words, the same as he had before but nothing happened.

"Something's not right," Carnick said. "I didn't feel that pull like I did last time. Like it was pulling that Darkness from me."

"Maybe there's none left."

"Or maybe you need something more," the king said. "Ren's magic is threefold. Dark, Light, and Elvin. You said you were connected to Violissa. Maybe he needs you both to awaken him."

A combination of his parents' powers.

"He would have ruled all the lands?"

"Yes, he is the end result of the Fates' prophecy, the one to ensure peace between our realms, well until Drakine showed up and changed our history."

She dropped her eyes, knowing her family was responsible and so she too carried the guilt of these crimes.

"Let's both try, Xali."

She placed her hand next to Carnick's then closed her eyes and spoke the words. At first, there was nothing, but then she felt it, that pull on the lesser powers within her. She felt the air escape her lungs as the force grew, felt the change in her eyes, knowing the power was transforming them. When she opened them, she heard the king respond, "I'll be damned."

But she couldn't speak, the flow of magic too intense.

Just as she thought she could take no more, she was thrown back as the case burst, just as it had with the king. This time, her landing was gentle, her magic cushioning their fall. She watched as the black mist flowed into a haze of white where the case had been. The room quaked, and she could feel power building. She stared at the haze as a form took shape, then she caught her breath as the most piercing blue eyes opened, beaming their brightness through the fog. As it dissipated, he came into view.

"Gods," Carnick mumbled.

He was the spitting image of his father but for the softness that shaped the eyes of a blue she didn't think she'd ever seen. Where his father exuded terror, the son was a calming presence, a welcoming one, emanating the same sense she'd felt when she'd seen the queen in her dream.

"Ren," the king said, embracing him.

"Father? Fates, you're alive. Where's Mother?"

"I haven't found her yet, and I can't sense her, she's blocked from me."

"Is she alive?"

"Yes, thank the Fates."

Relief filled his face.

"It's good to see you," the king said, holding his hands on his son's arms.

"Did you find Drakine?"

"No, there's a bit of a complication on that part." He turned and pointed to Xali and Carnick. Xali lifted her hand in an awkward wave.

"They're his people?"

"No, they're his heirs."

"But he had no children." Then his eyes went to the rest of her family. "They're all royals. Father, how long have we been asleep?"

"Ten thousand years."

His face fell. "That can't be."

"I'm afraid it is. Now, we need to wake Tynan and find the rest. We have work to do."

The king started to walk toward where his brother lay, but his son grabbed his arm.

"Paige?"

The king shook his head. "Only the three of us are known. The rest we'll need to find."

There was a glimmer of sadness before the son replaced it with determination, following his father into the next room. They stood over the case, looking in.

"Uncle," his son said. "I must say that's the most serene I've ever seen him. Are you sure we should disturb him?"

The king laughed, a disturbing sound that left her wondering if she should be happy or terrified.

"You two," he commanded, his scowl returning. "Wake him."

There was a moment of quiet while the two looked at each other as if having a silent conversation.

"Carnick," she whispered as they walked to the case. "Do you think they can speak in their minds?"

"I don't know. Anything's possible at this point."

They looked into the case, and a shudder passed through her. This one looked very similar to the others. His facial features had slight differences, but it was clear he was the king's brother. The same essence of terror exuded from his mere presence.

"Tynan only has Dark power."

She swallowed. Something about the brother gave her the urge to run away.

"He won't bite," the son said. "Well, if we stop him first, he won't."

"That's reassuring."

"You can't wake him, Father?"

"No, I can't even sense him. Can you?"

"No, I can't sense anyone. Looks like these two are the ones the Fates have chosen."

"Let's do this," Carnick said. "No turning back now," he whispered to her.

"No, there's not," the king said. Carnick had said it so low she couldn't imagine how he'd heard it.

Carnick placed his hand on the case and again spoke the incantation. Within moments, the black mist was pulling into the case like the tide pulling back during a nasty storm. Xali held her breath as the room began to shake, the magical doorway cracked, then shattered, the sound of the two in the other rooms could be heard fragmenting, and Xali wondered if the ones in the palaces were doing the same. The room was covered in darkness, and she was thrown back as the case exploded. Her landing was soft again, but debris hit her face before she could put her hand up to stop it. She heard Carnick land close to her.

As the dust dissipated and the darkness lifted, she could see the king and his son then a figure emerging from where the case had been. She didn't know why this one frightened her more than the others. There was something unstable about him that she couldn't place.

"I've been asleep for a long time, haven't I?" he asked, rolling his neck and flexing his hands.

"Ten thousand years, brother."

"And I thought your punishments were bad." He stepped forward. "Drakine?"

"Dead with time, unfortunately."

"Shame, I would have liked to have inflicted a great deal of torture to that one." He lifted his head and sniffed the air. "Why do I smell mortals?"

His eyes landed on Xali, and she couldn't help the shiver that ran up her spine.

"You look like him, and you smell like him."

"They're off-limits, Tynan."

"Going soft, brother?"

Xali thought she heard a growl from the king. "They're off-limits…for now. We need them to find Violissa. She's connected to the girl somehow."

His demeanor changed. "You haven't found Violissa yet?"

Suddenly, the room didn't seem so frightening. The king's face dropped as he replied, "No, I can't feel her. My connection to her is severed."

"Severed? She's not…she's not dead, is she?"

"No, she's calling to me," Xali said, feeling a strange need to reassure them all, even though she'd already shared this with the king.

"To you?"

Xali nodded. She noticed Carnick had moved closer to her.

"Why would Violissa call to you? Who are you anyway?"

The king's son stepped toward Xali.

"They are his kin."

He raised his hand, and Carnick blocked him. The blue of his eyes changed to the black of his father's.

"I would lower that hand before you lose it," he said. "She has a wound, likely from the debris."

His eyes softened to the blue, and Carnick lowered his hand but not before Xali noticed the shake in it. Why had the son's eyes changed?

As if hearing her thoughts, he answered. "All three powers run through me. As long as you stay on my good side, my mother's powers stay dominant."

She felt a tingling as a haze of arcane blue magic left his hand. She hadn't even noticed she was injured.

"You're healers?" Carnick asked.

He moved his hand to Carnick, Xali watching in awe as the wounds from earlier disappeared.

"My mother's side, yes. The Light is healing magic."

"Why would the great king want to rid the world of healers?"

"Good question."

"Great king?" the brother asked.

"Drakine apparently thought higher of himself than we imagined."

"Humorous. That weakling usurper dared call himself a great king?"

"He did manage to defeat all of us," the son said, moving away.

"Through trickery and only by trickery," the brother growled, eyeing Carnick. "You look like him. I should kill you just for that reason alone. Why are you off-limits if she's the one we need to find my queen?"

"He just woke you, Uncle, leave him be."

"Yes, Tynan, until we figure out why the Fates have chosen them, they remain under our protection."

He crossed his arms. "Fine, I'll leave him be, but why do I sense Darkness in him?"

"I don't know, but if I know my wife, she will." The king's eyes grew black.

He blasted the ceiling apart, causing Xali to jump. She'd expected the stone to come down upon them but was surprised to see flower petals raining down instead.

"Flowers, nephew? Not something that strikes fear in men's hearts."

"My mother would disagree."

The light of the moons from far above lit the room as Xali heard her mother yell for her.

"There are more mortals here?" the brother, Tynan asked.

"More kin of Drakine. They are of no consequence."

The words were cold and callous, and Xali prayed that didn't mean he'd already sentenced them to die. Sure, they'd done the same to her, but they were still her family.

"Are you not going to kill them?" she asked.

He gave her an irritated look as if she were an annoying bug.

"I have more important things to handle. Their fates will be dealt with when things are restored." He looked to his son and brother then said, "Bring them," before disappearing.

Fear coursed through her as the son reached for her arm and the brother for Carnick. The air disappeared from her lungs while the room faded from view.

Fifteen

Carnick lost his balance as his feet felt ground under them once again. For a split second, the world had disappeared, his body bombarded with feelings of angst. Then he was standing in the open air, the light of the moons shining down upon them, the ruins of the land beyond the guardian wall before them.

"What have they done?" the king's son asked. "It's all gone, destroyed."

His demeanor darkened with his mood as he took in the ruins.

"Looks like something I would do," the brother said.

"It's like this in the other realms as well. Nothing of ours still stands, no sign of our existence but rubble."

"Our people?" the son asked.

"Diminished greatly in numbers," the king said.

The air thickened, and the light from the moons appeared to dissipate.

"And no one has been punished?" the brother said through

gritted teeth.

"It was not my kin who did this, our ancestors are to blame, the grea…Drakine is to blame," Xali spoke up passionately.

"Did you and your kin not perpetuate the lie that we were dead? Did you not continue to persecute my people? To use us as fuel for your portals?" The king's eyes were black as the night around them, and Carnick knew if he had been a mere mortal, those eyes would have killed him.

"Not all of us. If we had, you would not be awake now. There are some of us who believe the ways of our elders, the ways they were sworn to protect and uphold upon taking their throne, are wrong. There are some of us who questioned it," Carnick said.

Xali looked at him, her eyes questioning.

"Our cousins all had doubts just as we did," he told her.

"Regardless, punishments will be given."

"The Dark king is the law," Xali said quietly.

The king studied her. "The only law."

He turned his back on them and tipped his head to the south. Carnick moved closer to Xali. She bristled, still angry at him for what she thought he'd done. Why hadn't he told her before this mess had started? Now, he might never have the chance. All he wanted to do was take her hand, to know that she still loved him. There was a part of him that wanted to protect her, but she didn't really need protecting. She'd stood face to face with the immortals and held her ground. If she had fear, she showed none.

"Do you feel that?" the king asked.

The others looked at him.

"My Darkbearers, I can feel them." He opened his hands, and thick black tendrils escaped. Carnick felt it deep within him, something answering the king's call, a part of him that understood it was being summoned. These were no lesser beings, Xali had been right. Their powers were beyond comprehension, beyond anything he and his kin had shared. There was a heaviness to the air; it was ripe with terror, and he saw Xali shiver.

Around the king, men appeared, one by one, from nowhere. Shifting, the king had called it. As each arrived, the Darkness increased, the air dense with terror that Carnick welcomed. Before long, ten men surrounded them. The king reined in his power, and there was a momentary silence before voices erupted.

Carnick watched as a sort of reunion took place. Arms were grabbed in a strange fashion that must have been some form of greeting. Questions abounded, some answered, many unanswered.

"Darkbearers," Xali said, repeating the word the king had said. "What?"

"The king's Council, the Darkbearers."

She didn't have time to explain how she knew this. A mound of ground erupted before her, encasing her and dragging her away. Carnick turned, seeing his family who must have found their way through the tunnel and used their magic to escape the chamber.

"No!" he yelled, throwing his magic out at his uncle and mother who both looked defiant. His aunt stood beside them, but Xali's parents kept their distance.

His uncle blocked his magic and aimed his power at Xali, his eyes vindictive with deadly intent.

"Punishment must be paid and this mess you've made, Xaliandri, cleaned up!" his uncle roared.

The king and his men fell silent. Suddenly, his uncle dropped to his knees, a pained expression on his face. Carnick's mother and aunt were cast back from him. Carnick knew he couldn't save them; they'd chosen to defy an immortal. They had chosen their fate. He aimed his magic at the prison that bound Xali, and it crumpled. As she fell over coughing, the king shifted in front of his uncle, picking him up with his magic.

"Crebant!" his aunt yelled before being pushed to the ground by a force Carnick could not see.

There was fear in his uncle's eyes. "Drakine was annoying just as you are," the king said to Crebant. "Full of himself as if he were one of the Fates, as if he were even close to any of us in power. Pretending to be something he wasn't. I made the mistake of ignoring him, assuming he'd crawl back to whatever distant land he'd come from. It cost me greatly. I won't make the same mistake again."

"You and your kind are heathens, worshipping false gods—"

"Uncle, stop!" Xali yelled.

"You have unleashed an abomination that should never have been woken," Crebant spat. "Xaliandri, you are no part of us, you side with the lesser ones, they will destroy every—" His words were interrupted by the sound of bones snapping. A glaze filled his eyes before his head fell forward, the bones in his neck broken.

Screams erupted from his family, and Carnick had to steady himself as his uncle's limp body fell to the ground. The king turned back toward his brother.

"He needed to shut up, and you were letting him talk too long. I made a decision," his brother said.

The king cocked his eyebrow, and an awkward silence ensued. Was Xali right? Could they really talk in their heads?

The king walked away from the body and back toward his men. "My kingdom, my decisions. He needed to suffer first," he muttered angrily at his brother whose body went strangely stiff. Carnick heard the pop of multiple bones, but there was no sign of pain. The king continued past him, the sound continuing. Carnick could see the disfigurement occurring in his brother's back then, as if healing, it would disappear. Finally, the sound stopped, and the brother relaxed. Carnick watched as his back straightened to normal again. He had broken every bone in the man's spine with no movement, no indication he'd even used magic, and the man hadn't even flinched.

"I guess that's what it means to be immortal," Xali whispered. He hadn't noticed she was next to him and released the breath he'd been holding.

"He just broke his back," he said incredulously. "Every bone, and he didn't make a sound."

The king's son came over to them. "To show pain is weakness for a Darkbearer, and weakness is not tolerated. You two are to come with me."

The men were all disappearing.

"And my family?" Xali asked, looking back at the others who had surrounded their uncle's body. His aunts were crying, and Xali's mother looked to be in shock. His mother glared at him and then at Xali with unforgiving, cold eyes.

"Can find their way home," the king answered as if they'd been standing right next to them.

Before they could respond, the son grabbed them, and the world disappeared. That strange, unsettled feeling overcame him for a moment, and then he were standing on solid ground again, Xali by his side.

"This is what they did?" the brother yelled, tendrils of power pouring from him.

"Now you know how Violissa felt," the king snapped.

"That was different."

"Was it? Different usurper, same outcome."

They glared at each other.

"Stop it, you two. Let's rebuild while the others search for Mother," the son said.

"They won't find her."

They all turned to stare at Xali.

"It has to be me," she said. "I'm sure of it. That's why she's calling me."

"Perhaps," the king said, his dark eyes studying her.

Quickly, he turned back to the ruins. It was still dark, and Carnick could only assume these were the ones that lie in Old Tenebron. He watched in awe as the dilapidated, weather-worn pieces of stone transformed bit by bit until, at the first hints of sunrise, a complete castle stood before them. It was massive in size compared to the sprawling palace to which he was accustomed. This towered like an angry serpent ready to engulf unwitting souls.

Now he understood why there had been a distinction between the name given to their residences and those of the immortals. He'd always wondered. Palace seemed too soft a word for the monstrosity that stood before them.

"Isn't this more the work of your Darkbearers?" the brother asked. "Why are we doing this?"

"Because they're out looking for the others."

"Carnick, are you seeing this?" Xali asked quietly, moving closer to him.

"Yes, they're taking back Tenebron. The provinces will be destroyed."

"Yes, they will," the king said, his hearing keenly sharp. He didn't bother to even look at them.

Carnick pulled Xali away, hoping they wouldn't notice.

"We need to get out of here, Xali. Now, before they kill us."

"And do what? Go back to the family so they can kill us? This is happening, Carnick, there's no stopping it."

"Then take us somewhere else, any place that will keep you safe."

"Worried about me suddenly?" she bit back. It stung, but he let it slide.

"Do that thing they do where you take us somewhere. Shift he called it."

"I don't even know how I did that, and I know I couldn't take both of us."

"She hasn't mastered the skill yet," the son said, suddenly next to them.

Xali jumped slightly.

"Don't flee, it will anger my father, and if he doesn't punish you, I will."

"This is a reality we have no part in, one where we don't exist. Everything we know is being undone. What will happen to us when they have no more use for us?"

"Decisions have yet to be made. I know my father well. Your

family would be dead if he felt they deserved it. You are needed, and he sees that. He doesn't test the Fates, none of us do any more. If they have chosen you, then you will remain."

"He killed my uncle."

"Tynan killed him, and he deserved punishment. We all saw into his mind, the injustices he had served our people, the plans of killing you both, of taking all of Tenebron as his own. He was guilty, and Tynan served a punishment my father would have given him. In reality, it was a quicker death than he deserved. There is no place for treachery in our kingdom."

"Now the fate of the rest of us awaits what?"

"My father's mood, my mother's return. My father is more balanced with her by his side."

"And what is his mood presently?" Xali asked.

The prince raised his eyebrow. "Not an especially good one. Without my mother, he's a bit unstable."

"More reason for us to go."

"I would not advise it. Look, as much as it bothers him, we need you." He sighed. "Everything we know has been ripped from us, we've woken from a sleep we didn't know we were in to find that everything we were for eons has been erased, kingdoms that have existed since the dawn of time are gone, our people on the brink of extinction, our lands divided and dying. The world has been turned on its head, a history that should have been is no longer, replaced now, leaving us with no direction as to what to do. I should have been king these last millennia, my ascension, my calling to the throne has passed by." He looked down at his hands. "Do I get that back? Will it happen now that ten thousand years have passed? Does our rule continue if it is lost?"

His eyes held a deep sadness.

"You worry that everything you know will be taken from you, but that's exactly what Drakine did to us. There are others, still missing who need to be found. My mother, her Council, my wife, my aunt, all still missing. We need you to find them. We need you to make things right again, to help undo what has been done, and I promise you I will do everything in my power to see that you and your family are safe."

Carnick didn't know what to say, the words had been honest, sincere. And they were true. What Carnick was feeling was what they were feeling. The things Carnick wanted to protect, the provinces, their people, his family were all things that had been stolen from the immortals. The kingdoms Carnick knew, everything Carnick knew, had been built on what had been stolen from them.

"We'll help," Xali said.

The light of the dawning sun caught in the prince's eyes, lending a layer of dimension to them. Below the brilliant blue, Carnick could see a purple sheen. He thought of his own eyes, the violet that speckled them. Perhaps they were not as unlike as Drakine had assumed, as any of them had assumed.

The prince's eyes grew darker, a deep shade of blue that bordered on black. They were looking beyond, behind them.

"No," he said, walking past Carnick and Xali as if the conversation had never happened. "We need to find my mother now."

Xali turned toward where the prince was looking. The concern in his voice was palpable, and when she turned, she understood why. The morning sun was unveiling a mass of brown, bitter land that now stood where a thriving field of green once stood. It stretched beyond into the trees whose dead leaves littered the ground below, far beyond what she and Carnick had found the last time they'd been here.

She felt the king's presence.

"Vi," he said, his voice laden with concern.

"The land is dying," the prince said.

"I haven't seen it look like this since I cast her out. It's as if the connection to her has been broken," the brother said.

"What connection?" Xali asked.

"My mother is the life of this world. Her power keeps it alive."

"And without it, the land dies."

Xali's mind reeled. For someone to have that kind of power…it was unfathomable. She had thought a spell perhaps, magic imbued in the land that connected her to it, but instead, it was her, her existence, her power that had caused the land to flourish.

"So, what does that mean?" she asked.

"Either the connection has broken…or…" The king hesitated as if he didn't want to say the words.

"Or she's dying," his brother finished for him.

Xali's heart raced. That couldn't be, not if they were all only asleep. "No, no, that can't be. She's been calling me, she's alive, I hear her voice."

"When was the last time you heard her?"

"I…I…" Xali thought about it. When was the last time she had heard her? At the ruins? Well before all of this? "I haven't heard her for some time."

The king cursed and ran his hands through his hair, pacing. She could see the worry on his face; it was as if another man had taken over him.

"I want to know everything you know about your history," his brother said.

"You know everything we know. Only the first born heads know anything more, anything about you," Carnick replied.

"How many are there?"

"Three now, my mother, Xali's father, and our aunt."

"Your aunt? You share the same aunt?" he asked.

"Yes."

"But you are a couple, are you not?" the king asked.

"Yes."

"We were," Xali corrected, "until recently."

Carnick's hurt eyes dropped.

"Hmmm, seems you two have differing opinions on that matter.

How are you related then?"

"We're cousins."

"Cousins? Distant?" the brother asked.

Carnick shook his head.

"What does this matter, Tynan?"

"I find it curious, appalling but curious. Is this the norm in your culture?"

"Only in the royal family. It keeps the magic pure. Stronger so they say."

Two of the king's men appeared.

"Keary, Eion, go with Ren. Ren, take the boy, find the ones he mentioned and bring them to us."

"Yes, Father."

Before the conversation could continue, the prince grabbed Carnick's arm, and they were gone.

"Bring her."

The brother took her arm, and the world disappeared for a brief second, unsettling her until her feet were once again on solid ground. She let the vertigo settle as she found herself in a massive room that looked like it may have been a meeting room. It eclipsed the ones her family used. No windows lined the room; in fact, there was no light but the ball of light that lit the setting.

A meeting table sat in the center of the room, engulfing the open space. The deep mahogany looked black in the dim light. Around its length sat twenty-four chairs. Xali's mind took it all in, calculating the total number of chairs quickly and then realizing the sheer power this room had held at one time.

"There were twenty-four of you? Twenty-four immortals?"

"Sharp mind," the brother said. "There are twenty-four who hold power but twenty-six in total."

Her eyes must have reflected her confusion.

"My son's wife and Tynan's mate are immortal but hold no magic."

She remembered his son mentioning the two women and

nodded in understanding. She was sure there was a story behind them, but this was not the time to ask. The others appeared behind her bearing Carnick, his mother, and Xali's father.

"You left the others there?" Xali asked.

"The others stay until I decide their fate."

She turned to the king.

"You can't leave them there. They don't know their way home, it's too far to walk anyway, they can't hunt, and there's no water. It's cruel."

He slammed his hands down on the table, which splintered into a multitude of pieces. Xali kept herself from jumping, instead, staring at the damage.

"I am cruel. You do not question me—"

"I will question you. This is my family."

"A family that was ready to kill you? Do not dare to question me. You are lucky you're still live, lucky any of them live. You are a weak mortal whom I've chosen to leave alive."

Xali bristled, his words a blow to an already fragile temper that had been bottled up for far too long.

"I am not weak! I am tired of being seen as the weak one. I have never been weak. I can battle and slay the fiercest of our warriors, I can best anyone in my family, and my magic is stronger than all of theirs combined. I will no longer submit to that title, and you will not name me so."

She'd drawn herself up, proud and strong, although still dwarfed by the two men before her, one who had now drawn his power.

"Should I kill her, brother?"

"No. You are bold, girl. I admire that. You remind me of my wife, and I can see why she chose you. You should watch that temper though, your eyes belie the Elvin within you."

His comment caught her off guard, but she had no time to respond.

"Your family stays where they are…for now. Keary, bring these two to me."

The one named Keary pushed her father and aunt forward until they stood before the king. Xali moved to go to her father's side but was stayed by Carnick who gestured to the king. He'd drawn his power as if facing an enemy. Her father met the king's eyes, and the tension could be felt as a thick layer on her skin. Xali held her breath.

"You will release my daughter and my nephew," he braved, his voice filled with authority as the head of his house.

The brother laughed.

"You are in no position to demand anything of me," the king scoffed.

"You will not harm them."

"No, but I may kill you for your insolence."

"Then I will die proudly."

"You are a brave lot," the king said. "Too many centuries under a false rule have given your family the assumption that you have some kind of authority here. You don't, I am the only authority, the only voice that determines the fate of anyone in this land. It is time you and your kind understand that you were once guests in my kingdom and that privilege was revoked the day your ancestor decided to strike against me. Now, you will live for the moment as long as you set your naïve bravado aside and tell me your history. I want to know how it came to be that I have awoken from a forced slumber to find my kingdoms in ruin and your family in control. What lies did Drakine spout and what truths have you been hiding from your own heirs?"

Xali's father looked to her, his eyes holding a mix of concern and anger. Or was it disappointment? She'd awoken the sleeping beasts, their enemy, and toppled the reign of her family with one swift move. She bit back her emotion as his eyes moved from hers. Her aunt kept her eyes averted as well, clearly too offended by her actions to even warrant a look.

"And our children? What happens to them if we tell you?" she asked.

"These two live either way. For now. Enough idle talk. I want the truth and know that we will see if lies are spoken."

He hadn't mentioned her cousins. Had they not discovered them yet? Were they safe? She had to assume they were since the king had not indicated any knowledge of them. He crossed his arms and awaited the truth, his brother walking to the corner of the room, his eyes an endless ebony that held his irritation. It was almost as if he'd needed to punish, and that ability had been taken from him.

Xali wondered at his mood. Were they all so volatile, so filled with a penchant for punishment? Or was it something else? What had the son said, their uncle's punishment was fair? Was it more a matter of justice? Justice for a crime or what they saw as a crime?

His black eyes met hers, boring deep into her soul, her breath sticking in her chest until that other part of her rose to meet it. He cocked his head and studied her, his lips forming a smirk until she drew her eyes from his, dropping them as her father began to speak.

"We will tell you all you want to know."

"Then start."

"Where?"

"From the beginning. As far back as you know. I want every detail."

"Fine," her aunt said, surprising Xali.

She'd expected argument that their history was simple, the story Xali had heard since she was a child. As her aunt began to speak, Xali realized that story had been an abridged one, created on falsities that bolstered their family's right to retain the throne. A stolen throne, overseeing what she now knew to be a severed kingdom.

"The story our people know is not the entire truth," she started slowly.

"No kidding," the brother mumbled.

"Tynan," the king commanded. Both appeared to have equal power, but the king had control, his word, his rule trumping his brother's. Xali wondered about the reasons for this. What was their history?

"Our land once was a separate land, lost in the middle of the waters that surround this realm. It was vast but dying. The favor of the gods could no longer be found, the vegetation turning over to sand until barely any food could be produced to feed our people. The great king—"

"Drakine was not a great man and will not be referred to as so in my presence."

Xali's aunt looked taken aback before Xali's father hastily replied, "Our apologies, habits are difficult to adjust so quickly after a lifetime."

"Adjust them or pay the consequences," the king commanded. Xali could see his aura shifting, growing darker with the passing moments.

"Drakine," her aunt continued, "decided to move the land. With his power, he forced the land to separate from its place in our world and to move in hopes of finding a new home."

"He moved the land?" the king repeated, looking over at his brother who nodded, the two seeming to share a memory.

"Your power gives you that ability?" Ren asked.

"No longer. Our line was always given one heir until we reached these lands. As the house was divided, so was the power. Diluted until finally there were eight equal parts."

The king began pacing, running his hand through his hair.

"The Fates punished them for daring to leave their realm. The minute that land connected to ours, he cursed his line," Ren said to his father.

"The minute he stepped foot on our land, he cursed himself and his line," the brother corrected.

"The holy land," Xali said, making the association. "The inconsistency in the place where it meets the shoreline of Old Tenebron."

"Old Tenebron?" the king said with a raise of his eyebrow.

"It's what your people still call the land to the west."

"Tenebron," he corrected.

"No longer exists," her father said. "It has been separated into the two provinces and Old Cirillia into two provinces."

Black mist spread from the king. "My lands are no longer separated. They will be restored to their original glory and your measly provinces dismantled," he said with what sounded like a growl.

"Like it was when Drakine forced his land to mold with the shoreline of Tenebron," Xali mused.

"The inconsistency you noticed," Carnick said.

"Yes, the land doesn't sit flush there, as if it were forced to meld with a foreign host."

The king eyed her.

"The holy land was never part of this realm. I was right," she said.

"It is an abomination that will be destroyed."

Her aunt inhaled loudly, "You cannot destroy our holy la—"

Her last word was cut short as a pained expression crossed her face, and she grabbed onto Xali's father.

"Stop!" Carnick yelled, rushing toward her only to be pushed back by some unseen force.

"Do not dare command me. Whatever lies Drakine fed your ancestors were just that. Lies."

Her aunt gasped for breath as if filling her lungs, the pain leaving her eyes, replaced with a quick flash of fear, something Xali had never seen in her aunt. It saddened her to see her strength diminished.

"Please stop, she's telling you what you want to know," Xali dared.

He turned his now black eyes to her, and she tried to cover the shiver that ran through her. He said nothing, merely stared at her as if he was looking straight into her soul. The intensity in that moment was like none she had ever experienced, and she prayed it would end soon.

Finally, he looked away, the breath filling her lungs again

"Continue," he ordered her aunt who was still holding onto Xali's father.

"You know the rest," her father told the king. "Drakine defeated you and claimed the realms his."

A growl escaped the king, and darkness filled the room.

"I would choose your words wisely," the brother said, his eyes now a deep ebony as well. "Defeat is a strong word and one we do not know."

"But he did defeat you, all of you," Xali said suddenly as a thought took hold. "But how?"

Razor-sharp claws ripped through her, and it felt as if her insides were burning. The feeling grew, and she gripped her hands tightly as the king's gaze fell to her once again. The pain increased twofold, and all she wanted to do was double over in agony and scream for it to end. The claws dug deeper, her insides feeling as if they were being shredded, yet the king didn't move. He was punishing her. Testing her. Defeat was something they didn't know, the brother had said. It was a weakness.

He was waiting for her to succumb to the pain like her aunt, to show vulnerability. She gritted her teeth and straightened against the pain that pulled her down. She wouldn't let him see her weakened.

Through clenched teeth, she said, "How did he do it? How did he defeat the undefeatable?"

The king tilted his head as if studying her, and then the pain ceased, the fire extinguishing.

"Hmm, you are a brave child, a foolish child, but a brave one." He looked over at his son and nodded, before Xali felt a cool tingling through her body, erasing the remnants of the internal fire. There was a mist of blue that she traced to the son, meeting his vibrant blue eyes.

"You can heal?" her aunt asked.

Xali tore her eyes from his and followed the mist to her aunt. He had healed her as well. She was staring at the magic with wonder. "But that's not something you can do. Your magic harms and only causes destruction.

The brother let out a laugh. "Lies of the father," he said. "They clearly left Violissa's power out of the stories."

With the name, the king softened for just a moment, enough for Xali to catch it, and as if he sensed her awareness of it, he turned his brown eyes to her. She watched in awe as they darkened, the black eclipsing the brown. He glared at her then turned back to her father.

"You didn't answer my question," she braved, praying he didn't kill her.

"Xali," Carnick whispered.

"Trickery. That's how. I'm sure these two can explain." He crossed his arms and looked from her aunt to her father.

"No, we can't. That secret died with Drakine, he never told his children."

"Then it stays buried with him. Now tell me the rest. How is it we came to be where Xaliandri found us and what lies have you fed my people?"

"Drakine thought it best to leave your bodies in the northern region, your advisors separated and buried far from you."

Xali wanted to bust in and accuse them of hiding more secrets, but she bit her tongue.

"He claimed the lands, punishing those who questioned his rule. Those who claimed their allegiance to the immortals were killed." Her father dropped his eyes. "Your people fought, they still fight to this day in small ways, but their numbers have dwindled. Talk of any of you is forbidden as it has been since the first day of Drakine's rule. Over time, you were forgotten, a history page in our lessons, Drakine ensuring that your legacy was a tarnished one. And none of us knew differently. You've been dead to us for ten thousand years, Drakine's history all we've been taught."

"But you knew, all of you," Xali interrupted. "You hid it from the people, from us."

He shook his head. "No, Xaliandri, we knew pieces, ones

handed down as each of us were sworn to the crown, sworn to keep the secrets, but we only knew what was told to us. We knew they were down there, knew the history had pieces left out, that they were still here, but that was all."

"You knew they were there, and you never told me?"

"We were sworn at our crownings, Xali," her aunt said, defiantly, "just as Carnick would have been. It was a burden to be carried by the first borns."

"Wait, you knew where all of us were?" the brother asked.

"Yes, we made rounds every moon change to ensure your crypts were untouched, your slumber undisturbed."

"Then why do you not know where my wife is?"

"You were tied to our doorways, we needed your power to remain connected to them. At least that's what was told to us."

"We were tied to your doorways," the king said.

"Mother is tied to the land," the son said.

"Mother?" Xali's aunt said.

"Did they neglect to mention me in your history?" he asked, his eyes turning a richer shade of blue.

"Yes," she said softly.

"Pity, since he's more powerful than we are," the brother said.

Xali couldn't hide her shock.

"Ah, so our history has been erased, brother, not even the prophecy survived."

"It did," she said. "They kept it hidden. The people, underground, protected from…from us. They know the consequences if they are caught, yet they protect it."

"How do you know this?" the son asked.

"I…" she looked at her father, the disappointment clear in his eyes. "Don't give me that look, Father. I've brought down our houses, I am the end of our family's reign, but it needed to be done, and"—she stood taller—"and I'm proud that the Fates chose me, that she chose me."

Her father and aunt both looked taken aback. She turned her

eyes back to the immortals, proud and strong, knowing her words were correct. She had been chosen.

"I befriended my sl…my servant," she corrected when the king raised his brow. "She told me that this," she pulled a blonde curl from below her silver hair, "was a sign that I was touched by the Fates." She then pushed her sleeve down to reveal the dark etchings that remained on her arm. "I think it isn't only the Fates that have marked me."

"Fates, indeed," the brother mumbled, staring at her arm.

"Violissa's tie to you is physical," the king said. He looked to the others and then back to Xali. "Your hair does not carry curls, does it?"

She shook her head.

"It's as if a part of Mother is revealing itself through her."

"But what of the etchings? Violissa has no such marks," the king said.

"That's not Mother, that's the Fates, the tie that binds them. Wherever she is, I would wager those same marks have imprinted on her skin." He met Xali's eyes. "Where is my mother?"

"I don't know. Do you, Father?"

He shook his head. "None of us do."

"But you knew where we were. Why wouldn't you know where she is? Why not check on her regularly? And why separate her from us?" the king asked.

"Power?" the brother suggested. "Too much concentrated in one place?"

"No," her aunt answered. "I don't think so. I once asked the same question and was only told that her magic was tied to something greater, something that needed her body elsewhere and far from the magic the other immortals held."

The king had begun pacing as if he were thinking as hard as Xali on where she was and why. What was she tied to that made her special?

He stopped, turning to his brother and son. "He tied her to the land. He knew her power, knew the connection, that's why he kept us all in stasis and why he separated her. He needed her separate, someplace he could continue to feed the land in her state without any chance of us awakening. If she was too close to me, if the power he was draining from us ever crossed, I would wake. She's somewhere out there in the land, the tie bonded to wherever he placed her."

"He knew? How would he know? Did we tell him?"

"We must have. He was so inquisitive, and Violissa so…"

"Naïve," the brother finished for him.

"You know she hates that word."

"Well, it's the truth, she was naïve to trust him, to indulge his questioning. We should have killed him the minute he set foot on our shores."

"Mother would say this was the Fates' doing," the son said.

"Don't spout that bullshit to me, Ren," the brother spat angrily. "Why would it be the Fates' desire to have us lose ten thousand years, to delay your ascension, to decimate our people?"

Just then Xali felt a subtle breeze.

Xaliandri, she heard, her eyes catching the king's as he turned to her. He'd felt it, too. Her presence.

"Because it needed to be done," he said.

"What?" the brother asked.

"What is it Violissa always says? The Fates have their reasons. Whatever their reasons, they wanted these people here, wanted Xaliandri to be born and to find us. As did Violissa."

He sighed and ran his hand through his hair, then turned back to them.

"We need to find her. If he tied her power to the land and the land is dying, then we don't have time to stand here bickering."

"Why would he tie her to the land?" her father asked.

"Because she is the land," Xali answered for them. "She is the key to this world, to the air we breathe, to the land our feet stand upon, to the grains we eat. She and the land are one."

"That's madness," her aunt said. "No one has that kind of power."

"The immortals do, Mother," Carnick said.

Xali looked down at her hands at the sound of his voice.

"So Violissa is asleep somewhere out there, and no one knows where she is?" the brother asked. "You made sure to keep an eye on us, but you left her without any thought. The one person who is keeping this world alive and no one thought to watch her?"

"We didn't know," Xali's father said.

"It would seem there is quite a bit you didn't know. Keary, Eoin, take them from my sight before I change my mind and kill them."

Before Xali could react, they were gone.

"Ren, take these two and find them quarters. They're no longer needed." He looked at Xali. "For the moment."

"I can help," she argued as Ren took her arm.

"No, you can't, no one can," she heard him say as the room disappeared.

Sixteen

The room shifted from Carnick's sight, his stomach rolling at the action. He wobbled a little when they landed in a dark corridor. The prince, Ren, dropped his arm and Xali's, then made a ball of light that lit the hallway. It floated in the air before them.

"This is where you'll stay," he said. "Don't get any ideas about leaving. A Darkbearer will be stationed at the end of this hall, and he will not hesitate to hurt you."

"That makes me feel welcomed," Carnick muttered.

"We aren't welcomed," Xali said sharply. "We're prisoners."

She didn't look at him. Instead, she asked the prince where her quarters were.

"Xali," Carnick said, grabbing her wrist as she began following the prince. She turned, looking down at his hand and then up with eyes full of anger.

"Xali, please."

She jerked her wrist from his grasp and walked away. He sighed, his eyes catching the prince's, who studied him as if he could see straight into his mind. He raised an eyebrow at Carnick then turned and led Xali away.

Carnick watched until they were too far to see then entered his quarters. The room was dark, but the moons offered enough light to see that it was large but sparse. Only the minimum furnishings could be found as if the room were a last-minute thought. It was a room, but Xali was right, they were prisoners. He sat on the corner of the bed and dropped his head to his hands. Too much had happened, too many events, too many revelations.

Xali had woken the immortals. Immortals they'd been told were long dead. Immortals who held power unlike anything they'd seen, anything they knew. All of it had been a lie. His entire foundation had been ripped from under him. He dropped back on the bed and stared at the high ceiling, his mind running through it all.

He'd always felt strong, sure of himself, confident in his power and his place in the world. His path had been a straight one, to join with Xali, take the throne when his mother acquiesced, to lead his province. That had been his destiny. At least, it had been. Now it was gone, all of it lost, even Xali who believed he'd betrayed her. A belief he hadn't argued, blindly protecting his sister.

Now, what was he left with? Nothing. Not even a sense of purpose.

He closed his eyes and thought about Xali. She had changed. It may have been her time in hiding, but he thought it might be something more. Something to do with all of this. She was special, he'd always been aware of it. Unique. His family had never appreciated it, but he had. Was this why she was different? What had the king said? She'd been chosen. Chosen by their Fates. A purpose far greater than he had ever expected.

Opening his eyes, he sat back up. She would change everything, she'd already begun. And what did that mean for him? For his family? For their people? Did he love her enough to watch as it all crumbled around him?

She'd been promised to him before she'd even taken her first breath in this world. He hadn't chosen her; they'd chosen for him. Did he love her enough? The words played in his mind as he opened his heart. Images of her flooded the places in his mind where doubt had crept. Her long silver locks, the flecks of emerald that adorned her eyes, the way she smiled at him that made his heart swell, the curiosity that had gotten them here in the first place, the need to question, to take risks, to pick her sword up even after the tenth defeat. All of her unique to everyone else in their family, and he loved every part of her.

Yes, he loved her enough to let it all crumble if it meant she was safe, happy, finally taking the role for which she was destined. He remembered back to the night of her birth, the two full moons becoming a brilliant emerald that had overcome the night sky. It was an omen they'd said. And it had been. She'd been destined for a greater path than the one their family, even the great king had chosen for her. This was her destiny, and he would be with her through every step if she'd have him.

He stared at the door, wondering where the prince had taken her, missing her presence. He would stand by her side as he always had, but did she love him enough to allow him to stand in that place?

As the prince walked her down the corridor, Xali's mind remained on Carnick. She missed him. As much as she was angry at him, she missed talking to him, having him by her side.

"Your mind wanders to your betrothed," he said as if he'd read her mind. "And your thoughts are troubled."

"My thoughts are troubled by much more than simply Carnick."

"Ah, but in this moment, he dominates them."

"It's nothing."

He stopped and turned to her, the light sphere pausing its

movement ahead of them.

"Things are not always as they seem."

"In this case, they are."

He studied her, his blue eyes sparkling in the light.

"He is not guilty of that which you accuse him."

"How can you know why I'm angry with him?"

"I cannot, but I can read his guilt, and there is none there. He is innocent of whatever reason you hold your anger."

He turned and began walking once more, leaving her stunned. She glanced back at Carnick's door, tempted to run back to it, but refrained. Instead, she turned toward the prince and caught up with him.

"Thank you, your highness," she whispered as they approached another door.

He was quiet for a moment.

"Ren, call me Ren" he said with a sad smile. "My wife is out there somewhere. I believe she'll sleep until my mother awakens. At least that's my hope…that she remains, that Drakine didn't find a way to kill her knowing she held no power."

She wasn't sure what to say, so she remained silent. He looked up, the blue of his eyes rich with emotion. "Don't let your anger keep you apart. If she were here, I would have her within my touch every chance I could. I wouldn't let anything steal another moment of time from us."

"We'll find her," she said quietly.

He nodded then was gone, a slight breeze left in the wake of his shift, the only evidence he'd been there. She looked back toward Carnick's door once more then entered her room.

It was dark, lit only by the moons that shone through the long window. Xali rubbed her arms against the darkness, wondering if Carnick's room had been this way. She found her way to the bed, her eyes quickly adjusting, and flopped down, weariness grabbing hold of her.

She dropped her head onto the bed and released the emotion

of the day. Drawing her knees in, she hugged them to her as her body shook with the fear that she'd pushed aside, the tears finally spilling. She'd remained strong through all of it, since the day she'd fled her family, but now that strength had abandoned her, leaving only raw pain and emotion in its wake.

What had she done? Let her curiosity unleash a chain of events that had run swiftly from her hands. Her uncle was dead, her family imprisoned, their titles stripped from them, their rule ended. And in their place, she'd seated the Dark king, an immortal who seemed to be his own law.

There was no going back, no ignoring the voice that had haunted her dreams, no obeying her family's traditions, no acquiescing to the shackles they'd tried to place on her. She would not sit by Carnick's side as he ruled his province, and her brother would not rule with Fairenth by his side. It was over, she had destroyed it all, and with her blind willingness to turn her back on everything, death would come—that of her family, of Carnick, and eventually her own.

She held her knees tighter as the realization settled upon her, and eventually, sleep dried her tears, taking her away.

A calm settled over her as she tipped her head to the falling snow, the coolness of it washing away the grief and self-pity. She stepped forward, the cold wet ground below her feet sending a shiver through her. She looked down at the feet that were now bare. A light purple gown sat upon her skin, touching her toes and dragging in the snow behind her.

She was dreaming, she had no doubt, and the thought gave her a sense of happiness. She'd missed her connection with the queen. Hadn't dreamed of her since she'd run away, only hearing the echo of her voice. In the dreams, there was a closeness to her, a oneness.

Xali looked around, only then noticing the long golden curls that lay upon her. She picked her hair up, no silver to be seen. But this wasn't her hair, it was thicker, softer than hers had ever been. Then she noticed the ring on her finger. Xali never wore rings;

she supposed one day she would have worn the ring of Carnick's house, but she disliked them. She studied the ring. It was delicate and beautiful. She let her hand fall, knowing whose ring it was and in whose body she now walked. With that thought, she let the queen guide her footfalls, aware that she was a guest in a sacred temple.

Around her, the snow fell, but she no longer felt the cold sting of it. She walked in silence, an endless world of white until she noticed the snowflakes change in hue, slowly becoming a vibrant emerald. The snow beneath her feet disappeared, the green flakes still falling but dissipating before reaching the ground.

What did it mean?

"What are you trying to tell me?" she whispered.

She came upon a cliff, noticing the dry ravine below, the split between the old realms. The snow stopped, and her eyes traveled past the ravine, north, surveying the land before her. Land whose color faded as the snow had, leaving in its place nothing but death and decay. The vegetation brown and brittle, the trees crumbling before her eyes, their remaining particles carried away. She turned to look behind her, the crunch of the grass below her feet warning her that she would find the same sight.

As she watched the last of the trees fade, she stared at the desolate wasteland before her.

"You are dying," she affirmed. "They were right and with you dies the land."

As she spoke, she felt the quickening of the queen's heart. Longing flowed through her.

Sinow, the name ran through her mind as a whisper.

Tears filled Xali's eyes, and her heart felt as if it had been severed in two, the intensity of it doubling her over. This was no ordinary heartache. This was something deeper as if part of her was missing. The emotion was drowning her, and she struggled to breathe.

"I will help him find you, I promise," she said through the tears.

Find me and the land will heal, my heart will heal.

"I promise, I will."

Sinow, the thought was as a scattered whisper.

"You miss him." As she spoke the words, the pain grew, but then it stopped, her heart swelling once more. A flurry of emotions and thoughts rushed through her, strengthening her heart. She tried to grasp it all as it quickly swept through her: love, desire, security, contentment, wholeness, oneness. The love she held for her husband somehow fortifying her weakened state. The grass below her feet softened, and Xali watched as a rich sage bled through the land before her, sprucelings climbing their way from below it.

Xali let out an astonished laugh as she took in the changes, the world flourishing once again.

"Love. Your love. It's keeping you alive and, with it, the land."

A breeze caressed her skin, and she felt the loss of her connection to the queen as she drifted from her dream, her eyes opening to the dark of the room.

She sat up, her mind a jumble of thoughts, the emotion of experiencing the queen's love for the king leaving her weak. She'd thought her love for Carnick was strong, but that was mere child's love compared to this. There was a timelessness to this, something ancient, weathered that gave it an endless depth, that made it incomparable and unbreakable.

There was a knock on her door followed by someone entering.

"The king has requested your presence," a man's voice said beneath the black robe that made him indistinguishable from the dark room. She knew better than to question. He grabbed her arm as she stood, and within seconds, she was standing in a dimly lit room. It looked to be a study or an office. He stepped away from her as she met the king's eyes, a rich brown carrying the emotion she had felt in her dream. She swallowed.

"You felt her again," he said.

She nodded.

He ran his hand through his thick ebony hair and paced. There was something different about him now that she was alone with him, a vulnerability she somehow knew he didn't often show.

"Why you? Why not traverse the Dream Realm with me? Why not pull me in?" he muttered.

"Dream Realm?"

He stopped pacing. "It's where she pulls you when you're sleeping. It's the realm between our world and the realm of the Fates. Few can traverse it, my wife being one of them. But she's always called me to it in dire circumstances, never another.

"Maybe she doesn't have the power."

"Then how does she call you?"

"Whatever connection I have to her maybe?"

He looked over at her, his eyes boring into her. She wanted to run from the weight of his stare, but she didn't, instead, standing her ground.

"It's the Elvin in you."

"You keep saying that, but I'm not Elvin."

"No, you're a mix of it, at least that's what Violissa thought." His face reflected a moment of pain when he said his wife's name, his eyes dropping. "What did she show you?"

She wanted to ask him more about why they thought she was part Elvin, but he'd moved past it. Narilen had told her something similar during her time in hiding but had never explained it. Yet another question left unanswered. He remained silent, his arms now crossed, awaiting her answer to his question.

"The land. It died, fading before my eyes. Before her eyes. It was like I was her, seeing it from her perspective. Feeling it. And you."

"Me?"

"She misses you. It hurt. So much pain, her heart aches. I've never felt such pain."

"She has," he said softly. His eyes lightened a shade, and the king was gone, replaced by a man who loved his wife, who needed her desperately by his side. Gods how could Drakine have done this to them?

The color in his eyes darkened as if he realized his moment of weakness, and the immortal king stood before her once again.

"What else?"

"I think you're what's holding her together, keeping her alive. Her love for you. I could feel it, she lets it replace the pain, it strengthens her, and with it, the land remains intact."

He dropped his eyes. "Our love has always kept us both alive."

"But you're immortals. You can't be killed."

"There have been times in our past when she was vulnerable, when we both were."

"How long is that past?" she asked, curious as to how a love could be so impermeable.

He brought his eyes up. "Are you asking how old we are?"

She nodded.

"The answer to that is one you may not wish to know."

"Why?"

"Because it would make your life seem small and insignificant."

"How old?" she asked again, annoyed that he would think her insignificant.

"With the ten thousand years you say we've slept, nearly thirty thousand years old."

Her mouth dropped, and in that moment, she did feel insignificant.

"Your ancestor stumbled into something bigger than he and his ambitions, throwing us from a path that should have been nearly completed, throwing us from a path that had taken us eons to find, destroying our peace, one we'd fought for with our lives. I'll be glad when we can both finally rest."

She didn't know what to say, her shock still holding her prisoner.

"Take her back to her room."

The Darkbearer grabbed her arm, and she was about to object when the king held up his hand to stop the man and asked, "Where were you in the dream, Xaliandri?"

She didn't know what to make of the sudden change.

Answering honestly, she replied, "The ravine at the divide between the old realms."

His brow furrowed. "There is no longer a divide."

"Yes, I was there."

"There was once a divide that severed our realms, keeping us apart physically in so many ways, but that divide was healed by Violissa eons ago."

"No, it's there. Carnick said it's always been there, ending in his province, but it runs dry."

He looked stunned for a moment. "Drakine's destruction ran deep, deep enough to have physically severed the realms again, fracturing a land whose divide had long been healed. Why is she calling you? What does it mean?" he said absently. "Thane, take her back and make sure she gets a deep sleep. She needs it."

Before she could protest, she found herself in the black room again. She felt the magic as the man cast it, slipping through her like a heavy cloak, blackness taking over as she collapsed to the bed.

Seventeen

Carnick stood before the massive doors, hesitant to enter. Behind lay a room of immortals. He still couldn't fathom that any of what he'd experienced the prior day had been real. Immortals. They were alive, they were here, and they'd taken over.

The king had acquiesced to Xali's request, and their family had been moved from the wilderness behind the guardian wall and to Carnick's home under guard by two immortals, Darkbearers they'd been called. He and Xali were to remain in the king's castle until the queen was found and their fate decided. Or so he'd been told as he'd woken that morning and dropped to wait outside the door until summoned.

He lingered in front of the door, voices coming from behind.

"We'll find her, Sinow."

"When? Why can't I feel her, Tynan?"

"None of us can."

"Father, she's alive. The girl is her connection."

"But for how long? She hasn't had any sign of Violissa since we awoke except that dream last eve that does not bode well. And the land…the land is dying. It can only mean one thing, we're running out of time." Carnick could feel the pain in his voice. "I need her Ren. I can't…"

There was silence, and then Carnick heard, "You can. You did before when she was gone, and you'll survive now, we will find her, I promise you."

"You're right. We'll find her. We'll find all of them. I'm not the only one suffering, I'm sorry. We'll find Violissa and, with her, Paige and Chastity. I'm sure of it."

"Is this what you've come to? Spying on people?"

Carnick jumped at Xali's voice. Regaining his composure quickly, he replied. "They told me to wait out here. Besides, I'm not certain this is the best time, they're having a pretty intense discussion."

"He loves her. It's intense, but it has something to do with some prophecy."

"Where did you hear that?"

"I snuck into a Cirillian village in our province."

"You did what?" He couldn't believe she'd been so foolish. "That's how you learned all that talk about the Fates? Gods, I thought you were simply talking to her, I didn't know you'd actually risked going to her village."

"It was before this mess, before everyone turned on me." She paused, momentarily looking down at her hands. "Why didn't you tell me, Carnick?"

"Tell you what, Xali?" he asked although in his head he knew to what she was referring. He wanted to hear her say the words.

"That you didn't tell them. That it wasn't you. Why did you let me believe it?"

"Because you were so quick to believe I would do such a thing. You didn't even hesitate."

"You wouldn't look at me—"

"It hurt too much, knowing what they planned. I would have thrown myself in front of their punishment for you, Xali. Would have given my life for yours. But you didn't need saving, you're stronger than me, strong enough to save yourself and so I stayed back."

She searched his eyes, regret heavy in her own.

"But you didn't believe that. You chose to believe that I handed you over to them, that I loved you less than I do." He couldn't help himself, the hurt from her action had been swelling. He hadn't had time to accept it until now, to own it.

The gray clouds swirled around her eyes, the emerald blinking in and out of sight.

"I'm sorry," she said softly. "I was scared and you…well, you weren't by my side. You stood with them."

"When have you ever needed me by your side, Xali? It's just like you said to the immortal king yesterday, you're strong. You don't need anyone's help, you're capable of anything, you always have been."

"No one sees me that way."

"I do, I always have."

She gave him a slight smile. "So where do we go from here?"

"Well, I think this is the moment I pull you into my arms and kiss you, forgiving you for thinking of me as such a cad."

Her smile widened. "I'd like that very much. I've missed you."

He pulled her into his arms and kissed her, just as he'd said he would, the feeling of her against him sealing the hole that had grown since she'd disappeared that day. He didn't want to let her go now that he had her back.

"Ahem, if you two are done." He heard.

Both he and Xali jumped at the voice. The prince stood before the now open door, his arms crossed. Xali recovered quicker than he, saying, "Sorry we were just…well we…good morn, Ren."

"Good morn, Xali, Carnick."

He turned and led them into the room, which was filled with

immortals.

"Ren?" Carnick whispered to her. "You're on a first-name basis now?"

The prince laughed.

"Only with my son," the king said, his eyes deep ebony.

"That really doesn't bother you? Kissing your cousin?" the brother asked from the corner of the room.

"Tynan. Watch your temper. They have different traditions than we have."

Unable to resist a comeback, Carnick replied, "Do you have your own realm to rule?"

"Ha! He wanted his own. In fact, there's quite a story behind what he wanted and what he has."

Carnick couldn't remember the name of the king's man who had said it, but he recognized the anger in the brother's eyes.

"Funny, Keary. Still don't like me after all these millennia?"

"It's a love-hate thing, Tynan."

"I'd hold your tongue before you lose it."

"Enough!" the king bellowed. "Xali, I want you to come back to the Elvin Enclave with me. Violissa has to be buried somewhere there, the place was fortified too well for her not to be. We believe her Lightbearers are somewhere under the remains of her castle based on what your family told us, but she should be able to wake them when we find her. My Council has been searching for them."

"Lightbearers?" Carnick asked, unsure of the term but remembering that Xali had used a similar term about his men.

"Her Council of immortals as you call us."

"I'm going with her," Carnick then said. "You're not taking her without me."

The king raised his eyebrow. "I thought you said she was stronger than you?"

Carnick couldn't hide his surprise.

"You're not the only one who can listen in on conversations."

"You heard the whole thing?"

"It was quite interesting…young love. What did she blame you for?"

Carnick tried to form a sentence, unsure why he was feeling incoherent.

"I thought he was the one who had turned me in to my family for having lesser powers. Handing me my death sentence."

"Hmmm, for one, they are not lesser powers. I think I'll have that term banned. Secondly, next time, trust him, trust his love for you. Take it from me, doubting it will only cause trouble and heartache."

For a moment, there was a tenderness to the man, something soft that spoke of the man behind the power. It was curious, and Carnick wondered what had happened in his life for him to say such a thing with the certainty of someone who had experienced it. The vulnerability was quickly replaced with a cloud of power, his eyes darkening to a rich black.

"There's something happening outside," he said. His eyes bore into Carnick and then Xali. "Your people."

He disappeared, followed by a few of the others. The son, Ren, stayed.

"Why would your people be here and who would they be? They'll be dead within moments if you have no answers."

"The cousins," Xali said, looking at Carnick for confirmation. "They're coming for us and our parents."

The ground shook.

"They have power?"

"Minimal against you."

He nodded and grabbed them both. Carnick landed awkwardly, taking in a scene that terrified him. His cousins had assembled, and they held a woman who looked to be from Old Tenebron.

"We won't let her go until we have our family back," Sartria yelled.

The brother roared. What could only be described as a tendril of black mist whipped from him and snapped Sartria who fell instantly to the ground writhing in pain. Mendol lifted the land to protect them all, but the king decimated it before he could even finish, walking confidently down the front stairs of the castle as the others threw their power at him. He had his sights on Mendol.

"No!" Xali screamed, running as the Old Tenebron woman ran toward the brother, her cousins not noticing as they were now on the defensive. The brother pulled her into his arms, his face momentarily filling with relief before it morphed to anger, and he pushed her behind him.

Xali had placed herself between the cousins and the king.

"Xali, move!" Mendol screamed.

Carnick stood, frozen, as his fear for Xali kicked in. Seeing both the king and his brother drawing their power, he ran toward Xali, unable to take his eyes from her. She brought her hands up, the land rising smoothly behind her to protect the others, the sky above turning gray and stormy, the wind whipping her hair around her.

"You won't hurt my family!" she yelled.

The king paused, evaluating her.

"You would dare stand in the way of my justice?"

His brother broke the soft hill of land she'd created, but it instantly reformed. He reached his power out toward Xali, but Carnick jumped in front of her, taking the hit that brought pain to every cell in his body. He ignored it, pulling himself to a crouch as a piece of that magic woke the Darkness in him, that same sensation he'd had when he'd woken the king. He let it fill him, and against every thought in his mind that said to break from the pain, he brought himself up to standing, facing the brother.

"Well, well. You two continue to surprise."

"You won't hurt our family, and you will not harm Xali."

"It would seem we are at a crossroads," the king said. "We cannot kill you, Xali—"

"We can kill him, brother."

The king put his hand up to stay him. "No, I think we need him still."

There was an awkward space of silence, the two looking at each other as if having a conversation, just as Carnick had seen them do before. It still surprised him, the depth of their abilities. How could they have been so foolish to think the immortals were weak?

"Lower your land shield, Xali," the king commanded.

The king's eyes lightened, the air growing less dense.

"You won't hurt them?"

"We will hear them out, then we will decide."

"That's not good enough. You've already stolen one uncle from us—"

"A man who deserved to die."

A cry could be heard from behind them as Ainia and Trevant realized their father had been killed. The ground lowered, a slight wave flowing beneath Carnick's feet. He turned to face the others.

"Carnick!" Fairenth ran to his arms, her small body shaking with fear.

Xali embraced her brother as Ren came over to Sartria who was still on the ground crumpled in pain. Carnick watched as he lifted the pain from her, healing whatever unseen damage the king's brother had done. The others looked on, their faces reflecting their shock.

"So, it's true, everything Xali said, everything you both said. The immortals were stronger." Herind stated.

"Are stronger," he corrected.

All eyes rose to view the immortals that stood before them. As Ren moved to join them, Carnick took in the sight of them standing before the castle; it was overwhelming, awe-inspiring. Their magic seemed to encase each of them like an aura of gray and black. No one could doubt the sheer magnitude of power these people had. They were gods of their own right.

"Everything we knew about them was wrong," Mendol said.

"Those are the immortals?" Fairenth asked, always a step behind the others.

"Yes, sister, at least some of them," Carnick responded. "And

Xali is helping to find the rest of them."

Trevant moved forward, holding his sister who was still crying. "You killed our father?"

Yes, we did," the king answered coldly.

"Why? Why would you do that?"

"Did he not intend to kill your cousin?"

"But she broke the law."

"Did she? Your father was a guilty man, manipulative and deceitful. He would have killed her, then Carnick, overtaken their realms, and warred upon your final house."

Trevant looked taken aback. "No, he…he was only punishing a crime against the family."

"Was he or did you see into his heart as I saw into his mind? Regardless, it is done, the sentence was fair. Now, before my brother kills all of you, like he wants to, someone tell me why you have his mate. I can already see what your intentions with her were as can he, so I do hope you are honest."

Mendol stepped forward. "You're the immortals?"

"And you're not talking," the brother said, his power swirling.

"We only wanted to exchange her for our family," Mendol replied. " We didn't know what had happened to them. My father and the others went off after Carnick. They knew he had snuck away to find my sister; she'd been gone so long. When they left, we all convened in my uncle's palace, awaiting their return. Then when none of them returned, the guards brought this woman to us. She'd been ranting—"

"I don't rant!" the woman defended herself.

Mendol looked as if he wanted to step back, but he didn't. "Sorry, talking about the Fates and finding people we'd never heard of, then when we pieced it together, a scout returned to tell us the Old Tenebron ruins had been restored. We knew Xali was involved."

"And you just assumed I'd sided with them and done what to our parents?" Xali asked, angered. "Had them killed? Had Carnick imprisoned? What were you thinking, Mendol?" Xali pushed him.

"I didn't think you'd done anything like that, Xaliandri! I thought you'd gotten in over your head! That you were in trouble. You took off that day, disappeared in front of us all! We haven't seen you, Mother has been worried sick, the provinces are on edge. No one knew where you'd gone, and then all of you disappeared. You don't think, Xali! You run on instinct and emotion, doing things your way, always shunning the norms, testing, questioning. And now… this is what you've done. One head is killed, you've unleashed the immortals, and what of our father? Our aunts? Did you think you could dig up the dead with no consequences?"

Xali looked hurt, and Carnick's heart ached for her. Mendol was right, but Xali was as well.

He looked to the immortals, but they were waiting, listening for her response, testing her.

"That's enough Mendol," Carnick said, wanting to take the pain from her eyes.

She put a hand on his arm. "He's right, Carnick. I left but not purposely and why would I return? They wanted me dead, all of them. I didn't know that I had anything to return to. We were living a lie, Mendol. Everything the great king built was on the back of his sin. This land is not ours, it never was, it belongs to them. Just look…he said they were dead, but here they stand after we woke them from their sleep. A sleep that fed the doorways to our provinces as the great king siphoned their power for his own use. He said they held lesser powers; you see that they don't. We are no match for them, their magic eclipses ours. It was a kingdom built on lies, built on the remnants of a kingdom lost. It was bound to crumble from the burden of lies. I simply toppled it first."

She kissed Mendol on the cheek and then walked over to the king and the others. "I stand with the immortals. I know what it means to us, but their Fates have called me, their queen calls me. I stand with them."

"They killed my father, Xali," Trevant said, his sister beside him.

"And your father, my uncle was a horrid man. He vied to have me killed, Carnick killed. He would have destroyed our family, our kingdoms if I had not first. And you know this to be true."

Carnick smiled inwardly. He was proud of her, just as he always had been. She'd spoken like a queen, and for a moment, he wondered if they would reward her for her loyalty, for waking them. Could there be room for her, for their people? Or would all of them be killed, enslaved just as the great king had done to their people?

He squeezed Fairenth's hand and then walked over to Xali. "I stand with Xali and with the immortals. It's what needs to be done, what should have been done centuries ago."

"Well, now that that's settled, the rest are mine," the brother said.

Carnick's heart dropped. It hadn't been the reaction he'd expected, but then again, these men were not cut from the same mold as his family, and he suspected mercy was a rare thing for the Dark king.

Xali shuddered at the words the king's brother had said. All of it had been for naught. They would be killed for threatening the woman she now knew was his companion, mate as they'd referred to her. Xali had thought it an odd term and wondered if it had meant they were not yet joined.

Now she waited, breath held as the king put his hand up toward his brother as if in a gesture to stop him. Ren moved closer to his father, and a strained silence ensued. They were talking in their heads again, and from the blackening eyes of the brother, whatever Ren was saying was persuading his father.

Carnick took her hand and squeezed it. She squeezed back; it was the only movement she could make she was so nervous. Finally, Ren walked toward her cousins. Xali felt Carnick tense and saw the fear in their eyes. Her chest burned from the breath captured within her lungs.

"As I will be king soon, my father has deferred the decision of your fate to me, against my uncle's advice. You may thank whatever false gods you pray to that I tend toward my mother's inclinations, for you will not suffer punishment by my hand this day. I offer you a choice instead, stand with Xaliandri and her betrothed, offer her your loyalty, offer her your trust. Help us, as she is to find my mother and the rest of our family. Xali is the key, chosen by the Fates, chosen by my mother who is struggling to stay in this world. For if you do not, then all of us will perish.

"Just as Xali is a key, Mother is the key to this world's prosperity, the foundation on which this land flourishes, and with her fading, so goes that land. You can see that for yourself. Look around and take in the dying land that will spread as she weakens. Your ancestor Drakine cursed us to sleep for too long. Tying my father's and uncle's powers to your shifting doorways as you call them and holding my mother separately, knowing if he truly found a way to kill her, the world would perish with her.

"He used her, used us, and built the world you know upon the lives of my family. Help me, help us undo the wrongs and find my mother and the others, my wife as well. Help us and I promise there will be a place for you and for your people in our world."

Silence followed, and then Mendol took a step forward.

"I will stand with my sister."

Xali let the breath she'd been holding finally go as one by one they stepped forward until only three remained. Trevant looked to his sister who still had tears from discovering their father had been killed. Then, he stepped forward and pledged his loyalty to Xali, saying, "I stand beside Xali. I always have questioned the traditions, the history as we all have. My father is dead because he couldn't see the possibility that what we had was false, that it was wrong."

Ainia took his hand. "I stand beside you, Xali. I don't think my father should have died, but I have seen the land, seen how the death has spread through the forests into the plains. I will put our people and this world before my heartache and stand with you."

Xali nodded then they all looked to Fairenth who remained the final one.

"What are you doing, Fairenth?" Carnick whispered.

Mendol extended his hand to her yet still she remained. She lifted her eyes and met Xali's; they were filled with fear and guilt. It had been Fairenth; she had revealed Xali's secret, a secret Mendol must have shared with her. That was why Carnick had stayed quiet all that time.

"I don't think Xaliandri will want me by her side," she said softly. "I'm sorry, Xali, I didn't mean to tell her, I didn't mean for any of this to happen. I didn't think, and it almost cost you your life."

Xali heard grumbling from the brother who was growing impatient. She glanced over at him, the woman still tucked behind him protectively.

"Fairenth," she said, "I know. It's all right. It was meant to be, all of it, for I would not have found the immortals if you hadn't betrayed me. And now, we move forward together. Take your place at my brother's side where I know you want to be."

"Will you have me by your side as well?"

"Yes, of course."

Fairenth extended her hand and took Mendol's, moving beside him. Xali felt Carnick relax.

"Well, that's no fun," the brother mumbled.

"Darkbearers, take them," the king said. "See that they are given shelter until we find Violissa."

Several shifted next to the cousins, and within seconds, they were all gone, including Mendol.

"Where are you taking them?" Xali asked, worried for their safety.

The king ignored her and began to walk away, followed by the others. Ren went to pass her, but she grabbed his arm. He turned sharply, his eyes darkening, but at the same moment, the wind stirred, becoming frigid, a sensation buzzed through her like an electric current, and she heard a distant, *Xaliandri*. She dropped his arm and stepped back, the experience leaving her shaken. Ren's eyes softened, filling with hope.

"Violissa," the king said, stopping and turning toward her. "I felt her. What did you see?"

His eyes were filled with a mixture of pain and hope, now a shade of soft brown.

"I didn't see anything, but I heard her. She's still out there, but her voice, it was more…distant, softer."

There was a shift in his eyes, subtle but enough for her to notice, sadness, longing, and, in that moment, she felt their connection, remembering Sianna's words, that their love was unlike any other. Part of a prophecy from the beginning of time.

As if he sensed her thoughts, the ebony filled his eyes, covering the softness. She swallowed as he studied her. Then he turned and walked away. She wasn't certain what had just happened.

Ren met her eyes. "My father does not like people seeing under the surface of the Dark king. He needs my mother, he needs balance soon, or it will be more than the dying land to be feared."

He walked off, following the others, leaving Xali and Carnick by themselves. She watched as they all disappeared through the castle doors. The weight of everything that had just occurred seemed to settle on her small frame. For a moment, she didn't know if her legs would hold her, and then she felt Carnick beside her. She moved her gaze to meet his, and as if he knew, he pulled her into his arms.

It felt good, secure, constant, and she wondered if she'd ever want to leave as tears threatened to spill. He kissed the top of her head, and she let herself relax, escaping from the crushing reality for just that moment.

"What have I done?" she whispered into his chest, doubt surfacing for the first time.

"You did what needed to be done, what you were meant to do."

"But our family, our rule—"

"Is over but our family remains."

"To do what? To be prisoners of the immortals for the rest of their lives?"

Carnick pushed her back so that he could look into her eyes. "Where has my strong, confident Xaliandri gone?"

"She's tired and…and scared."

"Shhh, this is your time, Xali. You were chosen by their Fates, our gods I believe, to free them, to bring them back because they're needed. Our family destroyed what once was, and now, the world's existence is threatened because of one man's greed. You were chosen to undo that mistake, and no matter the consequences, I will stand with you."

He gently wiped a tear from her cheek. "You know I don't think I've seen you cry since you were a small child. Always too stubborn to show weakness, trying to be brave, to be as strong as all of us. Now look at you."

"Family destroyer, tradition breaker, need I go on?"

He laughed. "No, not those things. I believe those are things in our past, from the life we knew, things we need to leave there. No, you are now one who walks with the immortals, history changer, child of the Fates."

As he said those last words, a breeze swept through her hair. "Hmmm," he said, his eyes growing larger. "I think they like that last title."

He brought his hand up and pulled her hair forward. Where before she'd only had the one golden cluster of strands, now her hair was a mix of silver and gold streaks, the silver deeper than it had been. She looked up in surprise, then as a subtle current went through her, she heard the voice again, *Xaliandri,* her name faded as the breeze drew away.

"She's calling me again, Carnick."

"Just now?"

"Yes."

"Amazing."

"I wish I knew where she was. You heard what Ren said, his father needs her just as much as our land does. Do you see the change in his eyes, in his demeanor whenever he talks about her? Their love is different, Carnick, deeper I think. Sianna mentioned something about a prophecy, and I think it binds them so that they can't live without each other, as if they're two pieces of the same whole."

"You took all that from a story your servant girl told you? And why was she even telling you that? She knows the penalty."

"Knew the penalty. And I sought her out, their people have kept their history intact, Carnick. Underground, hidden away so we would never find out. Their devotion to the Fates and the immortals was greater than our laws. But it's more than just the story she shared. It's something about the king, something about the way the queen calls to me. There's a longing to both of them."

"Then let's find her and reunite them. I hated being without you in the time you were gone, I can't imagine having lost you as long as they've been separated."

She smiled and kissed him, then took his hand and led him into the castle.

There was no one to be found when they entered. Xali found it odd as she and Carnick hadn't stayed outside for long.

"Strange," Carnick said in a whisper. "Where did they go?"

"I don't know," she said as they walked further in. "Do you think we can find where they took the others?"

"I don't even think I could find my way back to the room they had me in."

"I wouldn't try it," she heard from the right of them.

Xali turned to see the woman her cousins had found standing with her arms crossed. It was the first time Xali had really gotten to look at her. She was striking, her long ebony hair cascaded loosely down her back, her soft brown eyes held specks of gold, and her skin was a soft bronze the likes of which Xali had never seen before.

"Just because you can't see them, doesn't mean they're not here. There are several stationed throughout the keep until they build enough Scian."

"Scian?" Carnick asked as they followed her. "The rebels who fight our armies?"

The woman gave him a perplexed look. "Rebels? Scian are no rebels. They are the king's guard, special selected loyal men who are handpicked by the king to guard where he cannot."

"He had an army?" Carnick said.

"He did, but they were rarely used as you would think. Sinow and his Darkbearers along with Tynan are the force in this world."

She stopped and opened a set of doors, continuing into the largest library Xali had ever seen. She stood frozen in the doorway, taking it in. It wasn't so much that it was brimming with books, but the space itself was in such contrast to the rest of the castle. The windows were uncovered with their hangings drawn to the side, allowing the sun to stream through. The colors were light and calming, and throughout the room were soft chairs that welcomed one to sit for an extended time.

"Mendol would love this place," she whispered.

"This is Violissa's library. It's her place to sneak away when the Dark of the castle and the men in it become too much. I sneak in here occasionally because it's a better option, all that black and dust of the rest of the castle can bring you down," the woman said, plopping into one of the chairs, the skirts of her dress puffing around her.

"Ugh. I hate these things, so much material. That outfit you have on looks so much more comfortable. I'll have to nudge Violissa to see if we can change up the fashion. Seriously, eons of these things, and they never go away. It's like a land stuck in time."

Xali eyed Carnick as the woman rambled. It was as if every thought she'd had for the last ten thousand years of sleep was rolling out of her mouth.

"Who are you?" Carnick asked.

She stopped talking and looked up at them.

"I'm Chastity. Sinow told me to keep you company. I'd honestly rather be keeping Tynan company. Seriously, they said it's been ten thousand years that we've slept, and I can't even spend a few minutes with him? Not that that would be enough mind you, we'd need much longer." She rested back in the chair, staring at the ceiling. "Much longer. Ten thousand years. I can't even wrap my head around it. So long to be alive, to be asleep." She raised her head and shook it. "I need some time with Tynan desperately if it's been that long. Locked away for days. Damn Sinow for dragging him away when I just found him."

Xali felt a slight blush fill her cheeks as Carnick stifled a laugh.

"So, you two, you're a couple?"

"Yes," Carnick said.

"She blushes like she doesn't know you."

Xali felt the color deepen, wondering how she could get out of this conversation, and then she sighed. "That's because I don't. Second borns must remain chaste before the joining with their first born."

Chastity's brow raised. "Do first borns need to stay chaste?"

"No."

"Hmm, interesting class system, and I thought home had a crazy segregation system. Virginity is definitely a new one."

Xali didn't understand what she was talking about. "Home? Isn't this your home?"

"It is now, but it's not my true home." Her eyes drifted as if she were lost in memory. "My true home is in another world. It's been so long though, I'm sure it's changed. Honestly, I'm not even sure that world still exists. Hell, this one is hundreds of thousands of years old, so I suppose it could still be around."

"Hell?" Carnick asked as confused as she.

"Sorry, we talk differently in my world. Well, we do a lot differently, but that's another story."

"You're from a different world? Not province or realm but world?"

She smiled a knowing smile. "I see it's true you underestimated the power of the Dark king and his Light queen."

"The immortals can travel to different worlds? Other worlds actually exist?"

"The immortals? I like that name, and yes, but that's a long story for another day."

She rose stretching. "Now, tell me why Sinow stole Tynan from me so quickly. And why Sinow looks like he's on the verge of madness."

"The queen—"

"Violissa?"

"Yes," Xali answered. "They haven't found her yet."

Chastity exhaled sharply, her face falling, her lips forming an *oh* shape.

"We found the king and his brother along with his son, but that was mere chance. We don't know where she is."

Her eyes narrowed. "Nothing in this world happens by chance. If you found them, you were meant to find them."

She twirled a piece of her hair around her finger.

"That's why he looks off. Fates, without her…" Chastity stopped as if she didn't want to say the words.

"The world dies," Carnick finished.

She eyed him sharply. "That shouldn't be what scares you. It's what happens to him if she's lost that should terrify you."

Xali was afraid to ask what would happen; she'd heard Ren say something similar.

The air stirred as a Darkbearer appeared. "Chastity," he said, nodding to her.

She gave him a smile. "Thane."

"I have orders to take these two. We've found something."

"Violissa?" she asked, hopeful.

His face dropped. "No, her Council."

Before anyone could respond, he grabbed Carnick and Xali, then shifted.

Xali only wobbled a little this time, getting used to the sudden movement of shifting. She looked around to find that they were standing in a cave that looked similar to where they'd found the king.

"Where are we?" Carnick asked.

"Cirillia," Ren said, approaching them. "We found them buried in these caverns below my mother's castle. The Darkbearers were in a similar place below my father's castle."

"But how did you get down here? There were only ruins left of this place," Xali asked, running after him. He'd turned and started walking down a corridor.

"You're not the only ones who can move stone. My father is quite determined when it comes to my mother. Stone is nothing to him."

They entered an enormous room, ten slabs situated within. She caught her breath. Ten, just like the Darkbearers.

"Can you wake them?" the king asked, coming to her hurriedly.

"We can try."

"No," Ren said. "Carnick's power feeds from Dark magic. Only you would have the capability. These are Lightbearers, Light magic."

"Light magic? I don't know what that is compared to yours."

"Healing magic, calming. Here," Ren said, a wave of bluish energy freeing from his hand. It slipped over her skin, its feel cooling, gentle, relaxing. It was similar to the healing magic he had used but stronger, different, and something in her rebelled, the feel startling it, raising its defenses. It stirred, rising as the other part of her, the one to which she'd grown accustomed, welcomed the feel of Ren's magic. A battle ensued, the two parts of her vying to accept or reject the Light power.

"I'll be damned," the king's brother said as Ren withdrew his power.

"Nature and Dark. How can that be?" the king asked.

"Drakine's powers were always a mystery to us, a warped form of nature magic. Maybe there was more to it. Violissa seemed to think so," the brother said.

Xali managed to catch her breath, the internal battle settling. Two powers, just like the dream had shown her, just as the Elvin king had told her. What did it mean?

Everyone was looking at her, including Carnick; he was shocked by the revelation.

"What was that?" she asked.

"Your power's reaction to Light magic," the king said, looking from her to Carnick and then back to her.

"I'd surmise that she won't be waking the Light Council," the brother said.

"I'd have to agree with that presumption."

They turned and walked away, Ren following but throwing her a curious look back.

"Xali," Carnick said, reaching for her arm. "Your eyes, they grew dark, black almost, but those emerald sparkles were flickering throughout them."

"Black like yours now grow," she said absently, the words of the brother playing through her mind, *maybe there was more to it*. More to their magic, more to who they were. Nothing in this world happens by chance, the brother's mate had said. "I don't think we're just land movers, Carnick."

"I don't either. Whatever our line is, they are the key to finding out. They have a knowledge of our world that we don't have. Ours has been censored, abridged, you heard the woman, Chastity, say how old this world is. Why does our history begin at the arrival to these lands? What was it that the great king wanted to leave behind?"

"I don't know," she answered honestly, her eyes drifting to the king who was watching them as if hearing their words, "but I think you're right, they are the means to finding out who we really are."

Eighteen

Carnick let Xali's words settle. The immortals were the key to discovering their past. A past that had a definitive starting point, their history prior to coming to these lands brief and without detail.

He looked around the room at the lifeless bodies of what they'd called Lightbearers, all covered in white cloaks, their hands folded gently across them. He'd sensed the magic the son had demonstrated to Xali, the coolness of it, the calm peaceful feel that stood in contrast to the king's. His own power had reacted to it, tearing through him for release at the invasion, that same Darkness but below it, he'd felt another sensation stirring, one that sought to simmer the Darkness that had become familiar to him over the past moons.

It didn't appear to have as striking an effect as Xali's powers had, but he'd felt it all the same. Nature and Dark, the king had said.

The magic of his family had never been labeled, never defined as it now was with those words. Was their magic a blend of the same powers these immortals held? How could that be?

"The Light magic, it comes from your mother?" Xali asked, her voice breaking the silence of the room.

The son stopped and turned back to her. "I am my mother's son, so her magic flows through my veins."

The queen held two powers as well. The revelation stunned Carnick although considering what they'd just discovered about their own magic, it should have seemed a reasonable thing. Xali didn't appear as taken aback as he.

"Your mother holds nature and this Light magic? You hold the same?" Carnick asked.

Ren nodded. "And Dark, for I am my father's son as well."

He turned away, and Carnick caught the king's eyes, his look confirming Carnick's thought. A thought that had repeated since the moment the immortals had awoken. There was more to the immortals than anyone had imagined.

"But why? Why hold three powers?" Xali asked.

This time, it was the brother who was swift to answer. "You ask too many questions, like an annoying bug that needs killing. If your people had bothered to learn the history of these realms, you would know the answer to that question, understand the significance of Ren's place in this world. But you chose to erase that history, to wipe it from the minds of our people. Your questions do not deserve answers."

"The prophecy," Xali said, ignoring the murderous look that sat upon the brother's face. One which Carnick was tempted to shield her from. One that morphed to surprise when he heard her words.

"You know of the prophecy?" the king asked.

"Only what the servant girl told me."

He regarded her for a moment. "Then you would know that my son is the final blending of the three magics of this world. They will be one at his ascension to the throne then carried on to his heir and those beyond."

"Then where does our magic fit in?" Carnick asked, afraid to hear the answer.

"It doesn't," the king replied before turning his back on them.

Carnick sensed Xali's confidence slip, just as his own had with the words.

There was no place for them in this world, one that had been in existence long before the great king had waged war upon it. Great king? He was no great king; he had left nothing but a mess behind him, a legacy coated with deceit and lies. Left for him and Xali to clean up and for all of them to suffer the consequences.

If there was no place for them here, there was no future for them. No position of safety. He and Xali were now the servants, the lesser born working to an end that did not offer them shelter.

He looked at Xali as she observed the men, her stance tense as if she were readying herself for battle. He knew the look, the one she used to build her façade of the strong warrior in defiance of her lack of power.

He took her hand. "You no longer have to hide behind that wall, Xali," he whispered.

She glanced at him, her eyes stormy, the gray in them floating like storm clouds on the cusp of rain. She was the dichotomy between the brave battle-ready warrior and the wounded princess who'd been told she was less than everyone else, second born, powerless in every aspect. She was glorious and heartbreaking all at once.

Forgetting where he was, the moment only allowing for the two of them to exist, he brushed her hair back.

"You are no longer that second born princess you strived so hard to run from. In my eyes, you never were that person. You are a leader, Xali, it is you who will save our people, you who will save their queen. You have never been weak, never been less than who you are, the woman I love," he whispered.

He could see the change in her as the doubt washed away, a

smile forming as she leaned over and kissed him. Everything fell away, and for a moment, life returned to the way it had been, as he kissed his betrothed, the woman who would share his bed, share his throne, his life. Then as quickly as it had come, the thought fled, and reality returned.

"I still can't fathom it," the brother said, his voice breaking the trance and throwing them back into the tomblike cavern. "They're cousins. Does this not bother anyone else?"

"You don't even have a cousin, Uncle," Ren said. "Why should it bother you so?"

"It goes against the laws of nature."

"You go against the laws of nature, brother," the king said, "yet we keep you around."

For a moment, the mood was lighter as they all gave a quiet laugh, but it didn't last, the laughter dying quickly, the solemn mood returning.

"Keep your hands to yourselves and stop disturbing my brother's sense of softness. This isn't the place for it."

"And you never just felt the urge to kiss your wife?" Xali said defiantly. Carnick balked at her, wondering if she'd gone mad.

He felt the air turn as she fell to her knees, pain gripping her face.

"Let her be!" he yelled, throwing the land up below the king and throwing him off balance.

He recovered quickly, and Carnick felt the claws of power grip him. He balled his hands against the pain, his mind still on protecting Xali who was struggling against it, all the while holding back whatever reaction the king expected. *Weakness,* the word slipped through his mind. Pain was weakness to them. Show it, scream out in agony, and you lower your standing.

He bit back the urge to pass out as something within him broke, the sound of the bone snapping, tempting the scream he was holding in.

The king stepped forward. "I have shielded you from

punishment, girl, but your mouth never stays shut."

"You didn't answer my question," she said through gritted teeth.

Gods, what was she doing? There would be no staying their execution now.

The brother laughed. "Oh, I like her, brother. Don't kill her, let's keep her around just so I can see her grate your nerves."

"Don't make me punish you, too, Tynan," he growled. That was the only word Carnick could think for the deep rumble that had emerged.

The king picked Xali up by her neck.

"Leave her alone!" Carnick tried rising, but he was fighting, the pain too intense for him to move.

"I don't know whether you're brave or stupid," the king said to Xali.

"Both, but I prefer naïve," she choked out.

Her last word seemed to affect him, and the pain receded some.

"If my wife were here and not imprisoned by the recklessness of your people, I would kiss her every chance I had, but she's not. She's lost to me, dying somewhere with who knows how much time left. So don't you dare ask me if I ever have the urge to kiss her."

Carnick could see the emotion as he spoke, his hold on Carnick vacillating, loosening then tightening.

"I haven't held her in ten thousand years, haven't seen her, kissed her, touched her. Ten thousand years. So next time you think of asking me a question like that, think about not seeing your betrothed for that timespan."

He threw her, and Carnick feared she would slam into one of the sleeping men, but she rolled and caught herself, pulling to a crouched stance.

"You dare ask me something like that again, I will kill you both, regardless of your tie to Violissa."

He disappeared, the others all following, but the brother and son. They stayed silent, studying Xali who was trying to stand but fell back to the ground with a crash. Carnick had felt the grip of the king's magic flee with his absence, but the pain lingered. He didn't want to move for fear of collapsing.

"You two are certainly a handful," the brother said, crossing his arms. "I'd venture to say stupid is the word and not naïve nor brave. No one crosses Sinow or me and lives to see another day. Lucky might be the word for it. Lucky Violissa has chosen you, or you would certainly have died today."

"Why can we not question?" she asked, clutching her stomach. "I think he ruptured something."

"Because you can't, Xali," Carnick said. "You question all the time. Sometimes, the questions are necessary but this? The man's wife is missing, and you ask him that question? For gods' sake, Xali, use your head," he said angrily as a trickle of blood dribbled from her mouth.

She gave him a wounded look.

"He almost killed you, Xali."

"Heal her, Ren," the brother said. "Heal them both before they die, and your father takes his wrath out upon you."

"Is he always like this?" Xali asked.

"Again with the questions," the brother said as a cool tingling sensation weaved its way through Carnick. "Of course, he's a bit moodier now with Violissa gone, but he's a Dark king. He's violent by nature, it's in our blood to punish, and you were being insolent."

Carnick stood, the pain having washed away with the cool sensation. Healing magic. It still boggled his mind that they'd never known, but then there'd been a lot the great king had left out. Purposely concealing the imperfections, the wrongs he'd wanted to bury.

"Your magic heals but theirs harms," Xali stated to the son, Ren.

"Take them back, Ren. I'm tired of her questions and her statements of the obvious. I'll secure the Light Council."

"Her curiosity is the only reason we're awake, Uncle. It would behoove you and father to indulge it."

"Your father will indulge it when your mother is found. I will never indulge it."

"I carry the three powers of our world within me. The Dark of my father's ancestors, the Light of my mother's as well as the Elvin."

"She really has two magics in her blood?" Carnick asked, surprised. "And you carry them?"

"Just as you both appear to carry two."

Carnick's mind was still having trouble fathoming why they'd never been told more than one magic existed. Why their family wouldn't embrace such a notion. Unless they'd never known. And why was it the immortals seemed to think he and Xali carried two forms? This was the second time this idea had been mentioned.

"You seem surprised."

He looked at Xali whose expression was unchanged. "Did you know? Had you figured it out?"

"With my many unnecessary questions?" she returned, her voice carrying an edge of hurt.

"Xali—"

"No, I…" she trailed off as if remembering something. "I did, they told me. The Cirillians, they told me the history of them, their powers, the Fates. I'd forgotten that part."

"Take them, Ren."

"No, wait. There's something else I forgot. The Elvin, they told me. They live."

Carnick was stunned. The Elvin were a myth. Stories told to children to keep them away from the guardian wall. They were among the monsters that had been purged from these lands. Just as the immortals had been. Yet another story from the great king. When she'd mentioned them right before they'd discovered the king, he hadn't realized she'd actually seen them.

"They're alive?" Ren said, his eyes growing brighter.

"Yes, when I fled my family, they took me in. They sheltered me, helped me with my powers."

"Do they still have magic?"

She nodded. "Yes, but it's not strong."

"Why didn't you say something before now?" the brother asked angrily.

"I was overwhelmed, I'd pushed the knowledge back with all of these revelations. I'm sorry, I forgot."

"Where are they?"

"Behind the guardian wall."

"The wall…the Elvin Enclave. That's where Father is. But we've been there. Why didn't we discover them?"

"They're hidden, far back in the castle ruins, caverns that can't be seen."

"Ren, go," the brother said hurriedly. "You can find them. They're blood, their magic runs through you."

"Tell, Father. I'll take these two back first then meet him there."

"I can take you to them," Xali said quickly as he went to grab her. "I know where they are, take me with you."

"You're the last thing my father needs to see right now, but you can lead me to them." His eyes grew black, the air changing around them. Carnick looked to the brother to see if this change surprised him, but he found nothing that indicated this was not the norm.

He heard Xali whimper and turned back to see Ren's fingers on both sides of her temples. Her face wore a pained expression, her breathing short.

"What are you doing?" he yelled, running to her, but a force grabbed him and threw him to the floor.

A cry escaped Xali right before Ren pulled his hands back. She doubled over, holding her head in pain. Carnick pushed himself up and ran to her, no force stopping him this time.

"What did you do to her?" he asked, pulling her into his arms. Her body was trembling.

"I took what I need and…" He looked back at his uncle. "I saw what she's seen, the dreams with mother. It's her."

"Did you discover anything?" he asked, coming toward them, hope in his eyes.

Ren shook his head. "Nothing more than she's told us."

"Damn. I'll finish here. Take them and then meet your father."

"But…" Carnick started but was cut short as Ren grabbed them both, and he found himself back in the room he'd been in the prior night. Ren released them and disappeared.

Carnick stared at the empty space, trying to calm his spinning head, whether from the trip to the room or the whirlwind of events, he didn't know. With Xali still in his arms, he held her tight and prayed this would all stop soon. Then he wondered absently if he were praying to gods who were even real.

Xali fought the intense pain that cloaked her head, struggling to calm the shaking of her body. Someone had her, it was a familiar feeling, one she welcomed as she relaxed, the pain finally subsiding.

"Xali," she heard Carnick's voice, feeling his hand on her hair, the sound of his voice pulling her back.

She lifted her head and met his worried eyes. They were stormy with waves of black dancing within the violet flecks.

"Carnick." She brought her hand up to touch his face. Her world was crashing around her, but he was the one steady force, the one constant that never wavered. She reached up and brought his head closer, pulling up to kiss him. His hold tightened as he responded to her kiss, pulling her against him as if he never wanted to let her go. All else fell away for just that moment, life returning to their innocent bliss before she'd brought it tumbling down upon them.

He ended the kiss slowly, dropping his forehead to hers where he left it as they held each other, claiming those few more moments of peace before giving way to reality once more. His fingers traced the contours of her face, and she closed her eyes to his touch. Then the moment faded, reality rushing in as she opened her eyes again and took in the disheveled hair, the dirt upon his face, the stress that had edged its way into his features.

"I hate that I can't stop them from hurting you," he said.

Her heart ached at his honesty.

"I want to protect you, Xali. It's my duty, my role as your betrothed. It's what I should be able to easily do as…as the future king I once was. But I can't. No matter how hard I try, no matter how I want to."

"You don't have to protect me, Carnick."

"But I want to, Xali. I should be able to, and I never can. I've never been able to."

She searched his eyes, seeing the pain reflected in them. Bringing her fingers up, she traced his lips, letting her fingers wander down his cheek to his shoulders, then to his chest where they'd never explored, feeling the strength below, the tension.

"I don't need a protector," she said softly. "I only need you. By my side, holding my hand, my heart. Always there to protect it. I only need you, Carnick."

He brought his hand up and ran his fingers through her hair then tilted her neck, bringing her lips to his again. This time, there was a passion to his kiss as if the years of waiting for their union had built to this moment. She knew then that everything else could wait, that she only wanted to be with him, that the rest of their problems could fall to the wayside.

She gave herself over to him completely, no reservations, no traditions, no second born honor to hold her back. None of it mattered now. All that mattered was her love for him. As the world outside continued to fracture, she lost herself to his touch and feelings she'd only dreamed of as she'd awaited their union night, one they'd now likely never have, one that they would openly have this night instead.

Later that evening, as she lay in Carnick's arms, her mind and body at peace finally, she felt complete. He pulled her closer, snuggling his face into her hair.

"Why didn't we do this sooner?" she asked.

"Damned traditions," he mumbled, kissing her neck.

A thought occurred to her, and she moved so that she could see his face. His eyes were heavy, the storm clouds calm, a soft gray coloring them.

"Is this what you experienced with those other girls?"

"Really, Xali?"

"Really. First borns have no boundaries like second borns. I know I wasn't your first." The admission stung a little now where before it had never bothered her.

"Are you seriously jealous? Did I finally discover a weakness to you? Jealousy? You've never been the jealous type," he teased, kissing her neck.

"I'm not jealous."

"I beg to differ."

"I was simply curious."

He regarded her, then kissing her, said, "No, that is unlike anything I have ever experienced with another. Xaliandri, I love you and there has never been another whom I have loved. Others may have shared my bed but never my heart."

She could read the honesty in his eyes. "I suppose that makes me feel better."

He laughed.

"Have you always loved me, Carnick?"

"Ah, little Xali with so many questions. You are quite a bit younger than I, Xali. I can't say I loved you when you were an annoying child, all those questions. Trailing me and Mendol around." He laughed again. "You insisted on doing everything the older cousins did, your curiosity pulling you away too many times so that you'd aggravate them. I should have known then what a handful you'd be."

"So, I was annoying, and you didn't love me?"

"You were precocious, and I loved you for it, but I didn't fall in love with you until the day you bested me. Do you remember that day?"

"Yes, I was spending the summer months with you and Fairenth. You challenged me to a swordfight, confident that you'd lay me on my ass."

"Too cocky for my own good. What were you, all of sixteen? I was twenty-six, you were still but a babe. Standing across from you, it was then that I realized you weren't that annoying child anymore, that you'd blossomed, you were beautiful."

"So, you fell in love with my looks?" She wasn't certain what to make of his statement or how to take it.

He rolled his eyes. "No, I was enchanted, but then you drew your sword. You were strong, swift, strategic. During that fight, I saw who you'd truly become, unlike any other girl I'd known. You were different, unique, special, and when you laid me on my ass, your sword tip to my throat, I saw you, Xali, the woman you'd become, the power in your eyes. I knew then that I'd always loved you, and I fell hard. You were my equal, a woman who could rule my heart and my bed." With that, he winked.

"You saw all that with your defeat, an embarrassing one I might add?"

"Don't remind me and yes, I did," he replied, kissing her. "Now, my turn to ask the questions."

"You know the answer already."

"Do I?"

"I've always loved you, Carnick. For as far back as I can remember, even when you pushed me away. I admired you, your power, your wit. Every time our visits ended, and I was forced to leave, I hated it. The other cousins, they were harsh, their words stung, teasing me as my power failed to arrive, but you, you never did, you always stood up for me, you and Mendol. When you'd practice fighting with Mendol, I'd watch. I know it annoyed you, but I loved watching you. Even when he would decline, and you would train with the guards, I'd sneak out to watch, learning the strikes, the different moves. It was after one of your lessons that I remained behind. You'd left your sword, and I remember curiously trying to pull it from its sheath."

"I remember that," he said, laughing. "You were struggling, the thing was as big as you were. I'd returned to get it after the captain's scolding."

She joined his laughter. "But you didn't stop me. You picked it up, took my small hands, and wrapped them around the hilt."

She remembered that moment, the feel of the steel against her skin, Carnick's huge hands wrapped around her child hands. In that moment, she'd felt powerful and secure, the sword her weapon, Carnick her shield.

"That was the moment I knew there were two things I wanted in my life, a sword and you, and that with both, I would never again feel the sting of the cousins' tongues, nor the guilt of my absent powers. From that day on, I took every chance to master the sword. That day I bested you, I wasn't fighting you to defeat you, I wanted to show you what I'd done. I wanted to see the pride in your eyes. That I had power, strength, that I was your equal. You were the strongest of the cousins, and I knew if I could beat you, I would claim my place among them, and my place in your heart."

"That you did, Xali. You knew me too well."

"I knew what you wanted, Carnick. I knew that you didn't want me to be meek like Fairenth, part of me suspected you didn't want me to play the part of the second born." She stopped and thought about her words. "You didn't, did you?"

He gave her a sly smile. "Second borns are meek, they're trained to be subservient, it's boring. You had spirit, Xali, a fire in you that we all saw even as you were a mere babe. You mastered everything early and with this fierce determination. I loved that about you and knew they would try to clamp it down, to make you into that subservient second born they thought you should be. I did everything in my power to ensure they didn't bury it. I may have even gotten Mendol in league with me. I was only with you in short spurts, but Mendol and I are closest, and I knew he would help me, although I didn't think either of us expected this outcome." He sighed. The storm clouds in his eyes moving.

"I'm sorry," she said quietly. "I never expected for any of this to happen. I—"

"Yes, you did, Xali. You knew that if you kept pushing you would cause chaos and yet you continued."

She dropped her eyes, the happiness of the moment fading. He picked her chin up and gave her a smile. "And I wouldn't have it any other way. If we had it to do all over again, I would still follow you down this path. It was the right thing to do."

"I don't know now, Carnick. It's all such a mess. I fear none of us will live, that we will die by the Dark king's hands for the sins of our ancestors."

"Then we will die together. I will hold you in my arms as they kill us."

She swallowed, the thought overwhelming her. He kissed her nose and pulled her in against his chest where she relaxed, taking comfort in the power below her hands, the security she'd always felt with him.

"I don't think they'll kill you, Xali, you've been chosen by their Fates. Your role in all of this is still to come, and I think you'll be here to see the outcome."

His hand caressed her shoulder, her eyes growing heavy with the calm he gave her.

"And you?"

"I don't truly know. Perhaps you can sway them to keep me alive. If not, then I will die knowing I had your love and that you once lay in my arms."

"I don't like that outcome, Carnick," she said groggily.

He kissed her head. "Go to sleep, Xali. We'll worry on this in the morn."

She drifted off to the sound of his voice, the safety of his arms, contentment in her soul.

There was a sound. A loud rushing Xali could hear. She blinked, the dazzling sunlight temporarily blinding her. Squinting, she looked around, wondering where she was. Woods surrounded her on every side, lush with life and growth. Colors that only brushed the imagination layered the forest floor. She walked, urged on by the sound. Her feet, which she now realized were bare as was her entire body, sank into the damp ground. Looking out, she saw that a stream had formed ahead of her. It wound through the forest to a clearing she could see in the distance. She quickened her pace and reached the clearing, the stream growing in size. At the clearing, she could see the water shimmer, and kneeling, she scooped it into her palms. It was green, not a murky green but a beautiful clear emerald. She rose, the sound almost deafening. The clearing led to a cliff and from the cliff sprouted a massive waterfall, emerald water rushing from it to land in the river below. She recognized the land now. The ruins she knew now transformed into a glorious city, a castle built into the cliffside to her left, shimmering in the sun's rays. It was breathtaking.

"The Elvin Enclave," she said in awe.

As she spoke the words, the water dried up, the waterfall stopping its flow, all of it draining to the center of the city then disappearing into a hill that crested to complete the valley above, upon which she stood looking. The city below crumbled, the buildings turning to dust, the vegetation dying.

Xali's heart raced as the castle deteriorated until only the ruins she knew remained. A loud crack split the air, and her eyes were drawn to the center of the city where a marble wall had been split in two, its pieces now falling, shattering, and leaving only one discernable portion. The names Violissa and Sinow shone as brightly as starlight in the darkness that now shrouded Xali. She watched the names deteriorate until only the parts she remembered finding with Carnick remained.

The world shifted, and she was standing in a cavern, darkness submerging her until a vibrant emerald light filled the space. Hope filled her then quickly fled as she heard the rush of the water. It flowed into the cavern with a force that knocked her down. She struggled to get to her feet, but there was too much. It filled the cavern, leaving no space to breathe. Fear struck her as her lungs began to burn, the emerald of the water fading so that she could see nothing as she failed to escape. The burning in her lungs continued, and she was about to give up her fight when two brilliant green eyes lit the dark, streaks of gold streaming around them.

Xali sat up, gasping for breath and coughing.

"Xali? What's wrong? You've been stirring in your sleep," Carnick said, his voice layered in fear. "I couldn't wake you."

Finally catching her breath, she said, "I know where the queen is."

Nineteen

Carnick stared at Xali as she leapt from the bed and hastily threw on her clothes. Something she'd dreamt had rattled her.

"Slow down, Xali. Tell me what's going on."

"There's no time. I need to find the king," she replied, fastening her pants.

He rose and pulled his own pants on quickly, sensing he would soon be chasing her out of the room.

Concerned, he went to her, grabbing her shoulders. "What is going on, Xali? What do you mean you know where the queen is?"

Forced to stop adjusting her tunic, she said, "I know where she is, and I need to tell him now. She's dying, Carnick. Now let me go."

"We knew she was dying, Xali. It's the middle of the night, come back to bed, and we'll tell him in the morn."

She pulled from his grip. "No, she won't make it till dawn. See for yourself," she said, pointing to the window.

He looked curiously at her then walked across the expansive room, glancing back to ensure she wasn't slipping from the room without him. He pulled the heavy window hangings back, bulky things he'd never before seen hiding windows that had always stood open in his family's palaces. Looking out, he saw that the moons were bright and full above, their light casting through the clear sky to light the land below. The trees in the distance lay bare, their leaves shriveled and black on the ground below. The decay spread as far as his eyes could see, encompassing the land. He turned swiftly to her.

"How?"

"She's losing her fight," she answered sadly before finishing with her tunic. "Now, I need to find the king."

"You can't just barge out there and demand to see the king at this hour."

She gave him a determined look, pulled her long silver hair from under her tunic, hair that glimmered with streaks of gold highlight-ed among the curls, and then she headed to the door.

"Dammit," he muttered, grabbing his shirt and chasing after her. His mind barely registered the bareness of his feet against the cold stone as he wondered why the emerald fragments in her eyes appeared so striking.

"Go back to your room before I force you back," he heard the Darkbearer stationed in their hall.

"I need to see the king."

"You're not disturbing Sinow at this hour."

"Let her through," Carnick said, coming to stand behind her.

"How dare you order me, usurper's heir. Turn around and go back."

Carnick felt the Dark power before it struck him. Pain flared as the magic gorged him, but this time, he accepted it, feeling the Darkness that lay deep within surge in response. It grabbed the invasive power and used it to strike back, hitting the man squarely in the chest and throwing him backward.

Catching himself, he glared at Carnick, his power increasing. "I won't go gentle on you this time, child."

He drew his magic, but before he could strike, the floor below rumbled, the space around them shaking as Xali's own power erupted. The entire keep was quaking, the sound as if it would crash around them at any moment.

She drew her hand up, saying, "Enough!" and the man was sent crashing into the wall behind him, slumping unconscious on the floor.

Carnick looked at Xali, her eyes now enveloped by the green.

"I said we needed to go, it's urgent." Then she ran down the hall.

"Damn," he mumbled, running after her.

"Xali, you don't even know where you're going. You just knocked out one of his men. He's going to punish you."

She ignored him, continuing down the corridor. They'd only ever been shifted places, never having walked the entire distance from their rooms. How did she even know where the king was?

Carnick followed as she moved through the castle with the ease of someone who had walked the halls hundreds of times. He didn't know how she was doing it or where she was even going, but he followed as she led the way. She slid smoothly down the railing that lined the main stairs to the main level of the building then hopped effortlessly to the floor. He would have stopped and admired her moves if he hadn't been trying to keep up with her. Finally, she stopped in front of a closed door, throwing it open without touching it.

Catching up with her, he found the king standing, arms crossed as if awaiting her appearance. The king's brother stood in the corner of the room that appeared to be some sort of study. He was shrouded in black, the anger at Xali's abrupt entrance evident in his eyes.

"You knocked one of my Darkbearers out cold, something he

will be punished for in due time. Then you have the audacity to barge in on me at this hour. You'd best have a swift answer as to why I shouldn't punish you."

"I know where she is," Xali stated.

The king's demeanor changed, the shroud of black over his brother dissipating with her words.

"Where?"

"The Elvin Enclave, where the ravine flows through."

"We've checked the enclave, multiple times. In fact, my son is there now with the Elvin you neglected to tell us were alive."

"I don't have time to argue in defense. She's running out of time. See for yourself." She gestured to the window across the room, no hangings hiding the moonlit scene behind them. The brother walked over to it.

"Fates, Sinow."

The king furrowed his brow at Xali then went to the window.

"It's dead, all of it," the brother said. He turned to Xali as the king took it all in. "You had another dream."

"Yes, she's losing her battle." With her words, his eyes grew heavy with sadness before it was hidden behind a mask of power. "I fear she won't make it till morn."

"Then we find her now. The ravine once fed into the enclave at the castle ruins."

"No, that's not where she is. She's not at the waterfall, she's further in where it flows along the banks of the city."

"How do you know of the waterfall?" he asked.

"She showed me. She let me see the glory of the land before Drakine invaded it. The water has dried up, but it's not gone. It's wherever she is, and it's…it's drowning her," she said the words as if just realizing that was the case. "I don't have time to answer questions. She needs me. I need to find her now."

As the last word left her mouth, she disappeared from the room.

"She can shift?" the brother erupted. "Why was this not known?"

Carnick felt the grip of pain on his body but fought it, saying through gritted teeth, "It only happened once before. I don't think she knows she's doing it or how. The prince knows, he said she hadn't mastered it yet."

"Tynan," the king said, "summon the Council. I'll call Ren."

He walked toward Carnick, a far-off look in his eyes as if talking to his son silently. It was a strange effect, then his eyes refocused, and he grabbed Carnick. The room disappeared, and he found himself in the land behind the guardian wall, what the immortals called the Elvin Enclave. The place he now knew Drakine had hidden behind the wall he'd erected to hide his secrets.

Xali was on her knees trying to use her magic to dig the ground before her. It was something any of his family could have easily done, but her magic was distinctly different.

Carnick caught movement as Ren shifted with another man whose green eyes surveyed the scene before them. His golden hair reminded Carnick of the strands in Xali's hair. Moonlight hit the man's emerald eyes and lent them a sparkling effect. Elvin, he was Elvin.

Ren, Narilen," the king said.

"How can we help?" the man asked, not phased by the king's power. Royalty. Carnick remembered the king stating that only royal blood could tolerate his power. Was this the king of the Elvin? Carnick still couldn't believe they truly existed. Another part of the myths of the immortals. Had Drakine led a purge on them right after he'd defeated the immortals, leaving all knowledge of their existence locked behind the guardian wall? Likely, but he hadn't truly killed them all, had he? Carnick wondered how they'd survived.

"I believe this is in the hands of the Fates, and we are mere observers," the king replied.

"What is she doing?" the man asked, gesturing to Xali.

"Digging," Carnick replied. He walked over to her and placed a hand on her shoulder. "Xali."

"I need to get to her. I can't move the dirt." She stared at her hands.

"Is she under here?" the king asked.

Carnick helped her to her feet, her eyes still locked on her hands. "No. It needs to be cleared. The river must flow again."

"This spot needs to be cleared, Xali?" he asked.

"No, all of it. The river's path needs to be present."

Her eyes looked wild, frantic, and she turned, pulling from him so she could return to digging.

"Xali! Focus. You can't clear the river's path yourself."

He looked around, his eyes surveying the expanses of what was once river, a path of dirt that remained barren, traveling through the enclave for miles. He turned to the king.

"We'll need power, more than I have. We need our family."

The king eyed him then glanced at Xali, whose eyes were flitting, the green specks in them larger than normal. She was mumbling as if she'd lost her mind. The king disappeared as did his men, only the son and the Elvin man remaining. Carnick glanced at them.

"The queen is fighting, the girl fights with her, she is the tie that binds what remains of her soul to the world. She and the Dark king. Do not restrain her, let her go so that they both may return. Else, I fear they will both be lost," the man said, his green eyes deep with wisdom.

He released Xali's arms, and she wandered back to what had once been the river bank, staring at something unseen.

The king returned with the others, Carnick's family with them. His aunt ran to Xali, pulling her in even as Xali fought her. Carnick's mother looked as if she wanted to go to him but stopped short, the proud queen restraining her emotions. He turned from her as the king spoke.

"You have them, now find my wife."

Carnick nodded then turned back to his family. "We need to raise the riverbed. Anywhere you feel the land once held water, raise it."

They stared at him, no one moving. Xali's ranting stopped.

"Do it now!" she commanded.

"How dare you," his mother said. "A second born will not command me."

"She will, and you will listen, Mother. Xali is in charge now, and she is the only reason any of us are still live."

"She is the reason we are in this mess in the first place. She has destroyed us, and she should have been killed before this mess began." Carnick felt the king's power, but he was on his mother before it could hit. He slapped her hard.

She brought her hand to her cheek as the others silenced their reactions. Her eyes looked wounded, shock covering her face.

"You will not threaten my betrothed any longer. Our time is over, Mother. The only thing we can do is accept it and help find the queen. Only then do we have any chance of salvation for the crimes this family has committed."

He felt a hand on his shoulder and looked over to see his father. "Renia, do as Carnick says. The rest of us will spread out as far as we can to cover the riverbank. Son, direct us, we will follow."

Carnick couldn't help but stare at his father who had always been so meek, bowing to his second born status.

"Glad that's over. If you lot had taken any longer, I would have killed you myself," the king's brother muttered.

"He's right. All of you move. We're running out of time." It hadn't been the king who had said it but Xali.

His family spread out, taking position all along the riverbank. Carnick looked at Xali then moved to head out further. She grabbed his arm.

"No, stay close to me. I need your strength."

Her eyes were a blend of storm clouds and green. As her hands dropped, the sky darkened, and tiny snowflakes began to fall. As each touched her hair, it transformed, each curl darkening to a lush gold. The emerald in her eyes fought for dominance, finally overcoming the stormy gray that held the last piece of her. A sweet, lilac smell filled the air as she drew a breath, and Carnick knew Xali was lost somewhere within, for it was not Xali who now looked back at him. Her emerald eyes held an ancient knowledge and power that spanned to the ends of time. She gave him a small smile, her hand dropping from his arm.

"Vi," he heard the king say softly.

Her eyes sparkled at his voice, hope filling them.

"Go," she said to Carnick, a change from what she'd said only moments before, her voice no longer Xali's; it was like the gentlest breeze calming his soul.

Slowly, he walked away, his eyes still watching her. She moved gracefully to the king, her eyes softening, filling with longing.

"Shhh," she said, bringing her finger to his lips. Jealousy tore through Carnick, and then he reminded himself that although it was Xali's body that drew close to the king, it was not her. The feeling lingered however as she traced the king's face with the familiarity of a lover.

"I'm running out of time," she said, jarring Carnick from his jealous state. "I can't hold on much longer, the weight of it is drowning me, Sinow."

"Vi," the king said, "please tell me how to find you."

"Only she can wake me. She is connected to me now. She has always been. She must correct the wrongs, awakes us all, only she."

Pain filled his eyes, and Carnick noticed the small droplets of water upon Xali's fingertips that shimmered a vibrant emerald as they fell.

"She's drowning," he said.

She turned to him, tears of emerald shimmering on her cheeks. *Help me.* Her voice floated through his head, like soft petals.

She turned back to the king, her eyes locked to his then slowly she backed away, each footstep leaving a small trace of green water. Her hand lingered in the king's until their fingers no longer touched. Then, she turned from him and slowly walked toward the riverbed, the riverbed that had yet to be raised, for the family were all staring at this woman who now ruled Xali's body.

"She's using her last bit of power to control her, Sinow," the brother said, his voice soft for the first time, holding a sadness that was palpable. "To what end?"

"I don't know," the king said, his voice breaking.

Carnick ran to the riverside as she stepped into the dead traces of it.

"Now!" he commanded, pouring his power into it. His family followed his lead, the dirt in the ancient river's path rising. Xali walked through it, and Carnick heard the most glorious sound. She was singing. Xali rarely sang, unless forced to sing prayers for the gods. Her voice was pretty, but this was not her voice. This was something more, power, seduction, wisdom, the voice of the gods themselves. As she sang, he felt his control of the dirt release. She had taken over it, the dirt hanging in fragments in the air before them. She brought her hand up, and the fragments dissipated, shimmering until they faded from existence.

Carnick couldn't take his eyes from her. The green of her eyes seemed to light the space around her. The emerald droplets still spilled from her fingertips and splashed to the ground below. He listened as she sang of being carried under, drowning just as he'd said. The world around her seemed to be listening as well. The clouds above darkened, the ground below rumbling as though ready to explode, the trees swaying as the wind whipped around them.

"Fight, Violissa," he heard the king say.

Carnick glanced back at him. His eyes were on Xali, filled with hope, his body tense as were all the others. He felt the pull of power and turned back to see that she was aiming her power at the side of the cliff that overlooked the riverbed. What was she doing? She was straining as if trying to bring it down. But why?

Carnick studied the piece of land, noticing the inconsistencies with the places where it met the ridge. Inconsistencies like Xali had noticed at the holy land.

"It's not natural," he said, piecing it together. "It was made…

made by Drakine. Gods, she's trapped behind there."

The king's eyes turned to him, and he met his gaze, an understanding passing between them. The king was helpless in this, forced to take the role of bystander, something that killed him just as it would have killed Carnick. But Carnick wasn't. He and Xali had been thrust into this situation, whether by fate or coincidence, they were here, and both could help. He could help her.

He tore his eyes from the king and ran screaming to his family. "Tear it down! She's behind the land. Bring it down!"

He aimed his power at the cliffside, feeling his family join in. It shook, the magic that had created it straining to hold it in place until finally giving way to the rebelling magic that pulled at it. With a deafening crack, it exploded. He aimed his power at the large fragments of rock and dirt that were falling, breaking them to sand with the others. None of them had power over water, however, and he screamed as a wave of crystal green water collapsed upon the space where Xali stood, engulfing her. It rushed toward them all then narrowed, its rapid flow covering the riverbed. Carnick glanced back to see Ren's hands up, his eyes a rich sage. He held power over water, his mother's magic.

Pulling his eyes away, he searched for Xali to find she'd been lifted far above the billowing water, her voice still the queen's, her arms outstretched, fingers drifting through the span of the water. She aimed her magic at the opening, drawing the final remnants of the water out, then what remained of the false piece of land crumbled at her command, the water she stood upon settling, bringing her back down. In the air around her, the pieces of land floated until she turned them all into a delicate shower of flower petals that were swept away with the water, her voice fading, body falling. It was done. Carnick ran to her as the king and his men ran to the cavern that now lay before them. He lifted Xali's body from the water, limp and lifeless.

"Xali, please. Come back to me," he said, wiping the wet strands of hair from her face. Her eyes flew open as she drew in a loud breath and relief overcame him until an angry roar bellowed through the air—with it, the ground shook, and a mist of black shrouded them all.

273

Twenty

Xali gulped for air, feeling Carnick's arms around her, their usual comfort no help against the emptiness she'd felt with the fleeing of the queen's presence. As a pained cry split the silence, she scrambled to her feet. She was soaked, her feet and legs underwater. Flashes of seeing the water through someone else's eyes, of controlling it, passed through her mind, accompanied by a longing, a desperation to survive. The queen had taken over her body, but Xali had invited her in, letting the calm of her presence take hold of her, watching the world through her eyes, feeling her magic as it had never been used.

Now, there was an emptiness everywhere but in her heart, as if a small piece of her had remained.

Carnick's arms steadied her as she stood, and together, they watched the king emerge, his face a mix of anger and defeat. His brother and son flanked him, followed by his men, their faces all a twisted blend of power and pain.

In his arms, he held the limp body of what Xali knew instantly to be the queen, her long locks heavy with the emerald water that now flowed below Xali's feet. Her arms hung lifeless, but even in this state, her beauty eclipsed all.

Xali's heart lurched. She was dead; it had all been for naught. Xali hadn't found her in time.

"Gods, she didn't make it," Carnick said softly.

Xali met the king's eyes, and that small presence in her heart jumped. The emerald of the river shimmered, catching her attention. She pulled from Carnick's arms and ran to the king.

"No! Put her down, put her in the water!" she screamed.

The king's eyes darkened to a deep ebony. "She's dead. You and your lot will bother me no longer."

"Please," she pleaded.

"Father, how many times have you lost her only to have her return. The Fates are still speaking, listen."

He clutched the queen's body tighter to him.

"It was over. She should have been safe, finally left alone from their grasp."

"Brother, adrift does not mean secure. Listen to her. She may be the only hope we have, and whatever part she was to play has not been finished."

The king was quiet. He looked down at his wife, his eyes softening, the heartache of the man below evident for that brief moment. Then he turned his eyes back to Xali. When they met hers, she felt the pain, the desperation, the torment he carried, a man who wanted only to have his wife back no matter the cost.

Gently, he lay her in the water, her hair streaming around her. He ran his finger along her still face then rose.

"Nothing's happening," the brother said.

"Because she's not done," Ren said, looking at Xali.

Xali nodded, then swallowed her fear; this was her move. She'd been called to this moment, the power was hers. She moved closer and kneeled next to the queen, entranced at her beauty, the peaceful godlike presence she commanded even in death.

She called to the magic in her, to that strange presence in her heart, setting them both free, then touched the queen's hand. A current charged through her as everything appeared to freeze, a blinding light surrounding them both before its power sent everyone around them flying back with its force.

Xaliandri, the queen's voice whispered. Then, her eyes opened, and Xali was sent tumbling away. She caught herself and shielded her eyes to the brilliant white that shrouded the queen's body. The river water stirred, and the emerald within it snaked its way to the blinding light, slowly overtaking it until she was hidden below a cloak of green.

Xali held her breath, knowing she was witnessing the true power of the immortals and the Fates. The emerald faded as a voice cascaded over the land, its sound weaving through Xali's existence, claiming her heart, her loyalty, her allegiance. It flowed through her as no sound she'd ever heard, leaving a sense of calm and peace that she'd never felt. The emerald faded, and there stood the queen, her golden curls spilling down, the green of the water now sparkling in her eyes, her skin aglow with life and power. She raised her eyes skyward, and the clouds dissipated, the light of the moons casting a spotlight on her. Xali watched in awe as their light seemed to envelop her in ribbons that danced over her skin.

A burst of magic flowed from her, light and airy as it drifted past Xali and beyond the enclave. The queen's eyes met her son's, and Xali watched as she smiled and gave him a nod, another note fleeing her mouth. Within moments, he'd shifted.

The song continued, this time a sage stream of magic dancing from her, causing the ground beneath Xali's feet to shift. She pulled her eyes from the queen and saw the grass rise, color filling it, the trees beyond blooming with soft leaves that looked mauve in the moonlight. The crack of the wall in the distance filled the air, its essence transformed to tiny snowflakes that blew through the breeze. Xali felt Carnick beside her. She took his hand, taking comfort in his presence as the sheer power of the immortals played out around them, men in white capes appearing, all kneeling to their queen's voice.

She moved forward, toward the king, her song continuing with words that told of her endless love for him. When she reached him, she let her fingers drift along his face, his eyes lightening to a rich brown as she sang her final note and then kissed him. A calm breeze rushed through Xali's hair. The king pulled her closer, their kiss deepening, and Xali had to look away, feeling as a voyeur to such a tender moment. Her eyes landed on Ren who had returned with a woman, her lush auburn hair enhancing the pretty face that held eyes of shocking blue. He gave Xali a smile as he brought the woman tighter against him, her head resting upon his shoulder.

Xali looked at Carnick, feeling his eyes on her. They were filled with pride and love.

"You did it, Xali," he whispered.

And she had, but what had she truly done? What had it cost them? And what was the price left to be paid?

Epilogue

Xali paced the room, her nerves too taut to sit, her hands wringing with each footfall.

"Xali, sit. You can't keep pacing. We've no idea how long it will be," Carnick said, gesturing to the space beside him.

They were prisoners again, locked in Carnick's quarters in the Dark king's castle. She walked the wide expanse of the room, and as she passed him in the bed, he grabbed her hand, forcing her to look at him.

"It's been three days, Carnick. Three sun and moon cycles and yet nothing."

"They've been apart a long time, Xali. Perhaps they wanted time alone before they dealt with us. I know if you'd been lost to me for that long, I'd never want you from my arms."

"I need to know, Carnick."

He sighed, letting go of her wrist and standing. "We will know soon. The longer this is delayed, the longer I get to have you with me," he said, brushing a stray strand of her hair back from her face. He reached back, pulling her locks to the front and letting them run through his fingers. No trace of gold nor curl remained. They'd disappeared the night the queen had been found, their connection severed. As had the vinelike markings that had adorned her arm.

"I'm scared, Carnick," Xali whispered.

He gave her a small smile then laughed. "I thought nothing scared my Xali. You are the bravest woman I know, possibly the bravest of all of us. You faced the immortals, the lies that warped their memory, faced the wrath of our family—"

"And now I face my death and yours," she said.

"We don't know that. The queen said a decision would be made. She never gave any indication as to what that decision would be."

"In the king's eyes, there is no fate but death in store for us."

"You woke them all, Xali, you saved the queen. Your fate will not be death today."

"But what if yours is? And what of the others? Our family?"

"No matter how you pace the room, we will not know that answer until they summon us."

She searched his eyes, the gray sprinkled with storm clouds that belied his worry.

"This is your journey, Xali, your path, one on which I have been allowed to travel. If my fate is death, your path will continue."

"No—" she started, but he put his finger to her lips to stop her.

"Yes, you have been called, Xali, your purpose greater than any of ours. You will continue on no matter the sentence the rest of us are given. Your place is with the immortals. I have no doubt that their Fates chose you, and you will be rewarded."

She swallowed back her fear, pulling forth the brave façade she'd carried throughout her life, even though her heart was breaking below.

She touched his cheek and leaned up to kiss him, part of her wondering if this would be the last kiss they would share. She let her lips linger before slowly pulling back and dropping her head to his chest.

"It will be all right, Xaliandri," he said, kissing her head.

Their moment was interrupted as the door opened. Her heart pounded, and Carnick pulled her against him, wrapping his arms protectively around her as Ren entered the room.

"It is time," he said. "Your fate has been decided."

J. L. Jackola discovered her passion for writing in grade school when she wrote a short story that earned her a spot in a local writing workshop. She has been creating fantasy worlds ever since. When she's not weaving tales, she can be found logging miles in her running shoes, watching movies with her family, or curled up with a book. She resides in Delaware with her husband and three children.

To learn more, visit her website at www.jljackola.com.